Dear
The r
and dangerous, remember
to bring a torch and a lot
of hot tea!

CEDAR VALLEY

A Novel

DENISE WALKER

XOXO
Denise Walk

Cover design by Lydia Stewart

For the lost

ONE

They bring us in separately. Children in one entrance
and our parents in another. I find this a curiously cruel
tradition, being divided in these last moments. I am
with three others my age, two women and a man. The
women cling to each other, eyes red and swollen. The
man stands apart from us, his jaw locked and his fists
balled at his sides. He's not crying but staring intently
on the steel doors before us, determined to stay strong.
I can respect that. I am doing much of the same,
although my jaw is slack and my fists are relaxed. My
blood is rushing under my skin but it's not from nerves
or fear and my eyes are dry. No tears, not today.

The doors slide open and out step four Council
members, each bearing black robes for us. Their hoods
are up but I can see weathered faces beneath—they've
been doing this for a long time. I want to question

them, I want to know what they've seen but I hold my tongue.

One removes his hood, "Your parents have chosen to let you decide who shall go first."

"I will," I don't skip a beat. The women grasp one another more tightly, their breath ragged. A choking noise comes from the lock-jawed man as he attempts to control a sob. It doesn't work.

Without looking back, I leave them and follow the unhooded Councilman through the doorway and into the hall. Cold white lights lead us towards the Lifechamber, sucking all warmth from the tight corridor. I take my time moving forward. In a few moments my life will be forever altered. My feet kick up dust and I embrace the way it tickles my throat. This dust has seen much more than I.

We are met by another set of metal doors. The Council member gives me the black robe, "After these doors, please remove your footwear and place them in the drawer. Change into this robe and leave your grey one on top of your sandals. You won't need it anymore."

The black linen is cool in my hands. It symbolizes the beginning of transition, a new chapter. I run the fabric between my fingers and my heart beats faster.

"Are you ready?"

CEDAR VALLEY

I nod, eyes fixated on the robe.

"I'll see you in there. Congratulations," he gives my shoulder a squeeze and leaves the way we came.

When I near them, the doors open automatically to reveal a small room and I am faced with yet another set of steel doors. I slip off my sandals and place them in the metal drawer; its metallic siding seems out of place in the old stone wall. I do not hesitate to take off my grey robe; it's the colour I have worn all my life and I am done with it. I am ready to move forward.

I wrap the cool black linen around me and square the old one away. I face the last doors. They open and I enter the Lifechamber. My parents wait below in the sunken midsection, their beaming faces luminescent in the moonlight. I descend down a circular stone ramp, tracing the outer wall until I am beside them.

I think about this morning when we said our goodbyes. It is customary to have the whole last day to spend with our families, many of which spend their time teary and fearful—but not us. Instead of holding each other, weepy and distraught, we spent our day laughing and enjoying each other's company. We watched as the sun faded from burning orange to pink to deep, deep purple and that was the best goodbye we could have asked for. After our last meal, we came here, all three of us ready for what comes next.

I never gave much thought to decapitating my parents; I only knew it was something I would have to do. My twenty-fifth birthday has arrived and now we are here, me with my hands folded and them kneeling before me in the centre of the room. The council stands around us, unmoving in their beige robes. A pair of unfortunate looking girls flanks a steel doorway, standing unnaturally still, holding their breath to remain calm. Such weight is placed in this ceremony—it's seen as oppression, but it's not, it's liberation. Today marks my parents' death but we call it the Life Ceremony for a reason. Without these rules, without these sacrifices, life on this Earth would cease to exist. Not everyone can live forever but this way, humanity can.

Heads extended over the block, my parents smile at each other. I hear their voices from this morning:

"As you breathe death into us, we breathe life into you."

They brought me into this world and they will leave it having given me everything. If that isn't the true nature of love, I don't know what is.

I look up towards the arched ceiling. Moonlight pours down from a circular opening, bathing the room in cool grey. Metal reinforcements have been retrofitted to stabilize the opening. This building is old, the oldest in the entire city. I can imagine how our ancestors chose to build around this structure, preserving it as a centrepiece. Being inside such an ancient room is calming; I feel connected to the world and its history. Past, present, future; it is all intertwined. Here, everything is made of light stone, much like home and that is comforting. The long-dead masons' hands supported the stones beneath my feet and now these stones support me. I am not alone in this.

The closest member of the council hands me the sword. It is long, twice the length of my arm. It feels good in my hands, balanced, a perfect extension of myself. My fingers close around the ornate handle, the grip rough against my skin. The blade itself is not thick but I have no doubt it will do the job. Many before me have held this sword but I know it was made for me. The others were undeserving and weak. I have heard the stories of the infinite hacking needed to behead someone. So misguided. They let fear and grief consume them and that is not the way. This is a happy time—perhaps the most important moment of our entire lives.

"We love you, Arun." My mother's voice is sure and unwavering. My father nods along with her. They take their eyes off me to share a moment between themselves, their whole existence exuding love and admiration.

"I love you too," My smile matches the ones on my parents' faces. They take each other's hands as I square my shoulders and lift the blade high above my head. Feet planted firmly, I swing the sword over my shoulders in a wide arc. First my father and then my mother. Their heads roll away still smiling.

What they didn't tell me is how good it would feel. The life leaving them and flowing into me, it's electric. I want to stay here. I want to touch their gushing necks. All the lifeblood flowing from them is calling to me. One of the homely usher girls, somehow shapeless despite her fitted smock, brings me to a small adjoining room. There's no light save for a burning lantern. She moves to untie my robe but I grab her wrist. She gasps and my mouth softens—I want to do it myself. She nods and leaves, her eyes trained on the floor. She'll be back to retrieve me soon—I quickly shed my robe and look at my new self in the mirror. My face and neck are speckled in blood and I cannot bring myself to clean it off. They had to die so I could live. It is the circle of existence. The blood is still warm and when I touch it, it smears across my cheek. The excitement is affecting me in full—my heart is racing. I reach down and stroke the length on my shaft and the urge for release is hard to ignore.

She's back, pretending not to stare. She motions sheepishly for me to follow her through another set of steel doors into the Afterchamber. This room is brighter, each corner illuminated by candles. A vast, still pool rests in the middle and stretches from wall to wall. The ceiling is low; I am sure I could touch it if I tried. The air smells like dirt but something is different—every sense is heightened and as I breathe in, I can smell every mineral and taste every particle. The floor is wet under my bare feet. The stone has eroded here and the coarseness lends me grip.

The council stands across the water from me. The same member who gave me the sword now has a white silk robe draped across his arms. The fabric flows like a veil, and I know that through that pure white veil awaits a new world. I descend the steps into the pool and submerge myself. My parents' precious lifeblood washes away but that's okay, it has already become a part of me. I am new, and the world sees me as the man that I am. I step out on the other side and am enveloped by the white robe. Another council member taps on an electronic tablet, recording my status. I am new. I am alive. I am Holy.

TWO

All the lights were off in the house. Peter tried the front door but it was locked. "I don't think anyone's home."

"That's weird," Royal consulted his tablet. "They're on the list."

Peter moved to the window, cupped his hands and peered inside. Light from a fish tank basked the living room in blue but nothing moved.

The rest of their day had been uneventful. Each inspection had gone seamlessly; every family present and accounted for. This house was the last on their list. Located in a blue collar neighbourhood, the community was busy with people returning home from work. All around them cars pulled into driveways, children greeted their parents, and conversation flitted through the streets. But not this house.

Royal thumped on the door, "Police! Open up!"

His efforts were met by silence.

"Huh," Peter readjusted his duty belt. This was an anomaly; families selected for inspection were always notified in advance and required to confirm that they would be home during the allotted time frame. Inspections were a source of anxiety for most civilians and Peter had never encountered anyone with the guts to skip out on one. "I guess we'll just have to come—"

SMASH!

Royal's hand reached for his gun, "What the hell was that?"

Peter stared back through the glass, a vase lay shattered across the kitchen floor, "Someone's in there."

A muffled cry echoed from inside the home. Peter pulled out his flashlight and shone it through the window but its beam did little to illuminate the interior. The cries continued.

"A baby?" Peter racked his brain, "I thought they had a teenager?"

Royal pulled up their file on his tablet, "Yeah, their daughter is thirteen."

Peter keyed his radio, "Dispatch, this is Charlie-One. We need back-up at 569 Cormack Crescent. We have a possible Act Violation."

"You think that baby in there is an illegal?"

A knot formed in Peter's gut, "I really hope not."

Soon after, two units pulled up to the curb. Officers Harvey and Lamb stepped out of the first. They both had cropped brown hair and angular features. They looked startlingly similar. Nearly everyone assumed they were brothers upon first meeting them. Aside from being partners, they spent most of their spare time together doing things Peter could only guess at, perhaps going to the gym or sculpting each other's hair.

Out of the second car came a pair of detectives.

Royal nudged Peter's arm, "It's your parents."

Peter's father shed his black blazer to reveal a Kevlar vest over a light blue dress shirt. He unbuttoned his cuffs and rolled his sleeves up to his elbows. He scratched his salt and pepper beard then moved to help Peter's mother out of her jacket. As he slid it from her shoulders, she untucked her straight blonde hair and snuck a smile at Peter.

Peter couldn't help but smile back at her.

The six of them convened on the sidewalk and Peter briefed them on what had happened.

"So," Peter's father looked him dead in the eye, "Officer Holloway, what do your instincts say?"

Peter fought the chill off his back and matched his father's gaze, "They were on the list. They knew we were coming by for inspection. My instincts say that they're hiding out in there with an illegal second child." The words felt like poison in his mouth. He prayed he was wrong but the chill refused to leave his spine.

"Alright," Frank Holloway nodded. "Then that's how we'll run this. Peter, you're on point."

Peter signalled to Harvey and Lamb to take the back of the house while the rest of them would enter through the front. They unholstered their weapons and got into position. Thumping on the door again, Peter called for the family to come to them. If they would just give themselves up, this would be a whole lot easier. After roughly thirty seconds of silence, Royal braced himself and kicked the door in.

Once inside, they split up, clearing one room at a time. Peter strained his ears but could no longer hear the baby crying. He glanced around the main room— empty. *Maybe they're upstairs?* Peter veered up a white railed staircase, Royal hot on his heels. The second floor hallway had three doors, all closed. Peter slid against the wall, gun trained on the first door as his partner secured a hand on the doorknob. They looked at each other, listening for any movement inside the room. Hearing nothing, Peter nodded and Royal swung the door open.

It was empty save for an unmade bed and a dresser, the drawers of which had all been gutted. There were no personal affects in sight except a few boy band posters on the wall. Peter called out that the room was clear.

Royal led them to the next room which proved clear as well. The closet had been emptied and the walls showed square areas of discoloration where pictures had been recently removed.

They cleared the last door, a storage room occupied by three bulging suitcases. Peter swallowed and shot Royal a wide-eyed look.

"I guess your instincts were right," Royal sighed. "Looks like they were planning to defect."

Peter shook his head, "They must have thought they'd be out of here before we came by."

"If it weren't for that baby crying, we wouldn't have breached the house." Royal pulled out his tablet, "I'm going to take some photos and catalogue these suitcases. You okay on your own?"

"Yup."

"Be careful," Royal said without looking up.

Peter went back downstairs and into the kitchen. He stepped around the broken vase, "Kitchen's clear!"

Half eaten chicken salad sandwiches lay on the counter and the milk had been left out. To his right, the basement door was closed. He stared at it—*Jesus, they're always in the basement. Has no one cleared it yet?* Gun raised, he opened the door. Below him, the stairwell descended into darkness. Peter grabbed his flashlight and settled it under his gun hand.

"Police! We know you're down there!" His voice projected across the room, hanging there in the black space.

Foot after foot, he stepped down towards the cement floor. A creak sounded from his left followed by a soft whimper. He spun around, his light falling over a woman, a teenaged girl, and the baby.

"Ma'am, there's nowhere for you—" something hard slammed into the back of Peter's head. Pain cracked across his skull. He fell down the last three steps, his gun clattering to the ground. Head spinning, he blinked back the pain and scrambled to grab the weapon. His attacker kicked it away and pointed a revolver in Peter's face.

"I won't let you take her," dark features stared Peter down. It was the father. His voice was deep with a sharp desperate edge that compounded Peter's dizziness.

Something warm trickled down Peter's neck but he resisted the urge to reach for the back of his head. His heart was pounding. Blood pulsed in his ears. Peter reminded himself to breathe. He needed to remain calm if he was going to get out of here.

Peter eased to his knees, hands up, "We can figure this out."

The father's face was bright red and his arms shook. He paced manically.

Peter's gun lay in the opposite corner from the weeping family, too far for Peter to recover successfully; he was going to have to talk his way out. His opponent stood between him and the stairs—his only exit. He had just failed Policing 101: never let someone get between you and your way out.

"Sir," he kept his arms raised, "I'm going to be straight with you. You're in a lot of trouble here. We know you were planning to defect, and assaulting an Officer on top of that—"

"Tell them we're not here," his voice strained further, hoarseness cutting off the corners of his words. He cleared his throat and motioned to Peter's radio, "Tell them we're not here and leave."

"I can't do that." The baby was wailing now, "They'll hear her anyway."

The mother was crying too and holding her infant tightly, "You can't have my baby!"

Jesus, where is everyone else? Surely we are loud enough to draw attention.

"Against the wall," the father gestured to Peter with his gun.

Back on his feet now, he complied, "What's your plan here? Shoot your way out? You're outgunned."

"Tell them we're not here!" The father's dark eyes were wild.

Where are they? He heard footsteps above.

Peter's mouth was dry, "Your only option is to surrender. Put down the gun and I'll tell them you cooperated. I'll even let the assault slide."

The father clutched his temple and began pacing again, "And then what?"

Peter opened his mouth but no sound came out. He didn't have an answer for him, at least not one he'd want to hear.

Tears brimmed the father's eyes and he settled the gun under his chin. Peter wanted to lunge forward, he wanted to stop him, but he was frozen. He couldn't move.

"Daddy!" The daughter was sobbing, "Don't!"

"Listen to your daughter," finally, words formed. Peter struggled to keep his own voice from straining. "She shouldn't have to see this."

"We're dead anyway," his voice held a tone Peter knew all too well. It was the tone of defeat, the tone used by every suicidal person he'd faced. It was the tone he heard right before they took that final plunge. The father's clenched his jaw so tight, it trembled. He closed his eyes and squeezed back on the trigger.

"Wait! I'll tell them!"

His eyes flew open, his voice raw, "You will?"

"Yes, but you have to lower the gun."

The father's gaze flickered to his family. They stayed silent but Peter felt them willing the gun to be dropped. Arm still shaking, he lowered the weapon. Peter extended an arm to grab it but the father stepped backwards.

Okay, no more games. Peter kept his eyes locked on the father, he reached for his radio and keyed the mic, "Basement."

Bang!

The bullet slammed into Peter's vest, winding him. He toppled onto his right knee and struggled to find his footing. Before he could move, the barrel of the gun settled between his eyes.

Bang!

The mother screamed. The father's body hitched forward and fell into Peter. Pain radiating through his chest, Peter managed to slip out from under him before being pinned to the ground. Royal's gun was still trained on the father. Sweat dripping from his temple and whole body heaving, Peter collected the father's firearm along with his own. He placed two fingers to the father's carotid.

Nothing.

"Peter!" his mother's voice sounded from the top of the stairs. Detective Anne Holloway jumped across the room to be at his side. The rest of their backup filed into the basement, guns at the ready. Anne placed a hand on Peter's shoulder, "Are you alright?"

"I'm fine," he groaned and clutched his chest.

Frowning, she looked over his shoulder, "And him?"

Peter followed her eyes to the gunman and shook his head.

She raised her radio to her mouth, "Dispatch, we need medics to our location."

Harvey assisted Anne with the mother, handcuffing her once Anne had pried the baby from her arms. Beside them, the teenage daughter crumpled to the ground. She yelled out to her father, begging him to wake up. Lamb hauled her back onto her feet. He tried to walk her towards the stairs but her knees buckled. As she screamed for her dead father, Lamb carried her up the stairs, unaffected by her small fists pummeling him.

Peter's face hardened and he tore his gaze from the grieving family. In an attempt to block out their cries he focused on the pain spreading through his body. Royal placed an arm around Peter's torso and helped him up the stairs to the front lawn. Frank followed them all out, requesting a Medical Examiner over the radio.

Shortly after they made it outside, the ambulance arrived. Royal handed Peter off to the medic. She guided him up the ambulance steps and onto the stretcher. He took his uniform shirt off, the pain intensifying as he shrugged off his vest.

The medic pushed her sleek pink safety glasses to the top of her head where they became lost in her light brown curls. She snapped on purple gloves and took Peter's vest from him.

"You're going to need to take your undershirt off too," she smiled and extended a purple hand. "I'm Alex, by the way."

He shook her hand, "I'm Peter."

Removing his shirt was easier said than done; the pain would only allow him to get the fabric up to his shoulder line.

Alex held up a pair of pink scissors, "May I?"

Peter nodded and she cut off his shirt in one quick slice.

"That's gonna be one nasty bruise, Bro," Royal loitered in the doorway, staring at Peter's bare chest. He was smiling but his eyes were dark and wary, they still looked for danger. Peter's veins coursed with adrenaline and by the way Royal's hands were shaking, Peter was sure Royal felt the same. Behind him, curious onlookers huddled at the police line and peered in at them. Alex stiffened, afraid to move under the gaze of the crowd.

She cocked an eyebrow at Royal, "In or out?"

He looked over his shoulder at the every-growing mob then turned to wink at her, "Definitely in."

She rolled her eyes, trying to conceal a smile, and turned to Peter, "I hear your buddy here saved your life."

"I had it under control."

She fingered his ribs, making him cringe.

"Under control!" Royal threw his hands in the air. "Are you kidding me?"

The medic pulled her hair over her shoulder and gave Peter a smirk, "I'm sure you did."

Royal sighed and took a seat, smiling and shaking his head at Peter. He put on a strong face but Peter saw that he was rattled. Royal kept fidgeting with his shirt collar—a sure sign that he was nervous.

The medic placed her hands firmly on either side of Peter's rib cage, "Take a deep breath."

He obeyed. Despite his wincing, she seemed happy with what he could do. Instructing him to breathe normally now, she listened to his lungs with her stethoscope.

"What's the verdict, Doc?" Royal's hands still fidgeted.

Alex held up a large electronic square to Peter's torso and snapped an x-ray, "Well, Peter, nothing appears to be broken. Worst case is you bruised a few ribs. You'll be back to taking bullets in no time." She opened the cupboard above her head and grabbed her drug kit, "In the meantime I am going to give you some Toradol. It's a muscle relaxant."

A quick stick in the arm and a flower print Band-Aid later, Alex sent him on his way.

Once out of the ambulance, Royal shoved Peter, "Dude, what the hell?"

Winded from the push, Peter struggled to catch his breath, "What? You're the one who's manhandling a gunshot victim."

"I can think of someone who could use a good manhandling," he winked and nodded back at the ambulance. His demeanor had changed; his shoulders were relaxed and grin had broken across his face.

"The medic? Oh, come on," Peter kept walking.

"You mean *Alex*." Royal rocked back on his heels, "Why didn't you ask for her number! She was totally into you."

"Into me? Looked more like she was into you. Besides, you know how I feel about dating."

Royal smirked, "No one said anything about dating."

Peter glowered at him.

"Hey, you wanna grab a beer tonight?"

"I'm having dinner with my parents," Peter said. Seeing Royal's smile falter, Peter quickly backpedaled, "But I'll let you know once we're finished and maybe we could meet up then?"

"Sure, man."

"Hey, Royal? You really did save my ass back there."

Beaming, he went to clap a hand on Peter's shoulder but stopped himself, "I love you too, Bro."

They headed back towards their cruiser. Peter watched Harvey and Lamb stuff the family into the back of another squad car. Forensics wheeled the bagged and tagged suitcases towards their van while Peter's mother handed the baby off to a newly arrived social worker. To his parents, this was a victory; they had done their job, and they had done it well. But what Peter saw was a family forever ripped apart. He saw a family desperate to flee when they had no other choice. If they had been caught trying to defect, they would have faced the ultimate price—a price worse than this. But what if they had gotten away with it?

⚏

"That was the stupidest thing you have ever done," Peter's father glared at him from across the table. "Going down there alone? What were you thinking?"

The lecture had been going on for about twenty minutes. *Sure, it was stupid. Sure, I could have died.* To Peter there was a more pressing issue at hand.

He pushed his plate away, "What about that family? What happens to them?"

"Peter..." Anne's eyes saddened but her tone held irritation, "You know this."

"So, we kill the father, the mother is incarcerated, and her children are put into foster care, never to see her again?"

"It's better than the alternative. If they *had* defected and had been caught, we would have had to kill all of them."

"...all?" *Even the baby?* Peter hadn't thought that far.

"Yes. It's the law. Defecting has severe consequences for a reason, we want to discourage it in any way that we can. A married couple is only allowed one child. It's a system that works."

"Works?" his voice strained.

"Yes, works," she sighed. "Overpopulation is a serious issue. The world has too many people and not enough resources. Economies have collapsed, wars have broken out. The Earth was dying and something needed to be done. That's why we have the Act. Thankfully the worst of it was over before our time, but it's still a danger. We are still feeling the repercussions—the international ban on fishing, most of the forests being off limits. We're lucky that we don't have that in Cedar Valley."

"I honestly don't see how it could be worse than this," Peter grumbled.

"For God's sake, Peter, don't be so naive," his father cut at his chicken. "It's your job to enforce the Act. You of all people should see why it's so important."

The Procreation Act, commonly known as 'The Act' had been drilled into Peter's head during school and even more so in the Academy. It dictates the rules surrounding population control:

A) If a couple chooses to conceive, upon their child turning twenty-five years of age, their child must sacrifice them in a ceremony a.k.a the Life Ceremony.
B) Parents may only have one child.

C) It is encouraged for children to follow their parent's career path to minimize employment gaps.

D) A couple may waive their right to bear children however there is a minimum birth rate requirement per geographical region.

E) In the event that the minimum birth rate levels are not met, individuals of prime childbearing age are conscripted for non-voluntary conception. These individuals are allotted one year to conceive naturally and if unsuccessful, In Vitro Fertilization will be implemented. If still unsuccessful, the couple is passed over.

Peter shook his head.

It was Frank's turn to sigh, "No one is exempt, not even council members. If a couple wants a child, they know what they're signing up for."

Peter's stomach turned. Since his twenty-fourth birthday last month, he'd been plagued with nightmares of killing his parents, "Why did you have me? Why would you do that when it's literally a death sentence?"

"Son," Frank chewed on a piece of chicken. "We wouldn't trade having you for another hundred years on this planet."

Anne reached over and grabbed their hands, nodding, "We're so proud of you, Peter. Especially with your choice to join the police force. I know it can be trying at times but you're doing a great job."

Peter pulled away, "We should leave. Defect."

Frank nearly choked.

"Honey," Anne's eyes darkened. "Did you not hear me before? If they caught us, they'd kill us."

Peter was on his feet now, "And you expect *me* to kill you?"

She ignored his question, "It's not worth the risk."

Not worth it? "How can you even say that?"

Frank was livid, "Peter, it's not your job to agree with the law but it sure as hell is your job to uphold it."

Chest aching and tears stinging his eyes, Peter hobbled towards the front door.

"Peter, wait!" His mother called but he was already outside.

He slammed the door, immediately regretting it despite how angry he felt. He got in his car and drove home.

Peter had expected at least three missed calls from his mother. He checked his phone as he pulled into his lot—only one text message.

From Mom:

This is going to be a hard year for all of us. Love you, we'll talk when you're ready.

'Hard' didn't begin to describe it. That cold chill had made its way back to Peter's spine. Pocketing his cell, he forced all thoughts of death to the back of his mind and eased himself and his bruised ribs towards the door.

Out of all the places the government could have allotted him, this one exceeded all expectations. They had given him a few choices but from the moment he saw it, he knew this was the one. Beautifully landscaped, his third floor condo overlooked a park with a man-made lake. Most mornings he drank his coffee on his balcony and imagined he was alone. He envisioned being in the middle of nowhere, not in the centre of a big city. Calling Cedar Valley a 'big city' may have been reaching but it was certainly too big for him. He imagined the buildings falling away to be replaced by trees and mountains. That's what he wanted more than anything—just him, his parents, and freedom.

Peter locked his door, walked to his kitchen, and texted Royal.

Hey man, I'm just going to stay in tonight. Next time?

The Toradol hadn't touched him; each inhale caused his chest to burn. Peter reached into his refrigerator for a beer but blocking his six-pack was a fresh lasagna. He pushed it aside causing a sticky note reading, 'Love, Mom' to float to the floor. A new pang of guilt hit his chest. *She must have snuck it in here earlier today.*

Peter grabbed a bottle, popped the cap, and took a long drink. Reality and pain dulled a little more with each gulp. He didn't go to bed until he'd downed the whole pack.

THREE

Not five minutes into their patrol, the first call was broadcast over the radio. The Dispatcher's voice was robotic, words clearly annunciated and flat.

"Attention all units, assault in progress. Location north-west corner of Russell and Westin."

Peter reached for the dash radio to respond but Royal slapped his hand away.

"Nope," he said.

Peter surreptitiously rubbed the spot Royal had hit, "Am I missing something here? Shouldn't we be—"

"Nope."

"But what if—"

Royal braked hard at a red light. Harder than necessary. "There is no way we're going to that shit hole after yesterday. You know it's just two prostitutes fighting over their corner."

Peter's chest burned where it had strained against the seat belt. It was now tightly locked across his sternum. The goose egg on top of his head seemed to engorge, painfully. This time he wasn't shy to show his discomfort. "Alright," he said through gritted teeth. "We won't take it but under the condition that you stop beating the crap out of me."

The light turned green and Royal lifted his sunglasses to wink at Peter, "You got it." One eye on the road he hit the gas, sending Peter's sore crown into the headrest.

"Dick," Peter groaned. "I have a gun, you know."

Royal laughed, "I think I'll take my chances." He secured his sunglasses and continued to speed towards City Centre.

Peter unbuckled and loosened the strap. The moment he could breathe easily, he laughed too.

The streets were thick with morning commuters stuck on their way to their soul sucking nine-to-five prisons. Peter and Royal were trapped in the traffic too, but Peter felt free and light when he thought about his comparably reasonable hours. He'd rather die than only get two days off a week. *How the hell do they do it?*

The sun was coming up over the hills, hitting them right in the eyes. Peter flipped the visor down to no relief—the sunglasses he usually kept there were missing, they were likely sitting useless on his kitchen counter.

They crept around a turn in the road and they were mercifully cast back into the shadows of the buildings. The golden light bathed the unsheltered areas of the streets, crawling its way into tree branches and alleyways. Far ahead, the Temple's grand face was illuminated, its light stone exterior warmed by the sunlight. Peter hardly paid the Temple any mind but he did like to admire how it looked nestled up in the hills. Nearly every city had one, however not all were as aesthetically pleasing as the one in Cedar Valley. Most were located in downtown high-rises or converted condo buildings.

Despite the name, the Temples were not places of worship nor did they have any real religious affiliation; they were established as a place of healing and wellness—like rehab on crack, except free.

When the Act was put in place, a widespread need for mental health services surfaced. Some people still turned towards the church for support but Christianity had dwindled. As the population grew in places like India and China, Hinduism and Buddhism took the forefront as millions immigrated to North America. Yoga became popular and instructors were in high demand, on the same level as psychiatrists, both of which the Temples were swimming with. Many of them resided at the Temple along with their governing body known, archaically, as the 'Elders'. The Elders were responsible for the everyday operations like scheduling and staffing. Some of them still taught higher level classes or supplied more specific forms of therapy for the truly afflicted.

Warm and fuzzy psychobabble wasn't for everyone—Peter included. He'd like to say he gave it a try but that wasn't exactly true. The last time Peter was at the Temple was when he was thirteen. His parents enrolled him—against his will—in some anger management yoga bullshit. He'd been a rebellious teenager and trying to control him never worked well. They themselves hadn't been Temple-goers but there had come a time when police-based disciplinary techniques weren't working anymore and his parents thought meditation might help. Unfortunately, Peter never bought into *mindfulness* and *tranquility* like they had hoped. He continuously skipped his classes and once his mom and dad found out, they didn't force the yoga anymore. Eventually, after a few more torturous years, Peter calmed down on his own. Those memories in particular now gave Peter a jolt of guilt in his gut, they holed themselves in there like a rotten seed he couldn't dig out. He had been absolutely hellish to his parents, angry outbursts and malicious verbal abuse galore. He wished he could blame ignorant youth for those hateful years but that only made him feel worse. He deserved the remorse his conscience dealt him. Faced with their inevitable deaths, he would do anything to take back how he'd treated them.

The sunlit morning helped to force the past out of Peter's mind and he could look up into the hills, which were thick with cedars, and appreciate the

Temple's scenery. Like his backyard lake, the views provided a sense of isolation. With his abhorrent youth far behind, he could respect that the Temple was not a place of discipline but a place of peace and peace was something that Peter could get on board with.

Traffic inched forward, leaving space for their cruiser to pull up but Royal didn't advance. Peter gave him a moment to snap into motion but his focus was set out of the driver's side window. Peter gestured stiffly towards the windshield, "Uh, hello?"

Royal ignored him and rolled down the window. He was staring into the side mirror, at what Peter couldn't see.

"Royal," Peter's voice sharper. "Dud—" *Oh.*

A fluffy white dog came into view, its bright blue leash was attached to a long-legged blonde. Her curls reached the hem of her mid-thigh sundress and her skin was bronzed despite it only being mid-spring. Right when she was in line with the cruiser, Royal flicked on the siren then cut it short. She jumped and spun, eyes wide like she was worried that she was in trouble.

He leaned out the window, crooked grin plastered on his face, "Have yourself a good day there, miss."

Her stunned features burned her cheeks red. Her dog yanked her backwards, awkwardly forcing her away. "You too," she said through messed up hair that had fused with her lip gloss.

Royal winked at her and flicked the siren again, once, twice, then rejoined traffic. Peter rolled his eyes heavily but kept his mouth shut, glad to be on their way.

City Centre was focused around City Hall, an old building that had been built in the middle of the hills long before Cedar Valley came to be. Cedar Valley was a relatively new city, constructed when the rest could no longer hold any more people. City Hall had once been a bathhouse, nothing more than a secluded popular tourist destination. Now, restored and updated, its purpose was twofold. The newer expansion was home to the City Council. By day they saw to municipal needs and mayoral duties, but on many dark evenings, they oversaw the Life Ceremonies. Much of the bathhouses were kept intact and even some of the underground pools were used in the Ceremonies—used to wash the blood off after the visit to the slaughter house.

Cedar Valley beheads its parents. *Beheads.* Peter never could imagine that sword in his hands, his parents surrendering to death. His neck tensed at the thought, restricting his breath. A classmate had once whispered to Peter, "They can stay conscious afterwards, up to eight seconds." Those words had imprinted on his gut, making him sick nightly and plaguing his nightmares with scenes of his parents' heads staring at him with swollen eyes and gaping mouths that emitted wails of sorrow.

Decapitation was not what the Act had intended as a primary method but rather lethal injection. It worked for a time, until supplies ran out. Non-essential pharmaceutical production was halted and there was a shift in how things were done. Some places postponed Life Ceremonies until lethal injection could be available again, while others resorted to older methods. Worldwide, governments didn't interfere with any new means as long as the laws of The Act were upheld. Cedar Valley was formed right around the same time as the medical shortages and most of its original inhabitants were all members of a radical 'Save the Earth!' group. It was their own leader who suggested the beheading and he himself would be the first victim. The rest of Cedar Valley followed suit, the Ceremony becoming some sick rite of passage and despite lethal injection now being readily available, they never changed their ways.

The radio went live again with the robot Dispatcher's voice:

"Second broadcast for assault in progress. North-west corner of Russell and Westin. Any available unit required to respond."

"Royal, we really should—"
"Sir!" Royal's head was out of his window again, this time calling out to a sharply dressed man, suit, tie, briefcase—the whole shebang. Royal pulled their cruiser off to the right hand curb and swiftly left the vehicle.

"What the..." Peter shook his head, unbuckled, and followed his partner. A block ahead, Royal bent down, picked up a wallet, and continued to charge towards the man, all the while calling out to him. By the grace of some higher power, the man stopped and turned around before Royal had a chance to crash right into him.

"Sir! You dropped your wallet."

The man's face resembled the startled blonde's then melted into sheer relief, "Thank you so much, Officer."

"Have a great day now."

The man continued on his way and Royal slung an arm around Peter's shoulders as they walked back to the cruiser, "See, Peter? We're very busy. Good deeds are just waiting for us to seize them up! There are no good deeds down on Westin and I really can't let anything ruin my cheerful mood today."

"That's really too bad, Officer O'Leary."

Royal jumped back from Peter, eyes wide, "No!" He had accidentally keyed open Peter's mic when he'd put his arm around him. Now the whole squad had heard his disdain for Westin Avenue, including the Sergeant who was speaking over the radio:

"Dispatch, Charlie-One will be responding to the assault."

"Copy that," came the robotic voice.

Royal groaned and knocked his head back. He shuffled his way back into the driver's seat and grabbed the dash radio, "Ten-four, Charlie-One responding to Russell and Westin." He rested his head against the steering wheel, sighed audibly, and blindly flipped the siren on.

Westin Avenue was located in the far east of Cedar Valley, past an industrial sector where motels, pawnshops, and dollars stores dotted the pot holed street. Run down condos with peeling paint and broken windows lay just behind the main drag. Russell Way was right in the core. They passed a park that was nothing more than a dumping ground for unwanted shopping cart trash and meeting spots for hookers and dealers. Peter did his best to ignore all the sleeping bums and junkies outside his window.

"You can almost smell the misery," Royal's lips were pulled tight.

"I think that's just the sewers." For no reason in particular, Peter imagined that here the sewers were left grossly unmaintained. He pictured them overflowing at times of heavy rain and poisoning the streets. They never had, but if that should happen anywhere, it would be here.

"Shit, here we go."

Two prostitutes were rolling around on the sidewalk, one in a lime green dress and another with grown out purple hair. Royal brought the car closer and spoke through the external microphone, "Ladies, break it up."

They continued wrestling, the purple haired one dodged a bite to the arm and managed to secure herself on top of the other girl. Lime Green grappled at Purple's clothes. She pulled so fiercely that Purple's tank top ripped, exposing one of her breasts. Purple did nothing to cover herself but retaliated by landing a solid slap across Lime Green's face. Ear piercing shrieks ensued. Lime Green grabbed her discarded purse and slid it closer. She rummaged around and produced an eyelash curler.

Royal's scoff was amplified to the outside, "What are you going to do? Curl her to death?" his projected voice did nothing to prevent her from jamming the curler into Purple's side. "Oh, come on!"

Royal and Peter rushed over to them. Royal grabbed Purple around the waist to lift her backwards while Peter grabbed the curler out of Lime Green's hand. Purple was kicking and screaming in Royal's grasp. "Cut it out! Jesus."

Peter ordered Lime Green to roll onto her stomach. He reached back to grab his cuffs but she had something new in her hand. "Don't!" Peter turned away just in time to avoid the brunt of the pepper spray but Royal and Purple weren't so lucky. If Peter thought their screeches were bad a moment ago, they were nothing to how shrill they were now. He placed his knee against Lime Green's back and applied enough pressure to keep her on the ground. She tried to reach her hand back and aim her pepper spray at Peter but he snatched it from her grip.

"Get off of me!" she struggled under Peter's weight. He brought her hands behind her and cuffed her wrists together. "This ain't got nothin' to do with you, Pig!"

Peter hoisted her to her feet and was yanked forward and as she lunged herself in Purple's direction. Peter was quick to redirect her, using her own momentum to stuff her into the backseat of the cruiser.

The rest of the scene was a mess. Royal handcuffed Purple but was barely hanging on to her. Peter expected her to run but she slumped out of Royal's weak grasp and onto the cement. Hands unavailable, she attempted to rub her burning eyes on her shoulder which only made it worse. Sobs shuddered through her chest and she repeatedly cried out, 'You bitch!' between ragged breaths in the direction of the cruiser.

Peter opened the trunk and fished out two eyes flush bottles from the first aid kit. He radioed for another squad car to come and collect Purple. Royal grabbed one of the bottles and poured it liberally over his face, muttering, "I told you, I fucking told you," to no one in particular. Peter then helped Purple's tank top back over her exposed breast. He tilted her chin up and rinsed her fiery puffy eyes while snot and tears dripped on her shirt.

Peter had to drive back to the precinct. By the end of the ride, Royal had used three flush bottles and a squeeze pack of lubricating eye drops, all the while not saying a word to Peter. After carting their hooker into booking, Peter offered to take care of their paperwork but received no more than a grunt from Royal. His eyes would have recovered by now so Peter knew he just needed time to cool off; he wasn't lying when he said Westin would dampen his mood—it had made him downright sour.

Peter finished up his report and was hankering for a drink. He figured sharing that rain checked beer would be a good way to smooth things over with Royal. He looked for his partner to invite out but he had already disappeared from the station. Feeling annoyed, Peter decided to grab a six pack on his way home to keep him company.

FOUR

Growing up, my mother used to tell me, 'Ari, you are the Sun, and beneath you is only sky'. She was right. I've never felt higher that I do right now. I've lived at the Temple my whole life and now, standing in the gardens overlooking the city, I know. I am the Sun.

Everything here is made of stone; the pillars, the arches, every wall. Last night I was awarded my parents' room and it is magnificent. I was also presented with a midnight blue robe—the colour donned by those who have completed their Life Ceremony; the next step through transformation. Now everyone knows. I am Holy.

To my knowledge, no one else has experienced this elation after the Ceremony. If they had, it would obvious: every twenty-five year old would be singing from the rooftops and basking in their new found energy. From this I have concluded that I am special; I am the only one that's worthy and that means I have a duty. I mustn't let this power go to waste.

I am making my way to class when I see her. Selene. Dark skinned, raven haired, gorgeous Selene. She's practicing inversions in a sunken grove. I stand behind a large cedar—I don't want to disturb her. She is so small, but so strong. In a perfect handstand, she lowers herself down to her forearms—each muscle working in sync yet serving its distinct purpose. Selene bends her legs backwards into the most controlled scorpion pose I have ever seen. She reminds me of my mother. I looked it up in the Temple library: the name 'Selene' means 'Moon'. If I am the Sun, she most certainly is my Moon.

"Ari?"

I turn and am greeted by one of the Elders.

He smiles at me, "Congratulations on your Life Ceremony."

I dip my head and thank him.

"Your parents were important members here and will be dearly missed. However, I have no doubt you'll do a fine job in their stead."

"Thank you," I make eye contact. That means something coming from an Elder.

"Are you coming to class?"

"Yes, are you teaching?"

He nods, "I'll see you in there."

He leaves and I return to studying Selene. She has brought her toes to the crown of her head. Any other person would feel envious of her ability but I only feel deep admiration. Her eyes are closed, her breath is even. She seamlessly shifts her legs into charging scorpion—one forward and one back. My god. I tear myself away from her; if I don't leave now I won't make it to class.

There is only ten of us in this class, which I like—it's more intimate. Large classes feel so cramped and impersonal. To really connect to the Earth, I need my space. I place my mat in the centre of the room directly in front of the mirrored wall, the ultimate spot. I join the others in *savasana*; corpse pose. I have always found it a strange name, 'corpse pose'; yoga is about life, about connecting to the Earth and drawing energy from it—not death. The thermostat is set to forty degrees, making me sweat even while lying still. My legs spill off the sides of my mat and my palms face the sky. I wish Selene were in this class. I wish she were on the mat beside me, stretching her hand towards mine.

CEDAR VALLEY

I need to focus. I clear my mind of all thoughts of her.
The humid air provides restriction to my breath, a
sensation I adore and a challenge I yearn for.

The Elder from before enters the room. Wrapped in his
deep green robe, he welcomes us. As he leads us
through our practice, I feel stronger. My parents'
lifeblood is inside of me, powering me through my
poses. Not once did I fall out of crow pose or experience
pain in my feet. I am strong. I breathed death into
them, and they breathed life into me. I am new.

Dripping in sweat we all meet back in *savasana*. My
hands rest on my belly, my breath easy.

"Thank you for sharing your practice today. May you
take this peace and love into the world. Namaste."

On his way out, the Elder crouches next to me,
"Beautiful practice today."

He could see it too. He could see how strong I've
become. I will take this peace and love with me for it is
all I feel. I want more. I take it with me on my way to
my parents' room—a room I graciously accept as mine.
I pause in the gardens where I overlook the city. I am
disappointed that Selene is nowhere to be seen but I
won't let it dishearten me. Something so small will not
take away from how alive I feel. I've never felt so
energized in my life.

My new room is down a long stone hallway that borders the back of the Temple. My door is the first one in and I cannot wait to get inside. I slide my new key in the lock, swing the door inward, and am instantly comforted by the familiarity of this place. The main room is wide and decorated simply. Walls curve up to high ceilings, smooth grey stone consistent throughout. Directly across from me is the balcony which is completely open to the outdoors—the perfect place for meditation. The balcony overlooks a grand valley, lush with cedars. However, the balcony is only a close second to my favourite feature—the bath: a sunken rectangular pool in the middle of the room, each side faceted with a waterfall style tap. It is the epitome of serenity. I've always loved this room and now it is mine. I have received what I deserve.

I sit down on the edge of the bath, legs dangling. I close my eyes and imagine my parents here with me and for the first time, I miss them. They would be proud of me. My heart feels heavy and that heaviness spreads up into my head and down my arms. It's like their lifeblood is draining from me. No, that can't be right, can it? I killed them only yesterday. I breathed death into them and they breathed life into me. I am new. At least, I was.

I don't know why this is happening but I do know that I don't want to feel like this. My skin is crawling and itchy, I feel as if I am covered in mud. I have never felt this disgusting before. Is this what depression feels like? Sadness is foreign to me; I've never had a reason for it. It's getting worse by the minute. It feels like the walls are closing in and the ceiling is threatening to fall on me. The drastic change in my mood is making me nauseas. I have to do something, but what?

I close my eyes and I see my parents kneeling before me. The blade is in my hands. I am standing above them, lifting the sword over my head. My muscles fill with power. I swing down, their heads roll, and I relax. My heart lifts. I open my eyes and breathe in.

But then the memory vanishes. My chest seizes. I gasp for air.

There's a knock at the door. I am so heavy I can barely drag myself to open it. It's one of the young women who reside here. She wants to exchange my towels for clean ones. Too slowly, I retrieve mine from the washroom and hand them to her. Can she sense my weakness? The lifeblood is leaching from my pores making my heart ache. She's leaving. My body feels like lead and my skeleton begs to collapse to the floor. With her back to me, she loads her cart and pushes it out the door. I ask her to come back. Before she can fully turn, I close the space between us and her face collides with my hand. I slam her head against the stone wall. She slumps into a pile and I drag her body to the edge of the pool. The back of her head gapes open, blood oozes out. Dare I? I smear my hand along the wound, staining it red. I touch it to my face and my cheek melts into my palm. I grab a knife from my bedroom and quickly return to her. Slipping into the bath, I crouch below her. I torque her head to one side, exposing her pulsing carotid—she's so malleable. The edge of the blade is against her flesh and I slice her open, sending her eyes open too, wide. Everything opens wide. A small gasp and then a waterfall of red showers me. It gets in my mouth which is parted in a smile. Her eyes fade and my pulse quickens. This is it! I feel better already. I wait until the bleeding slows to a drip and I lay down in the pool. I breathed death into her and she breathed life into me. I am filled with peace and love. Who knew so much fit inside that tiny little body?

FIVE

Peter wasn't sure which hurt more, his pounding head or his bruised chest. The regret of having six beer before bed settled into his stomach as a twist of nausea. He knew he should stop drinking before day shifts but somehow, he never remembered the consequences. Nearly late for work, he ambled into the change room and made a beeline for his locker. Royal looked up from tying his boots but quickly averted his gaze, apparently still upset about their last shift. Before Peter could reach his locker, another officer clipped his shoulder. Sharp pain radiated from his sternum to his back.

"Watch it," Peter snapped.

The officer turned to face him, his chest puffed, "Excuse me?"

Peter mirrored his body language, "Did I stutter?"

Royal flanked Peter. *Friends again, are we?* The rest of the half-dressed platoon was on their feet. Peter's opposition towered over him, jaw jutting forward. His vest read, 'Officer Banks'. Peter had never seen him before and assumed he was one of the new transfers.

Banks nearly spat, "I don't let Catalysts speak to me like that."

"What the fuck did you just say to him?" Royal lunged forward. Peter tried to hold him back but his bruised ribs inhibited his reach. Though Royal was smaller than most of their coworkers, he was equally as fit as he was feisty. He knocked Banks to the ground and clambered on top of him. He was reeling back to throw a punch when Sergeant Pearl stepped into the room.

Everyone froze. The Sergeant didn't say a word, he just stared into Royal's soul. He climbed off of Banks and reversed into the lockers, hitting them with such force a pair of sneakers fell from the top narrowly missing another officer. Pearl's gaze never breaking, he stepped out. The whole room remained silent as they finished gearing up for the shift.

Peter placed a hand on Royal's shoulder, "Thanks, man."

"Forget that asshole," he said as he brushed dust from his knees, avoiding eye contact with Peter, undoubtedly embarrassed about his passive aggressive behaviour yesterday. Peter threw him a smirk to let him know that everything was forgiven. *No prostitute could ever come between us.*

They headed in for parade, aiming for seats as far from Banks as possible—he was seated next to another unfamiliar officer, this one beefy with dark spiky hair. As Peter passed them, Banks glared and tilted his head towards Spiky Hair. The two of them shared smirks directed at Peter and Royal.

Pearl assumed his position at the front podium, "We have a possible missing persons case."

Peter sat up straight. The screen behind The Sergeant lit up, displaying a picture of a smiling woman with blonde curls that framed her face. She reminded Peter of the medic who had helped him.

"This is eighteen year old Melissa Grant. She was last seen at the Temple where she lives and works." His eyes tore into Royal, "O'Leary, Holloway, Alvarez, and Banks, head to the Temple and see what you can find out."

Royal groaned and leant into Peter, "He's sending us to the Zen Den to talk about our problems."

Peter kicked him while stifling a laugh.

"Something funny about a missing woman, Officers?"

They stammered a string of 'No, sir's and 'Sorry, sir's.

"Good," his eyes still on Royal. "You'll report back to Detectives Frank and Anne Holloway. I want the rest of you on the streets. You're dismissed."

The platoon dispersed. Peter received another smug look from Banks as he and his beefy partner,

Alvarez, walked by them in the parking lot. Peter shook his head and slid into the driver's seat of his squad car.

"You okay to drive?" Royal shuffled in beside him, "You're lookin' a bit rough there."

"I'm fine."

"Okay, well you'd better find us some coffee on our way out to the Temple. Serg probably tasked you to this because he knew no one would ever shoot you at the Zen Den."

"Yes, coffee," Peter's head still throbbed. He ignored Royal's smartass comment and pulled out of the lot, "Isn't the Temple a strange place for someone to go missing?"

"Hey, man, anything is possible but it's definitely the first case I've ever worked out there."

"Me too."

They pulled off the main road and into a parking lot. Royal's face lit up when he realized Peter had chosen his favourite coffeehouse. The coffee was okay but Peter knew it was the baristas that Royal came for. Peter decided to stay in the car. Through the glass, he watched Royal program his number into a brunette's phone. Peter pulled out his tablet and opened up the Melissa Grant file. His parents had added some more info, limited at this time, but one line stood out:

Family status: Orphaned

His chest ached, and not from his bruise. That poor girl. He wondered what had happened to her parents. Time with parents was so short—to have them ripped away even earlier... Peter shuddered.

A to-go cup was thrust in his face. He graciously accepted it.

"Hey, Royal?"

"Yeah, bud?" Royal took a long drink of steaming coffee, unflinching despite the heat.

Peter looked down, "What do you think Banks meant by calling me a Catalyst?"

"Dude, he was just trying to rile you up."

"But that would mean—"

"It means nothing. Let's go."

Royal was probably right but Peter couldn't shake the pit in his stomach. Chalking it up to his hangover, he started back down the road.

The drive to the Temple was a pleasant one; the city fell away and tall cedars sprang up around them. Peter rolled down his window and breathed in the clean, fresh air. His head felt clear. He knew then that they would find this woman.

The gardens were better than Peter remembered. Flowers in a million colours bordered every path and tall stone pillars lined the main walkway. The cedars extended up from the road, filling the land. It was windier up here on the mountain, if you could call it that, but the breeze was warm and carried the smell of the roses and lavender. He thought about what his mother had said about some forests being off limits to the public. Being up here amongst the trees made him rethink his opinion; they *were* lucky.

Crushed shale crunched beneath their boots as they walked towards the arched entrance way. A man who looked to be in his sixties met the four of them; he was balding, the remainder of his short hair formed a crescent on his scalp. His slender frame was draped with a cedar green robe and his feet were wrapped in leather sandals.

"Welcome to the Temple, we are thankful that you are here," he didn't offer his hand but rather kept one palm cupped over a fist held tightly below his sternum. "I am Michael, an Elder here at the Temple."

Banks pressed to the front, "Sir, I am officer Banks. Can you tell us about Miss Grant?"

Peter caught Royal rolling his eyes.

"Melissa lost her parents last year in a dreadful car accident. She was in the back seat. Poor dear saw the whole thing. She came to live here after that."

Peter's stomach churned, "Sir, I am Officer Holloway and this is my partner, Officer O'Leary. What is her role here?"

"Melissa, along with many like her, work on upkeep. Cleaning, gardening, and the like."

"So," Alvarez's voice was sharp. "Her parents die and you turn her into a maid?"

Peter twitched but Michael's face remained unmoved, "She chose her own path. She likes the work."

Alvarez's tone didn't change, "Who reported her missing?"

"I did, after her friend came to me."

Royal's eyebrows raised, "May we speak to this friend?"

Michael gestured for them to follow him, "She's in Melissa's room."

Melissa Grant's bedroom was small, grouped together with the others, dormitory style. A young mousy woman with chestnut hair sat on Melissa's bed. When she saw them, she jolted upright and sprung to her feet.

Michael stepped to the side, "This is Sarah."

"Thank you, we'll take it from here." Peter shook his hand and let him leave.

Royal placed a hand on the woman's shoulder and sat her back on the bed, "Sarah, what makes you think that Melissa is missing?"

"We had plans after work last night and she never showed. I went looking for her and I couldn't find her anywhere. I thought maybe she made plans with someone else and forgot about me so I went to sleep—"

"Does Melissa have many friends?" Royal crouched down beside her.

"Well, no—I mean she's pretty shy," her eyes welled. "Oh god, I'm her best friend, I should have told Michael sooner."

"Hey, hey, hey," Royal gave her his best puppy stare. "You did everything right."

"She's never disappeared like this before," her tears spilled over. "What if something's happened to her?"

"Is there anywhere she would go? Anyone she could be with?"

Sarah shook her head.

Peter cleared his throat, "We're going to figure this out. What kind of work was she doing yesterday?"

"She was delivering fresh towels to all the rooms."

"Where would the last room on her list be?"

Michael reappeared in the doorway, "That would be the North Wing. I'll take you."

Royal offered to stay with Sarah and look around Melissa's room. Banks and Alvarez joined Peter in following Michael. Peter kept a few steps behind, not trusting his back turned to those two. Michael led them across a stone terrace with arched walls that opened up to look over the valley. Warm air teased the back of Peter's neck.

At the end of the terrace, the walls closed up to create a dark hallway. Candles lined the south wall and illuminated the doorways on the opposite side. Peter peered down the hall, the end was so far he couldn't see it.

"Alright boys," Alvarez wandered ahead and called back over his shoulder. "Let's get canvassing. Banks and I will start on the far end. Holloway, why don't you start here?"

"Yeah."

Alvarez's tone made Peter feel like he'd been handed the short straw despite their workload being identical. He watched them go and waited until their footsteps had faded before approaching the first door. He had raised his hand to knock when his phone beeped. It was a message from Royal:

Found something. Get your ass back here and let those punks do the footwork.

Gladly.

Royal met him outside of Melissa's room, "Where's Sarah?"

"She's still in there," he hiked a thumb towards the closed bedroom door. "Look at this. The last few pages."

Royal thrust a black journal into Peter's hands. He fingered through the indicated section, his brow creasing. Peter looked to Royal who shook his head and sighed.

"After you," Royal said, gesturing to the door.

Peter shoved the door open and stared down at Sarah. Her doe-eyes wide with confusion. He dumped the journal into her lap.

"Melissa has a boyfriend?"

Sarah looked from the pages to Peter, eyes wide, "What? No."

"I thought you were her 'best friend'?" Royal crossed his arms.

"I am! She never mentioned any guy to me."

"Look at what she wrote. She never mentions him by name but it's *very* descriptive."

Sarah cast the journal away, "I don't know who it is!"

Peter exchanged a look with Royal and stepped closer to her, "Sarah, you may think you're protecting Melissa but this could be what helps us find her. We need to know."

Sarah's eyes welled again, "Okay! Okay. I don't know who it is exactly, she never told me which one, but it's one of the Teachers."

"*Teacher*s?" Royal's voice held a hint of cynicism. Peter knew what Royal was insinuating but Sarah didn't seem to catch on.

"Yeah," she dabbed her cheeks with tissue. "I'm sure you've seen them, they all wear the burgundy robes."

Royal rolled his eyes and tried a firmer tone, "What exactly do they teach?"

"Most of the meditation and yoga classes."

"Where can we find them?"

Sarah looked up at them, "The North Wing."

Peter cocked an eyebrow, "I'll go."

Walking briskly, Peter pulled out his radio and keyed the mic, "Alvarez? It's Holloway."

"Go ahead."

"Looks like Miss Grant was romantically involved with one of the Teachers who live in that wing you're in."

"Got it."

Peter reached the first door again and knocked. A man around Peter's age answered. He had olive skin, a clean shaven head, and round yet masculine features. He was attractive—just the sort of guy an eighteen year old girl would go for. His green eyes softened when he saw Peter, and he extended a hand.

"Hello, I am Officer Holloway," Peter shook the man's hand. He had a firm grip, something that Peter always believed leant to the character of a person. A weak handshake always seemed insincere and noncommittal. Besides, grabbing a limp hand always reminded Peter of soggy bread.

"I'm Arun," he smiled. "Would you like to come in?"

"Thank you."

Arun led Peter to a gorgeous open balcony where its stone floor dropped off into a spectacular view of the valley. There was nothing but trees and hills as far as the eye could see. Peter could picture himself way out there, calm, quiet, safe. He noted a magnificent pool in the middle of the room. Perhaps the Temple wasn't an awful place after all.

"Sir, we're investigating the disappearance of a young woman who resides here, Melissa Grant." Peter handed him a picture of her, "Do you know her?"

Arun stared at the photo, "No, I am afraid not."

"She was reportedly changing the towels along this wing when she went missing last night."

"No one came by for mine. You can check if you'd like."

Peter nodded and poked his head into the bathroom, the racks were bare and the hamper was full of used towels.

"There's evidence that she was involved with one of the Teachers here, so I'll need you to be honest with me. If you're protecting yourself, sir—"

"Oh, I'm not a Teacher. I only moved into this room last night. It belonged to my parents."

Peter's nausea returned. His eyes fell to Arun's robe—it was dark blue. *How did I miss that*? Long ago, when he was at the Temple, he had asked his parents about the few wearing that same blue robe. They told him they were people who had recently participated in the Life Ceremony and had yet to assume their late parents role here. It was a symbol of transition.

"Oh, my mistake, I—"

"May I see that photo again, Officer Holloway?" Peter handed it back to him. "Now that you mention it, I think I've seen that young lady coming out of my neighbours room. And not during work hours."

"Thank you, Arun," Peter walked back to the door. "You've been very helpful."

"Please, call me Ari."

The neighbour's door was already open. Inside, Alvarez stood over a towel cart and was scanning it for prints. Banks was questioning a male in his thirties. However, 'questioning' was a loose term.

"So, is taking advantage of grieving teenagers your regular M.O.?"

The Teacher looked only mildly annoyed, "She's eighteen."

"Are you sure that's young enough for you?"

"What are you implying?"

"Oh, sit down," Banks pushed him down by his shoulder.

The scanner beeped and Alvarez turned the screen towards Peter, then towards Banks. The fingerprints were Melissa's.

"Okay, so let me get this right, *Teacher*," Banks now gripped the suspect's robe. "Melissa comes here during her rounds, she doesn't want to do what you want her to so you kill her."

"What!" The teacher's mouth gaped. "You think she's dead? I didn't even know she was missing!"

"Wow," Banks took an exaggerated look around the room. "Where's your boyfriend of the year award?"

Peter stepped towards the towel cart, crouching down to inspect it, "Is that blood?"

Banks twisted the Teacher around and shoved him face first into the wall. "Oh, yeah. You're coming with us."

Banks cuffed him and handed him off to Peter. Holding the Teacher strained Peter's bruised chest, making him cringe. Banks noticed and Peter could have sworn he saw him smile.

Banks and Alvarez stayed behind to collect evidence while Peter rounded up Royal to take their suspect back to the precinct. Thankfully, the Teacher allowed Peter to walk him down the hall with ease. However, the Teacher saw this as a great opportunity to rattle off all the reasons he wasn't responsible for Melissa's disappearance:

"I love her."

"I have no idea where that cart came from."

"She was supposed to be with Sarah, have you talked to her?"

"I wasn't even here!"

Blah, blah, blah.

Ari poked his head out into the hall. His presence silenced the Teacher. Peter nodded to Ari in appreciation, but Ari's face remained stony. Peter sensed his discomfort, the muscles in his jaw flexing to hold back emotion. Not only had Ari just killed his parents, but his neighbour was a potential murderer. Well, potential kidnapper; without more evidence, Peter had to assume Melissa Grant was still alive. Nevertheless, Ari was having an awful week. Peter hoped they would find Melissa soon and bring ease to both their minds.

SIX

My god, the authorities are stupid. That cop walked
right past where I bled her dry. What was her name?
Melanie? It doesn't matter now. How people get caught
by those fools is beyond me. It was so easy. I cleaned up
with supplies from her own cart and removed her body.
What an experience that was; despite her small frame
my muscles ached under her weight. Maneuvering
through the underbrush was a bit awkward but what's
life without a challenge? I knew exactly where I would
bury her. Very few, if any, Temple residents go into the
forest; the terrain is geared towards someone with
agility and stamina, someone like me. I like it out there.
Meditating amongst the trees is a true delight. Burying
her there was the obvious choice.

Once I had returned to my room, I snuck the towel cart
into Benjamin's room—complete with the fresh towels
she had given me and a splash of her blood. I'd seen her

leave his room before, bashful, hair a mess. Everything fell into place and the police marched him right off, handcuffs and all. It was too easy. It was way too easy.

And the best part? With him gone, the Elders needed someone to fill his spot, and who better than I? Michael presented me with a new burgundy robe. I was sad to let the navy one go, it was a sign of my achievement but this one is better. Some would say 'by a stroke of luck' I've been promoted to Teacher but it's not luck, it's me. It's the lifeblood. I breathed death into her and she breathed life into me.

The sun is low in the sky and I am about to begin teaching my very first class. I feel on top of the world; excited and accomplished. I close my eyes and engrain this moment in my mind. I lay out my new mat at the front of the room, the mat that my father presented me on his last morning. I had decided to save it for something as special as this. I couldn't have known it would come so soon.

My class is made of more than twenty and I am the focus of their attention. All of my students lay flat on their backs in *savasana*. I sit before them, placing one leg on top of the other. I invite them to bring their focus into the room and to begin concentrating on their breath.

"Long deep inhale through the nose, find pause at the top of the breath then exhale through the mouth. Bring your hands to your stomach, let the belly rise and fall with each breath. Three count inhale, three count exhale."

The entire room is breathing for me.

"Start to wiggle your fingers and toes, stretch your arms over your head and stretch your feet to the back wall. Full-body stretch. Bring your knees to your chest, let them fall to your right. Place your left hand down and push yourself up onto your hands and knees."

The room moves with my commands; they are all marionettes controlled by my voice.

"Coming into cat-cow, place your hands under the shoulders, knees under the hips. Inhale and arch your back. Look up to the sky."

My eyes stop on a brunette to my right. Her back arches deeply. Her plump lips part as she looks up, trying to control her breath, shy.

"Lead with your tailbone and send the navel high, exhaling into cow."

I control the curvature of her spine.

"Now kneel back, sit bones on your heels. Spread your knees as wide as your mat. Inhale, stretch your arms forward. Exhale, surrender into extended child's pose."

She makes eye contact with me as she lowers.

"Arms reach forward, forehead rests on the mat. Plug your shoulder blades down your back. Don't be afraid to come into the breath. I want to hear all of you," I want to hear her. "Fill the entire torso with air, long exhale through the mouth. Breathe into where you feel tension and let it go. With every breath, sink your hips back towards your heels."

I can hear her breathing now, loudly to impress me.

"That's it."

I move my puppet through sun salutations and vinyasas. The sweat begins to drip, rolling down her legs, her neck, pooling there in a backbend. I guide her from warrior two into a wide-legged forward fold.

"Feet spread far apart, hands on hips, and fold forward. Keep integrity through the spine."

My god, she has the most perfect ass. I walk over to her and place a hand on her lower back.

"Straighten your legs and lift up through the knees," I tell her. "Place your palms on the floor."

"I can't," she shakes her head. Her whole body shudders, "I'm really tight."

Oh, I bet you are. My pulse is racing. She tries again but can't quite bring her palms in line with her feet.

I nod and leave her be, "Take as many breaths here as you need and we'll meet in lotus pose."

Once everyone is seated, I can feel her eyes on me. Her breasts jut forward as she straightens her spine. I move them through a series of floor poses, finishing in *savasana*.

"Stay here as long as you would like. Come back into the evening feeling refreshed," I bring my palms to my heart. "Namaste."

I exit the room, cool air brushes my skin. Slowly, my students amble out after me and file into the change room to shower off. I wait for each of them to finish and wish them good night. They thank me for the practice and leave but the brunette stays behind. She tells me how much she enjoyed having me as a Teacher and how great I did. She can't take her eyes off of me. I fight the urge to laugh. Pathetic, a little extra attention and she's hooked. She bats her eyelashes and tells me that the evening classes are her favourite. She likes watching the sunset as she leaves, she says, hinting. She's not wearing a bra, on purpose of course. She could not be more obvious.

"My chambers open to the west. The view of the sunset is impeccable, if you care to join me?"

She says yes. Did I even need to ask?

My balcony doesn't open to the west, not that she notices. She mounts me almost immediately. Her kisses are sloppy and ill placed. Her hair is wet from showering but her skin is still sweating; it's sticky and salt tickles my nose.

She breathes into my ear, "I've never slept with a Teacher before."

No one cares, dear.

She pulls her shirt over her head, her breasts bouncing. She tears off my robe, too harshly.

"Be careful."

She flashes her dead eyes at me, "Do you want me or not?"

I pick her up and take her to the bed my parents conceived me in. This bed has life. She slides off my waist cloth to reveal my flaccid cock. Her eyebrows twitch downward but she grabs it anyway, trying to coax it up, yet I won't respond to her clumsy touch. She straddles me again. My face is stiff.

"Everything alright? We don't have to..."

I tell her that I am fine. I try kissing her, cupping her breasts.

"Your parents..." her eyes sadden. "I heard."

My dick hardens momentarily. Did she notice?

"I don't want to talk about that," I lie. "Let's try something else."

"What's that?"

I pull off her shorts, no panties either—desperate, "Meet me in the bath."

She bites her lip and nearly skips to the pool. So eager. I follow her, climbing into the tub. She doesn't notice the knife tucked behind my back. I hold her neck in one hand, drawing it back. She moans as I trace my other hand between her thighs, making her open up for me.

Eyes closed, she whispers, "Aren't you going to fill the tub?"

"Oh, yes."

I place my hand over her mouth. She screams into my palm when I fuck her with the knife—a little dramatic for my taste. I slit her throat just like the first, silencing her. I love how high she makes me feel.

SEVEN

Peter handed Royal another beer and closed the cooler with his foot. Royal cracked open his can and took a long gulp then grabbed a stick and began poking mindlessly at the fire. Peter sank into his plastic lawn chair, the ground shifted under his weight as he looked up; this was one of the few places in the city you could actually see the stars. The two of them had stumbled upon the little clearing a few years back while training for their police physical. They'd been crushing beer out here around a fire ever since.

"That barista ever call you?" Peter asked.

"No," Royal flashed a devilish grin. "But she will."

Peter shook his head and looked back up at the stars.

"When are you going to find yourself a nice girl, Pete?"

Peter's grasp on his beer can tightened, metal crinkling, "Not gonna happen."

"Why not? I'm not saying you've gotta marry her or anything. Just live a little!"

"Oh," his voice sharpened. "So I can accidentally knock her up and spend the next twenty-five years looking forward to my kid slaughtering me?"

"Dude," Royal rocked back in his seat, his eyes narrowing.

Peter stared at his hands, "I think Banks was right."

"About what? About you being a Catalyst?"

"Yeah."

"Oh, come on! You've gotta let it go. How could he possibly know that?"

"I don't know. Maybe his parents told him."

"Let me get this right," Royal shifted forward and leant one arm on his knee. "You think that your parents were forced to conceive you. *Your* parents."

"Yes. Maybe, I don't know."

"Well if you're a Catalyst then so am I. We're the same age, Dude. Was there even a population drop at that time?"

"I don't know," Peter thought for a moment. "You're eight months younger than I am. A conscription period could have ended before you were conceived.

"Maybe you should—"

"Royal," Peter looked him straight in the eye. "I can't kill them. I can't."

Royal was silent. His face was doused in empathy, alit by the fire. Peter focused on drinking his beer for fear he may start crying.

"I want to defect," it felt strange to admit to him. "I want to take them away from here and never look back."

Royal remained quiet but Peter could see the wheels turning inside his head.

"They would never go for it," Peter ran his hands over his face. "They would never break the law like that."

Royal's eyes locked with Peter's, "What if we break it for them?"

EIGHT

The brunette wasn't enough. My hands are shaking. I need another one. Two parents, two girls; how haven't I seen that before? It's so obvious.

Night has fallen completely. I am compelled out of my room, over the terrace to the Atrium, and out to where the Gazebo is. A meditation class is just letting out. The Teacher blows out the candles and bows to his students. I can sense their blood beating beneath their skin and I am drawn closer. I wait in the cover of some cedars. I know being here is risky but I cannot bring myself to care. I feel the life leaching from me, slowly but surely. I need to kill again.

Most of the students leave in groups or pairs but there's one girl, one mousy girl with chestnut hair and she's headed this way. She's small like the first. I shift my body to make sure she cannot see me. I hear her slow, tiny feet approaching, shuffling through the grass. She's perfect. Her footsteps grow louder and she's right beside me. I reach out, one hand on her mouth, the other around her waist and I slam her to the Earth. She's perfect.

I wait until the class fully dissipates and by then bringing her back to my room is easy. No one else is out at this time; all the classes are finished and everyone is at home. I lay her head over the edge of the bath and I walk to the bedroom to retrieve my knife.

"Where am I?"

She's awake. She turns and sees me, armed. She's on her feet and she's panicking. She runs for the door but I'm faster—I block her way. She screams for help.

"Be *quiet*."

She spins and runs past the bath and towards the balcony. Where's she going to go when she gets there? There's nowhere for her to go. I run after her. Someone is sure to hear her. I need to silence her. Nearing the ledge, she twists around to face me. Knowing she's trapped she tries to scream again but all that escapes her is a constricted yelp. Her face contorts in fear.

"I said, be *quiet!*"

She's inching backwards. She's trapped but she's not stopping, any farther now and she'll—

"Stop!"

A long shriek follows her as she topples over the edge. Her scream ends with a sharp *crack*. Dumb bitch. Now I have to haul her damn body back up here. I look around, the night is still and silent. No one heard. I breathed death into her and she breathed life into me. Or did I? I've felt no release but rather a sick feeling in my stomach. My cock hangs limp beneath my robe. Fucking bitch.

Knife in hand, I tiptoe through the Atrium and out onto the landing beneath my room. She's there, her neck is rotated too far and the side of her face is caved in. Once mousy features have now distorted into that of a rat's. Dark, beautiful blood blooms from her head and my anger dissipates. Her life is breathing into me.

We won't make it back upstairs. She'll make a mess— the chance of being noticed is too great. Besides, she's already bleeding for me right here. I know now that no one heard her because I am the Sun. This is exactly where I am meant to be. I drape her over one shoulder and as I do, I feel her shattered ribs crunch and grind. A sharp wheeze sounds against my back as she struggles to inhale.

She's breathing. I listen closely, to be sure. Her staccato stridor makes my heart skip—she's still alive.

I drop her to the ground. Her wheeze becomes strangled and her breath turns to gurgles as she chokes on her blood. She stares at me with one uncrushed eye. She tries to scream but she can't, her jaw won't respond; all she manages is a low moan. Her blood is on my neck and my breath catches as I touch my fingers to it. I reach them into my robe—finally, I'm hard. I watch the right side of her chest rise and fall while the left remains motionless. Her limbs, too, lay awkward and still—she's so broken she can't even move. No matter, I don't mind helping her into the woods.

Her blood drips down my back and my anticipation grows. I can barely contain my excitement. I am caught between rushing forward and savouring this journey. There's something about how her heart beats her blood onto my skin that is so intimate. We are becoming one. I want this to last forever but I know she is fading fast. I cannot let the fall kill her, her life will be mine. I walk forward, the mouse angled over my shoulder and ensnared in my claws. My pace is even and steady though my heart flutters beneath my ribs. We are so close now.

It is peaceful out here. Just us and the night. The only sounds are her raspy wheezes and the soft breeze rustling through the leaves. I count the trees. One, two, three... here we are. You'll fit in nicely here, little mouse. There is a spot just for you right beside the brunette whose grave is still fresh. The dirt is dark and I can smell the Earth from here. I gently lay the mouse at the feet of the trees and get to work. I use a thick fallen branch to dig a home for her, just like I did the others. I know I need to work quickly, her breath is becoming more shallow now. Her life will be mine. I need it.

Her grave is dug and just in time, it seems. I can barely feel a pulse as I pick her up and cradle her close. We lay down in the hole together, her body resting against my chest. I inhale and look up at the cloudless sky. I breathe it in as I slit her throat. Her life is mine. It spills out of her and onto me and I can't resist any longer. I shift her to the side so I can wrap my hand around my cock. With her beside me, I barely need to touch myself before my life spills onto her. We are one.

NINE

Peter's memories of last night were fuzzy, the conversation blurred by beer. He remembered the beginning of the evening but couldn't recall much after Royal's proposition. He had suggested that they break the law. *Was that it? Had he gone into detail?* The idea had tugged at Peter's mind all morning. He needed to find out what Royal meant.

The locker room was dotted with people getting ready for the shift ahead. Peter cornered Royal as far from the others as he could, "What exactly did you mean, 'Break the law?'"

Royal looked confused, "Uh, you do know that defecting is *against the law,* right?" He pushed past Peter to grab his uniform from his locker. "Good morning, by the way."

Peter followed him and leant against the metal shelving, "Jesus, of course I do. I meant how are we going to pull it off?"

He lit up, "You wanna do it?"

"Of course I want to," Peter lowered his voice as a co-worker passed them. "How?"

Royal buttoned his shirt, "I have a plan."

"Go on," Peter's eyes narrowed. He noticed a twitch in the corner of his partner's mouth; Royal was trying to keep a straight face.

"Let's just say I picked up a drunk one night who told me about a *pretty convincing* escape plot," a mischievous smirk snuck across his lips.

"Royal," Peter warned. Royal had a tendency to joke around at Peter's expense and this was quickly becoming one of those times.

"Seriously, that dude knew way too much for his own good," Royal whistled, his grin growing larger. "Conspiracy shit."

Peter grabbed his things and shut his own locker harshly, "Never mind."

"Oh, come on, Pete! You know I'm just fucking with you."

Peter glared at him.

"Okay, okay, games aside, I really do have a plan," he was grinning like a lunatic now. "Do you trust me?"

"No."

"Atta boy," Royal clapped Peter on the shoulders and left for parade.

Peter put on his uniform and walked towards the parade room. He passed the holding cells where an officer was uncuffing the Teacher and handing him his affects. Peter's brow furrowed. "You're letting him go?"

"Yeah, he's got an air-tight alibi. He wasn't anywhere near the Temple all night; he was at some sort of retreat the last few days. And there's more, you better go talk to Pearl."

Peter nodded. He remembered the Teacher rambling about not being there when Melissa disappeared. Peter wished he hadn't blown it off as bullshit; he could have saved them all some trouble.

The parade room was full, he was one of the last to take a seat. Sergeant Pearl was at the front. The screen behind him showed enlarged photos of Melissa Grant, a brunette who looked to be in her early twenties, and Sarah.

Sergeant Pearl had just opened his mouth to speak when Peter cut him off, "What happened to Sarah?"

"Sarah Preston is missing," Pearl said, addressing the whole squad. "Along with Madison Shaw," he pointed to the brunette.

Peter's heart sank. He snuck a glance at Royal, whose grin had completely disappeared. Peter knew what they were both thinking: they'd seen Sarah only yesterday, how could she be gone too?

Pearl continued, "The Teacher we arrested, Benjamin Wys, was away the night of Melissa Grant's disappearance and he's been here during the others. We're releasing him now."

"Do we have any other leads?" Banks asked. He sat near the wall with his arms folded.

"No."

"So, we're back to square one," Banks sounded just as pissed off as Peter felt.

"I've created a task force made up of the four of you who went to the Temple yesterday. Detectives Holloway will lead the team. You'll be in charge of figuring out what's going on there. I wish I could dedicate more resources to this but we're stretched thin enough as it is. You can set up in the conference room."

Peter stared up at Sarah's picture. Dread spilled down his back, prickling each vertebrae as it went.

Pearl had turned to a pile of paperwork, stacking it evenly between his hands. He looked up and stared at the unmoving squad. "What are you waiting for?" Pearl pointed to the door. "Let's go."

The platoon filed out the room. Wary of the location of Banks and Alvarez, Peter tugged Royal's shoulder down, "Should we really be participating in this task force when we're... you know."

"Well, we can't very well say, 'No'," Royal said, his voice barely a whisper. "We can't draw any suspicion our way. Besides, it'll take us a while to set everything up. Better help as much as we can for now."

"Alright." Peter nodded to Harvey and Lamb as they passed by.

Royal walked around the bullpen, pausing a few feet from the conference room door, "But I am going to get the ball rolling on this before you chicken out."

His devilish grin was back.

Peter rolled his eyes and allowed himself to smile too, "I wouldn't have it any other way."

The conference room's large table was spread out with pictures, copies of statements, DNA records, and all the evidence they had so far. The four of them sat down and looked towards Detectives Frank and Anne Holloway who were at the front of the room.

"Now," Frank pointed at the third woman's photo. "You know a little about Melissa Grant and Sarah Preston so I'll start with Madison Shaw."

Peter studied her picture, scouring his brain for a memory of her, "I don't think I saw her yesterday."

Frank shook his head, "You wouldn't have. She attended an evening class that started at 1830 and ended at 1930. She was reported missing by her boyfriend when she didn't return home afterwards. And before you ask, O'Leary, he's got an alibi too; at home with friends all evening."

Royal had opened his mouth to speak. He closed it and took out a notebook, looking amused as he jotted down what Frank was saying.

"We can't be sure these three girls disappearances are related, especially in the case of Madison Shaw; there's no discernable link between her and the others. But Melissa and Sarah are best friends—it'd be one helluva coincidence if they weren't connected."

Alvarez tapped a pen on the table, "Do you think they might have just run away together?"

"That's one possibility," Anne said. She turned to Royal, "You spent time with Sarah yesterday, how did she seem to you?"

Royal cleared his throat, "Normal for the situation. She was worried about her friend."

"Yeah," Peter added. "Although, she was definitely focused on hiding Melissa's relationship with Benjamin Wys."

Banks leaned backwards, "Do you think she was covering up an escape plan and you mistook worry for deception?"

"No," Peter frowned. "It was definitely about reputation." *Escape plan*; Banks used an interesting choice of words. Peter had been so focused on the briefing, he had let the idea of defecting slip to the back of his mind. His palms began to sweat, he shifted uncomfortably in his seat. He prayed Banks didn't notice his changed demeanor.

"Okay," Frank pointed to Sarah. Her photo was a high school graduation picture, her bouquet of roses were tangled in her brown curls. "Sarah Preston was last seen leaving a meditation session at around 2200. She was reported missing when she didn't show up for work this morning. Other women from her dorm can't confirm if she ever made it back to her room but it appears her bed was never slept in."

"We're assuming she was taken between the two places," Anne placed her hands on her hips.

"That's a narrow window," Banks said. "Seems a bit risky, doesn't it? No one saw anything?"

"Unfortunately, no one saw anything in regards to any of these women."

"How is that possible?" Royal asked. "There's got to be upwards of a hundred people who live there, not to mention the Cedar Valley residents who attend classes."

Peter consulted a file in front of him. "Like Madison," he said quietly.

"So our suspect nabbed two women in one night," Banks said. "He's bold."

"He?" Alvarez cocked an eyebrow.

"Assuming these women were kidnapped," Banks leaned forward now. "We're looking for a man. Most predators who go after young, beautiful women are men."

Frank wrote 'Kidnapped?' on the board and underneath it, 'Male'. "What else?"

Banks glanced over the files in front of him, "There have been no ransom demands, correct?"

"Correct."

"Then he's either keeping them or killing them."

As much as Peter didn't want to admit the fate of these women, and as much as he disliked Banks, he was probably right.

"Our only lead is a dead end," Peter said, feeling defeated. He tried to clear violent images of the women's dead bodies from his mind.

"Well," Banks continued. "Two of the girls went missing right after class and Melissa disappeared in the

North Wing where all the Teachers live. What do those have in common?"

Peter didn't like the condescension in Banks' voice but chose to ignore it.

"Teachers," Frank wrote it across the board. He didn't seem to notice Banks' attitude, either that or he was ignoring it just like Peter. "That's where we'll start. Who was teaching the yoga class that Madison Shaw attended?"

Peter flipped through more pages, "It says here: Arun Sinclair. I spoke with him yesterday and he told me he wasn't a Teacher. They must have promoted him in the wake of Wys's arrest."

Alvarez scoffed, "That's convenient."

"And he was the one who told me that he'd previously seen Melissa Grant leaving Wys's room."

"Be careful," Anne warned. "That could easily be circumstantial. Wys admitted to his relationship and Sinclair could have been the obvious choice for the Temple."

"That's true. He did recently have his Life Ceremony," Peter pulled out his tablet and scanned the system for the exact date. "This past Sunday. It was only a matter of time before he assumed his parents' roles. It says here they were Teachers as well."

"Okay, so what about Sarah?" Frank asked.

"Uh, says here the meditation Teacher was Mitchell Braun."

"I'll send a couple of squad cars to pick them up," Frank sat down. "Go get yourselves some coffee."

Once they were out of the room, Peter faced Royal, "Not having to pick them up ourselves? That's new."

"I guess that's the perks of being on a task force," Royal's eyes shifted. "Listen, you grab the joe and I'll meet you back in there."

Peter nodded. He had no idea what Royal was up to but he was eager to find out.

Banks and Alvarez were in the break room filling up Styrofoam cups with fresh brew. Peter stood patiently, empty cups in hand while Banks took his sweet time with his—most likely to piss Peter off. But then Banks extended his hand, took Peter's cups, and began filling them for him.

That's interesting. He braced himself, ready to step out of the way if Banks decided to throw the scalding liquid in his face. But nothing happened, Banks only handed back the cups.

Peter accepted his full coffee, "Good ideas in there, Banks."

"Yeah," he didn't look up while he sat down beside Alvarez. "Let's not fuck it up."

Peter's parents were still in the conference room chatting quietly at the front. They stopped talking when he entered.

"Sorry," he turned back towards the door. "Am I interrupting something?"

"No," his mother smiled. "We were just discussing how it's nice to be working together, as a family."

Peter felt guilt sink into his stomach. It began hollowing out a space to live. "I want to apologize about the other night. I—"

"No apology necessary," Anne walked over and gave him a hug. "We understand."

Peter hugged her back, "I'm happy we are working together, too."

Frank's phone rang. He took the call outside, shuffling past Royal, Banks, and Alvarez, who had since returned. Royal threw a wink at Peter as they sat back down.

Frank poked his head back in, "The Teachers will be here in about ten minutes. Peter, you have rapport with Sinclair, you and O'Leary set up in Interview One. Alvarez, Banks, you take Braun in Two."

Peter and Royal leant against the two-way glass in the observation room.

"What did you find?" Peter kept his voice low. His mind buzzed with anticipation, he couldn't wait for Royal's update.

Royal shifted closer, "You know those old safe houses they used to use?"

"Yeah?"

"It took a bit of digging but I found a list of inactive ones. We can hide out in one of those."

"That's perfect," Peter couldn't contain a smile. He hadn't fully believed that Royal would come up with a viable plan. At least, not this quickly. *Inactive safe houses? Brilliant.* "Now we just have to get there."

"Dude," Royal nodded knowingly. "U plates."

"Undercover Plates? People actually use those?" Peter thought they were just a rumour spread by overzealous cops.

"Yeah, my parent's used them. They—"

Used? Past tense? "Aren't your parents still undercover? Like, no-contact undercover?"

Royal shook his head, "They got back last week. But yeah, the U plates, they put them on the undercover vehicles they're using. To a civilian, they're normal. To a cop? Not so much."

"What do you mean?"

"If a cop scans the plate, a warning populates saying that the vehicle is involved in an undercover operation and poof—they leave you be."

"Okay, great," Peter nodded. "Thanks for helping out with this."

"Don't thank me yet," Royal winked at him. "Thank me when we're at the safe house."

Peter raised an eyebrow, "We?"

"Yup. Me, and my parents. I'm not about to let you go and have all the fun."

"Alright," he was hesitant about Royal risking his life to help him, not to mention his parents' lives but the idea of having Royal's help the whole way was hard to hate. "We're going to need a truck or van if we're all going to fit."

"Easy," Royal grinned. "Impound."

Through the glass, the interrogation room door opened. Ari was guided to a chair facing them. Peter noted he was no longer wearing the deep blue robe; instead his robe was burgundy.

Peter looked at Royal and offered him a hi-five, "Let's do this."

They left observation and joined Ari who greeted Peter with a small smile, "Officer Holloway, nice to see you again."

"Likewise," Peter flopped down into his seat while Royal leaned against the wall. "Ari, this is my partner, Officer O'Leary."

Ari extended his arm and shook hands with Royal, "How may I help you, Officers?"

"You've probably heard there have been more disappearances from the Temple," Peter lay out the pictures of the three women.

Ari looked down at them, "Ah, yes. Strange, isn't it?" His face twisted in confusion.

"Indeed it is. There's never been a missing person reported from the Temple before."

Ari touched the photos, "The Temple is a place of peace."

"Supposed to be," Royal crossed his arms and placed his right foot against the wall. "That middle one? That's Madison Shaw. She was last seen leaving your yoga class."

"I only just took over for Benjamin, I'm not sure what I can tell you about her."

"Did you kill her?"

Ari's face remained contorted, "You think she's dead?"

"We can't rule it out."

"I thought you arrested Benjamin?"

Royal switched his feet on the wall, "Turns out he wasn't anywhere near the Temple the night Melissa went missing."

"Poor things," his expression softened. "I do hope you find them."

Peter clicked his tongue, "You didn't answer his question."

Something glinted in his eye, "No, I did not kill her, or any of them for that matter."

Royal glanced at Peter, "Where were you after your yoga class?"

"I went back to my room and didn't leave until morning. I practiced some meditation out on my balcony."

"Can anyone corroborate that?"

Ari blinked, "Yes, Michael was with me for the majority of the evening. I assume you've met him?"

"Yes, and we'll be in contact with him," Peter gathered up the photos. "You're free to go."

Ari stood and headed for the door. Royal blocked his way, "Don't go leaving town, we may have more questions for you."

"I wouldn't dream of it," He pressed past Royal who let him pass. "Good day, Officers."

Before Peter and Royal could leave Interrogation One, they were met by Alvarez and Banks.

"Anything from Braun?" Peter asked.

"Nah," Banks sighed. "He was teaching classes when Madison disappeared and was met at the end of his meditation class by his wife who didn't leave his side for the rest of the night."

Alvarez shifted his weight back on his heels, "And Sinclair?"

"I'm not sure. He states that Elder, Michael, was with him for most of the evening. We'll have to see how long that was exactly. Maybe he still had time to take the women."

"You think he did it?"

Peter bit the inside of his cheek, "I don't know yet."

TEN

Talking about my girls was thrilling. It was like it was all happening again. I touched their faces laid out before me and I felt them giving me life. I forced my expression to sadden for police but believe me, I was smiling on the inside. They even bought my lie about spending the evening with Michael. Whether he verifies it is a test, one that I know he will pass. I am worthy and he knows it; he will support me.

I know that I cannot kill again for a while. Even though I've given myself an alibi, the police are getting too close. I need to let the trail run cold. Today I will settle for visiting my girls again, out here in the valley. It's far enough that no one would stumble upon it but close enough that if I stare out from my balcony, I can pinpoint where they are. There isn't any discernable clearing where I buried them. I know by the groupings of trees. One, two, three, here they are. I know these woods. The underbrush is thick and the terrain is unforgiving. One would not fare well in here if they were unfamiliar.

The journey out is well worth the effort. The scratches and bruises obtained are proof of my dedication. I take my time gazing at the ground where the mouse took her last breath, where her blood soaked the dirt. I sit at their feet and meditate. I feel their bloodless bodies draining the last bits of life into the Earth and the Earth channels their life into me. It hums beneath me, surging up into my soul. I breathed death into them and now they still breathe life into me. My body feels light. Being with them is enough to sustain me until it's safe again. They will keep me alive. Completely at peace, I turn my face up to the sky. I am the Sun.

ELEVEN

"I found us a vehicle. Classic non-descript van, you're gonna love it."

"Okay," Peter said through a yawn. Royal had insisted they meet at the coffee shop before work, unholy hour be damned. "We've got the hideout, the getaway car, now we just need to find a way to get them to come with us."

"They'll never come willingly," Royal stared at the brunette barista from their corner table. "We've established that."

"Well, we can't just beat them unconscious."

"No," Royal took a sip of his coffee and rolled it around his mouth. "But what if we sedate them?"

"How do you propose we do that?" Peter tipped his cup, burning his tongue.

Royal shrugged, "Just drink your coffee."

Peter debated arguing with him, he even opened his mouth but Royal stuck a finger up, signalling him to be quiet. He pulled out his phone and dialed.

"Who are you calling?"

"Your dad. Hello, Sir? It's Royal O'Leary."

Peter frowned.

"Sir, I'm with Peter and he was just saying how maybe we should circulate photos of the women to local hospitals, in case they turn up there?" He paused. "Okay, sounds good. Thank you, sir." He hung up and place his phone in his jeans pocket.

"*I* was just saying?" Peter smirked.

"Hey, you need all the brownie points you can get if we're going to pull this shit off."

Peter placed his still full cup on the table, "True."

"Let's go clock in and hit those emergency rooms!" Royal led the way out, slowing to gaze longingly at the barista.

Peter chuckled but didn't comment. If Royal wanted to memorize her face, all the power to him.

The first hospital they visited was eerily quiet; the waiting room had a mere two people in it. A unit clerk played solitaire on her tablet while the triage nurses gossiped quietly between eruptions of giggles that were loud enough for all to hear.

Royal sighed, shaking his head, "This'll never work."

Peter tailed him around the ER, "What exactly are we doing?"

"Come on," Royal handed the photos over to the unit clerk with a quick explanation. "Let's try another."

As they approached the entrance of the next hospital, they were nearly mowed down by a beat up sedan squealing towards the Emergency Room. After the car jolted to a stop, a middle aged man bolted from the driver's side and threw open the passenger side door. A frail woman who Peter assumed was his wife spilled into the man's arms, gasping in pain.

Peter rushed to help them but was flung to the side by a team of nurses pushing a wheelchair. Within seconds, they had her loaded up and wheeled inside, husband frantically bounding behind them.

Royal beamed and patted Peter's shoulder, "This place is perfect."

Peter followed him past an overflowing waiting room and towards the nursing station. They watched the wheel chaired woman and her husband disappear into an assessment room. Further along, a doctor barked orders at a team of nurses and respiratory techs who thumped on the chest of an elderly man. Next to them, a mother desperately tried to calm her screaming child. Royal pulled out a set of photos and handed them over to Peter as his eyes scanned the room. They rested on a red-headed woman in pink scrubs near a supply closet.

"Ginger," Royal pointed to the nurse. She was bent over a chart, phone pressed up against the side of her face. "Distract her."

He gave Peter a reassuring pat on the back and disappeared into the crowd. *Distract her? From what, exactly?* She was wrapping up a lecture to a lab tech who had messed up some blood work; to Peter, she seemed pretty distracted already.

He cleared his throat and approached the desk, "Uh, excuse me?"

She didn't look up, "Triage is at the front, you'll have to register there."

"No, uh, I'm not a patient."

"Family services is down the hall," she slammed the phone down, seeing Peter for the first time her lips formed a thin line. "Oh, god, sorry Officer."

He channelled his inner Royal and flashed her a smile, "That's quite alright, miss...?"

"Jenna," she smiled back at him, her stern expression melting away.

"Jenna, I'm Peter. We're investigating a string of missing women. Have any of these women come into your E.R.?"

She took the photos from him, looked at them quickly and shook her head.

"Their names are on the back," he reached a hand over the desk to point.

She flipped them over and entered their names into the computer, "Nope, never came here, or any other hospital for that matter."

"Oh," Peter's heart felt heavy. Even though this trip to the hospitals had been part of some *scheme* Royal cooked up, he had hoped they would find something pertaining to the missing women. "Well, thank you for checking."

"I'll flag their names so if they do end up here, we'll notify you," Jenna gathered up a stack of charts and began to turn towards the supply room. "Good luck."

Royal stuck his head out of the supply room and signaled to Peter that he needed more time.

"Jenna?" He had to think quickly. *What would Royal do?* The answer came quickly and before he could stop them, the words fell out of his mouth, "Would you like to have dinner with me sometime?"

Setting the charts down, she smiled again, "Sure."

Shit. "Really?" Peter's neck began to sweat.

She scribbled on a green sticky note, "Here's my number."

Peter accepted it, holding it in his hand like it might disintegrate. Royal's glowing face appeared behind Jenna, he held his thumb up—whatever he had done had gone well.

"Goodbye, Officer Peter."

"Goodbye, Nurse Jenna."

She walked through the doorway Royal had just come from. Royal waved his eyebrows at Peter and they walked briskly back to their cruiser, evading bloody noses and intoxicated homeless men as they went. Once back in the car, Royal was grinning at him like a madman.

"What?"

"Dude, did that hottie just give you her number?"

Peter felt the sticky note burning in his pocket, "I don't know what you're talking about."

Royal punched his arm, "That's my boy!"

Peter rolled his eyes, "What were *you* doing in there?"

"Check it out," he opened up one of his pant leg pockets, revealing a stash of vials and syringes.

Voice hushed, "What the *hell* is that?"

"Sedatives. Midazolam to be precise."

Peter's neck sweat was back, "Do you even know how to use those?"

"Yes," Royal's grin never faltered.

"I don't even want to know."

"No, you do not," he pat his leg. "So, we're doing this thing tonight?"

Peter took a deep breath and nodded, "Tonight."

The rest of the team was already in the conference room when they got back. Frank threw Peter an expectant look.

He shook his head, "The hospitals were a dead end."

Frank nodded solemnly, "At least they'll be on the lookout now. Banks, tell him about Michael."

Banks swivelled in his chair, "We contacted him and he denies being with Sinclair the other night. He had no idea what we were talking about."

Peter clicked his tongue, "Innocent men don't lie."

Royal rolled his eyes at him, "You hear that line on a crime drama?"

"He could have other motives for lying," Anne warned again. "It doesn't mean he's responsible for these missing women."

"He's still our best lead. He has no alibi and Madison Shaw was last seen with him. If we can get a warrant, I am sure we could find some sort of evidence in his room."

"What makes you think he had them in his room?" Banks crossed his arms.

Peter shrugged, "You got a better idea?"

Banks raised his eyebrows but stayed silent.

Anne pulled out her phone, "I'll get on the warrant. It'll take some time."

With the warrant in motion, Peter was hopeful that the investigation would head in the right direction without them. However, his stomach knotted with the realization that he'd never learn the fate of these women.

"I've set up a media conference," Frank added. "I think it's time we get the help of the public. The press should be here any minute. Alvarez, go talk to Admin to get a tip line set up and the rest of you, man the phones. We should expect calls by the end of the hour. Someone must have seen something."

As predicted, the phones started ringing as soon as the clock turned to 1400. Most callers had little to no information, they just wanted to know if the women had been found yet. There was even a handful of 'psychics' who claimed to 'see' where the women were. The only helpful caller was a man from the Temple. He stated that he was woken up by a scream followed by a *thud* at approximately 2230hrs the night Melissa Grant and Sarah Preston went missing. He said the scream was definitely female but he couldn't make out where it had come from—it had 'echoed throughout the valley' and when he looked out his window, he couldn't see anyone and never heard anything after that.

Peter logged the man's statement into the computer and printed it off for the conference room board. He stepped back, taking their progress in, or rather lack thereof. He couldn't help but feel like there wasn't much hope for these women. He turned his attention to the floor beyond the conference room; it was littered with desks, cops, and the odd civilian filling out reports. This had been his whole life for the last four years and overnight it would become nothing more than a memory. Shuddering as he swallowed, Peter sucked down the last bit of his office coffee. He looked into his empty mug, at least there was one thing he wouldn't miss.

In the locker room Peter stripped from his uniform, capturing a mental image of himself as a cop. He hung up his duty belt and left everything in his locker save for his gun and badge.

Royal came up beside him, voice low, "You ready to leave this place for good?"

"One last thing," Peter held Jenna's number in his hand. Breathing out slowly, he crumpled it and tossed it in a trash bin. "I'm ready."

TWELVE

Peter knew they had to wait for nightfall to set things in motion but he couldn't go home. He couldn't wait alone, staring at the clock and counting the hours by the rising level of anxiety in his gut. He had followed Royal to his shabby red sedan, its interior obsessively clean but the exterior was dented and rusting. Royal had opened the passenger door for Peter, not questioning why he was tagging along.

Royal's south-end townhouse was squeezed in between two nearly identical homes, their only discriminating feature was their colour schemes. Most were combinations of earth tones but Royal's was light blue with cream shutters and front porch railing.

Peter lounged on Royal's sofa, taking in the comforts of familiarity while Royal ran around, excitedly throwing clothing and various items into a duffle bag. He disappeared up the stairs and came back down with a black backpack. He opened the pantry, grabbed a box off the second highest shelf—he couldn't reach the top one—and brought it over to the sofa. He took a seat and opened the box: it was filled with alcohol wipes, tourniquets, and packaged IV supplies. He produced the stolen Midazolam from his pocket and set it in the box. Peter watched Royal as he unwrapped sharp needle tips and screwed them on to the syringes. Hands steady, he broke open an ampule of Midazolam and began to suck up the medication. Royal kept his eyes focused on his task but smirked, knowing he was being watched.

Peter rolled his eyes. Royal showed no sign of nervousness; Peter wished he could say the same for himself. His palms were beginning to sweat and he couldn't sit still. "You got a beer?" He hoped a bit of booze would cut the edge off.

"Nope," Royal slowly shook his head from side to side. He capped the syringe and placed it in the backpack.

Peter wiped his hands on his pants as he looked around for an alternate crutch. His eyes landed on the Midazolam, "Well, if we're not drinking, you might as well teach me how to use those things."

Royal placed one hand on his heart and the back of his other against his forehead, feigning a swoon, "I thought you'd never ask." He laughed at himself then picked a few already full syringes. "Okay, I've got a few practice ones for you."

Peter's eyes bulged, "You really expect me to drug myself?"

"No," Royal laughed again, this time at Peter. "It's just saline."

Peter wiped his hands again and cautiously accepted the 'practice' needle, "Are you sure it's saline?"

"Yes, here," Royal came and sat down on the sofa beside Peter. "You can use it on me first."

The syringe felt awkward in his hand. He stared at it, then at Royal. "How? Where?"

He smiled at Peter's hesitation. "Thighs or glutes would be ideal but that may be difficult to get to on our 'rents," he winked and rubbed an elbow at Peter. "We'll use the deltoid instead."

"Okay."

Royal rolled up his sleeve and pointed below his shoulder, "Frame the muscle with your thumb and index finger and hold the syringe like a dart."

Peter obeyed.

"Now just stick it in and plunge."

His hand wavered, "What if I hit the bone?" The image of such made his stomach turn.

"Oh, not a chance with these pipes," Royal flexed and kissed his free bicep.

That comment was enough for Peter to jab him.

"There ya go!" Royal didn't flinch from the needle or Peter's mild aggression. "Easy as pie, right?"

"Actually, yeah."

Peter moved to throw the needle away but Royal stopped him, saying, "We need to take all of the supplies with us, garbage and all. No evidence left here."

Peter nodded.

"You wanna to try again?"

"Nah, no need to waste them."

Royal gathered up everything and stashed it in his backpack. He slung the bag over his shoulder, grabbed his duffle, and headed for the door. Peter turned in his seat, "Where are you going? It's still light out."

Royal cocked his head, a smile cutting across his face, "You really think we'd leave Cedar Valley without going to the clearing one last time?"

Peter had been too anxious to even think about the clearing. Now that they were headed there, his nerves eased up. He jumped to his feet, grinning, "We're stopping for liquor on the way."

"Duh."

Royal looked fondly around his home, nodded to himself, and led the way out to his car.

〽

Royal left his beer untouched as he stoked the fire, scorched logs breaking away to make room for hungry flames. His face was slack and the night darkened the creases of his fallen expression. Peter could see that the reality of leaving their beloved clearing behind had started to touch Royal. Peter could relate; having a place to unwind and forget about the world even just for a little while had been vital to his mental state, but it wasn't something either of them had taken for granted. Peter cracked open a beer and drank in the bittersweetness of their last night there.

"We'll find another place," Peter said hoping to lighten the mood.

Royal allowed a small smile and nodded, "A better place. One where you can *really* see the stars."

Excitement sparked in Peter's chest. *Now that was a nice thought.* It was finally dark out but tonight clouds covered the sky, not even the moon shone through; the only light came from the fire. He wanted to believe his own words and hoped that their safe house really would provide a place like this. *That was the point, right? To find a better sliver of the universe.*

He asked Royal where exactly they were going.

"And ruin the surprise?" Royal's eyes reflected the flames, making them gleam mischievously.

Peter glared at him.

"Alright, I'll give you a hint. I don't want to tell you everything because honestly, Pete, it's safer that way."

Peter played with the tab on his beer can, "What do you mean?"

"If you don't know where we're going you've got plausible deniability; I could have kidnapped you as well."

The tab snapped off, slicing Peter's thumb. "I would never let you take the fall for this."

"It was my idea," Royal chewed the inside of his lip.

"And I decided to do it. It was just supposed to be me and my parents."

His face fell again, "You don't want me to come, Pete?"

"No, of course I do," the words felt strange in his mouth, loaded like a half truth. It was hard to imagine life without his best friend but it was harder to imagine him going down for this. Part of him wanted Royal to stay behind; it was safer. A larger part knew that he couldn't deny Royal a chance to save his parents too.

Royal fidgeted with his neck collar and looked at Peter warily.

"Really, we're in this together."

His expression didn't soften.

"That includes taking joint blame if we're caught. I'm serious."

He wrung his hands and stared into the flames. "Fine," he said but Peter knew he wasn't being sincere. Peter didn't press the subject anymore; if it came to it, he would confess and Royal wouldn't be able to stop him.

"So, what's this hint?"

Royal's eyes swallowed up the fire, his excitement returning. He leaned forward and whispered, "The mountains."

"The *real* mountains?"

He nodded, "I chose the most remote safe house."

"Good thinking," Peter could hardly contain his joy. The real mountains put Cedar Valley's tree covered foothills to shame. They were about 150 km away to the east. Giving up the clearing for the fresh aired seclusion of the mountains was a fair compromise.

"That's all I am going to say for now."

Peter gave a quick nod. He could make do with daydreaming about the mountains.

"Ready for phase one, then?"

Peter stared up at the clouds, pretending he could see the spread of constellations behind them and breathed in the clearing one last time, "Let's do this."

�📿

The impound yard was walking distance from Peter's condo, just a few blocks farther than the Police Precinct. The lot was dark, lit only by tall sporadic spotlights. Despite the late hour the gate was open. Royal started towards the guard house but Peter grabbed his sleeve, "Are we really going to be drugging this guy? What if he reports it and they find it in his blood or something?"

"Pete," Royal shook his arm free, "the best part of Midazolam is that it induces amnesia. He'll wake up, won't remember a thing. He'll think he just passed out or fell asleep or whatever."

"Okay," Peter said, letting his partner continue through the lot. Royal had yet to lead them astray but the further into their plan they went, the margin of error grew exponentially. He again wondered how

Royal knew so much but still didn't question him. For now, he'd have to settle for following behind him.

The guard was middle-aged with a round belly and a balding head. They greeted him by flashing their badges.

"Hello boys," he stood, adjusting his belt. "What can I do ya for?"

Peter handed him a case file, "We want to see if you've still got this vehicle or if it's been demolished."

"Not a problem," he took the file, sat on his bare-bones swivel chair and began single finger typing at his keyboard. The process was painfully slow; he stared, eyes squinting at the screen, searching, then down at the keys like it was his first time typing. Back and forth he stared, screen, keys, screen, keys. It took all Peter had to keep from looking over at Royal and rolling his eyes.

"Ah," the guard smiled contently at himself. "It's still here. You boys need to take a look at it?"

"Yes," Peter fought to contain his impatience; he crossed his arms tightly across his chest, as if constricting himself would keep it in. "Please."

"Sign here," he placed a clipboard in front of them and turned his back. "I'll grab the keys for you."

Peter pretended to reach for a pen while Royal slinked around the desk and stabbed the guard in the arm with a syringe.

He cried out and spun around, "What the..."

Royal shrugged his shoulders, syringe tucked behind his back, "Mosquito?"

"No," the guard advanced, eyes on Royal's hidden hand. "You drugged...me..."

They backed up until they were against the wall. The guard slipped forward into his chair and his head slumped onto the desk. Peter gave him a small nudge but he didn't move. He was out cold.

"Poor chap," Royal capped and pocketed the needle. He motioned to a steaming mug beside the keyboard, "Should've had that second cup of joe."

Peter grabbed the discarded keys and noted the van's location on the computer screen, "I can't believe that worked!"

Royal was already in the doorway, "Let's go."

"How long will he be out?" Peter gingerly closed the door behind them.

"Few hours, hopefully."

"Hopefully?"

Royal shrugged again, "I ain't a doctor."

The van was easy enough to find, each row clearly marked. Upon laying eyes on it, it was apparent that it was in no way Peter's vehicle of choice. The exterior was rusty and the wheels seemed too small for their wells. There was a long, deep scratch along one side and the painted-over rear windows were a particularly classy touch. Peter opened the passenger side door which hung loose on its hinges and took a few tries to get it to shut again. The interior smelled musty, the fabric seats were threadbare and sagging from wear. Peter wondered if it would even run. Royal hopped in the driver's side and twisted the keys in the ignition. The engine sputtered and grumbled but it indeed, eventually, groan to life.

Royal drove the van back to Peter's condo and dropped him off, "I'll be back at two."

Peter nodded. He slammed the van door and watched it drive off down the block. He walked up to his building for the last time, he checked his mail for the last time, and he walked up the stairs for the last time. A sense of calm washed over him; there was something sobering about knowing he'd never see this place again.

Slowly, he packed a bag, every item intentional; enough left behind not to rouse suspicion. He yearned to finish all the beer in his fridge but that too would be unrealistic. He needed his apartment to look lived in. Besides, he needed to keep his head for their plan to succeed. Reluctantly, he settled for packing half of the cans. He made himself the only thing he could cook: french toast, and left the dirty dishes. Peter left laundry in the dryer and left a cup of coffee in the microwave. He flopped down onto his sofa chair and took in everything around him as he mentally prepared for Royal to return. He stared out across the small lake through his open curtains and imprinted it in his mind. That lake had been his solace. Soon, he wouldn't need that. Soon they would be safe for good.

THIRTEEN

The shrill ring of his phone woke him up. How he had managed to fall asleep was beyond him. Royal was back. Heart pounding, Peter grabbed his duffle bag and stashed his gun in the back of his pant waist. One last look around and he was gone.

Peter slid open the side door of the van to throw his bag in, only to find Royal's parents passed out in the back. He shut the door quickly and quietly, hoping that no one saw. He slid into the passenger seat and settled his bag on his lap.

Royal sized him up, "You packed light."

Peter ignored him and looked in the back, "I thought we were going to grab them together?"

"I was too, you know," grinning madly, he shook out his arms. "Antsy."

"I suppose it saves us time," Peter sighed. "Did it go okay?"

Royal made a smoothing motion with his hand, "Seamlessly."

Peter spent the ride to his parents' house trying to slow his heart rate using Royal's parents' even breathing as a reference point. The reality of their situation still evaded him. *Are we actually doing this?*

All the lights were off at the Holloway House. Royal dimmed the headlights and backed the van up to the garage. As quietly as possible, they crept their way to the back door. Not allowing himself to breathe, Peter unlocked it and closed it behind them. The back hall was lined with family photos, most of which were from when Peter was a child. Now was when it hit him—this was his childhood home and they were leaving. He would never see this place again. Peter ran his finger along the frames, once again breathing in the bittersweet air.

They climbed the stairs, careful not to make them creak. He heard his father snoring from down the hall. His parents' bedroom door was ajar—*yes!* He remembered trying to surprise his mother with breakfast in bed on her birthday only to be foiled by the loud door latch. His disappointment had caused him to lose grip on the tray, coffee spilling and ruining the pancakes. The partially open door was a godsend.

Royal signaled for Peter to take the left side of the bed, and he'd take the right—Mom's side. He handed Peter a syringe and he pressed open the door. They moved like ghosts to opposite sides of the room.

Unable to see each other, Peter relied on the sound of Royal's breathing to navigate their timing. *Inhale, exhale, inhale, and jab! In and out.*

The needle went in easily. Peter held his breath, anticipating his parents to wake but Frank only snored deeper and turned over. Anne didn't move at all.

Flashlights drawn, Peter gathered up some clothes while Royal dug through the washroom for toiletries. Two full packs later, they charged back down the stairs. They threw the bags into the van, mindful not to hit Royal's parents, and headed back up again.

"Let's take my dad down first," Peter said.

Frank was tall and stocky—definitely a two man job. Peter hooked his arms under Frank's and Royal grabbed his legs. Apart from nearly toppling down the stairs, they got him down without incident. Anne was much easier to carry; with a little effort Peter could have hauled her out himself.

After organizing the unconscious like some sick puzzle, Royal chucked himself into the driver's seat. "Okay if I drive?"

"Go for it," Peter looked back at the house. He tapped the hood, "Just give me a minute."

He slipped back into the house. He couldn't deny his parents one family picture. He grabbed his favourite, a photo of them on a Christmas Holiday in front of a giant decorated tree, snow falling all around them.

The picture had been taken after Peter had graduated the Police Academy, his parents wanted to celebrate so they planned a winter getaway to the mountains—the same mountains they were headed to now. They took him to a sleepy little village that had donned every street and square with lights. It was one of the most beautiful things Peter had ever seen.

The thought of having more winters like that one calmed Peter. He joined everyone in the van, stuffed the photo in the glove box, and nodded to Royal to start the engine.

It had begun to rain, the asphalt was slick and reflected the streetlights. The wipers on the van were terrible, leaving streaks of water across the windshield. Traffic was light but Peter jumped every time another vehicle passed them by. He tried to cover his skittishness by turning in his seat to check on the parents.

"Relax," Royal cooed. "They're fine."

If only Peter could relax, "You know they'll kill us, right? If we're caught."

"Not if *they* kill us first!" he jerked a thumb backwards, chuckling.

Peter exhaled sharply, "Can you be serious for just one moment?"

Royal took a second to compose himself, rubbing his lips together to stifle anymore chuckles, "Okay, yes, it's possible that they'll kill us."

"But it's worth it," Peter said to himself. He stared at Royal, "It's worth it, right?"

Royal nodded, squinting through the rain.

Peter felt his breath start to catch in his chest, "Won't they think it's suspicious that we're all gone at the same time?"

"Maybe the kidnapper got us," Royal was laughing again.

Peter shifted in his seat, "Oh, really? All six of us?" He didn't realize he'd raised his voice until he noticed Royal's expression darken. Royal looked at Peter out of the corner of his eye but didn't say anything. Peter stared out his window. There were no more street lights and the rain made the visibility minimal; the unknown felt even more daunting. He gripped his duffle bag and hoped his nerves weren't showing.

They stayed silent for a while before Royal said, his voice low, "We'll cross that bridge when we get to it."

Peter held the bag tighter, "Feels like we're kinda in the middle of that bridge right now, buddy."

"You trust me, yeah?" Royal's face showed no sign of amusement.

"I thought we decided we were in this together. Quit it with this plausible deniability."

He shook his head so slightly, Peter almost missed it. "Just trust me."

He had better have a plan.

They had just passed the city limits when a low groan sounded from the back seat. Matthew, Royal's father, was beginning to wake.

"Shit," Peter spun around, his heart in his throat. "What do I do?"

Royal reached for the glove box and calmly handed him a syringe, "Just dose him again."

Shaking, Peter plunged the needle into Matthew's arm. *Shouldn't this get easier every time?* Matthew became still again and Peter's shoulders relaxed.

"You good?" Royal craned his neck.

"I'm good."

Ahead, Peter saw the Municipal Gate. A chill entered his gut and sweat began to form on the back of his neck. They were the only vehicle here, all eyes would be on them. *This was it. The moment of truth.*

Royal's face was stony. He instructed Peter to cover the parents with a blanket and began to slow the van, "We're going to be okay. The U plates will work and they'll let us go through."

Peter wasn't so sure. His back was cold from sweat. "What if they look in the back?"

"They won't."

"Don't do anything stupid. Let's just get this done."

Royal pulled up between two booths. He rolled down his window to greet the Provincial Control Officer. The Officer had eyebrows that hung heavy over his eyes, accentuating the dark crevices that lined his sharp crooked nose. At first glance, he seemed young but a closer look revealed wrinkles that had been obscured by a scruffy mustache.

"Good evening," Royal said brightly.

"Where are you headed?" The Officer's voice was monotone.

"The prairies," he pointed east. "Have you been?"

Don't push it, Royal.

The Officer's brow creased but he kept his voice flat, "At three thirty in the morning?"

Peter could hear the gears turning in Royal's head as he came up with a story for them. *Just say, 'Yes'. We don't need a crazy explanation.* He stared at the back of his skull, telepathically telling him to keep it simple. *We have the plates, anything extra will draw attention to us. We don't need an elaborate story.*

"Gotta get a head start! My buddy here's got to surprise his girlfriend," Royal pat Peter on the chest.

Peter fought a grimace. This was the exact kind of stupid ass story he wanted to avoid.

Royal continued, hands gesticulating towards the mountains, "She's been on field placement there for Agriculture. Boring, I know, but today is her birthday, so you know, here we are."

Whether the Officer bought the story or found it suspicious was unclear; his facial expression never changed and he didn't ask any more questions. All he said was, "I'm going to scan your plates."

Peter held his breath. Two large bars with scanners came down from the booth, one at the front of the van and one at the back. A white light slid across the bars. The Officer peered at his computer screen.

Peter noticed his eyes narrow ever so slightly. *Did the U plates work?*

The Officer handed Royal a green plastic card, the shape and size of a credit card, with 'APPROVED' written across it in white block letters, "This is your travel permit. Display it on the dash. It's valid for a week."

"That's perfect, thank you."

Peter's body relaxed, he could finally breathe. *We did it.*

The Officer exited the booth, "I just need to take a quick peek in the back."

Peter was winded. The van vas suddenly void of oxygen; he couldn't breathe. He opened his mouth but his vocal cords were frozen. He looked to Royal for direction.

"Is that really necessary, Officer?" Royal's voice held an edge of panic. He tried to cover it up by slowing his words, "We have a long drive ahead of us, we really should be—"

"It'll only take a moment," the Officer interrupted. Hunching in the rain, he walked to the back of the van, "Please come open it up for me."

Peter was shaking. Royal undid his seatbelt and opened his door. Peter's eyes grew wide from spying a gun in Royal's right hand. Peter mouthed, 'What are you doing' at him. *Was he going to kill him?* Peter looked around. The other booths were dark and empty; their Control Officer was the only one manning the gate. *No witnesses.*

Royal shrugged and stiffly exited the vehicle, whispering, "Stay here." Peter closed his eyes and listened. He heard the crunch of wet asphalt under Royal's feet. He heard him drag his hand along the side of the van, his fingers squeaking when they found resistance. He heard the even breathing of their parents and he prayed the darkness would conceal them enough even though he knew it wouldn't. He heard Royal's muted voice making another excuse and the Officer interrupting him again. A soft metallic clink let Peter know the latch had been unlocked. *Oh, god.* Peter imagined Royal behind him, slowly peeling open the latch, gun at the ready. *He'll see the bodies and Royal's going to kill him.* The back door opened.

Bang!

"Oh, my god," Peter fumbled with his seat belt. *He shot him. He really shot him.*

"Oh, damn it all to hell!"

Peter froze. The voice wasn't Royals; it belonged to the Officer. A hand smacked against the van and the Officer spoke again, "It's that damn bear. It keeps getting into the garbage bins."

Peter still couldn't move, he was suspended with one hand on the door handle, one on the dash, his ass lifted off the seat. *He's alive.* The bang hadn't come from the rear of the van but from ahead of them, near the woods.

The Officer moved around the van past Royal's window, leaned into his booth and retrieved a rifle. He stared at the dark tree line, eyes alert, "You two had best get out of here so I can deal with this. Bears can be unpredictable."

The Officer continued forward. As soon as his back was turned to them, Royal snuck back into the driver's seat and stashed his gun in the center console. Peter noticed sweat dripping from Royal's temple. His face was gaunt and his hands were trembling. He gripped the steering wheel to steady them.

The Control Officer reached into his pocket and produced a key card. He swiped it over a sensor on the exterior of the booth. The scan bars lifted up. The Officer nodded to Royal who shakily placed the van in drive and rolled forward into the night.

Neither of them dared to talk until the Municipal Gate was far behind them. Peter watched Royal; the farther they drove, the more his hands began to relax. Colour returned to his white knuckles and eventually they started to idly tap the wheel.

Peter was the first to speak, "I thought you were going to kill him."

Royal stopped tapping and his shoulders tensed, "So did I."

Peter didn't respond, the silence had allowed Royal to calm down and he didn't want to provoke him further. Instead, he turned his focus to the rain. His ears were starting to pop. Had it been dry and daylight, he was sure he would be able to see the mountains lining the highway. Their ascent had been gradual but there was no question they were nearing their destination.

Royal reached across Peter and back into the glove box. He pulled out a tablet and handed it to Peter, "We should almost be at the turn. Can you take a look and let me know?" His voice was too soft for Peter to determine any emotional inflection.

Peter turned on the screen. A bright green light blinked on a map, tracking their location. A blue line traced the route Royal had laid out for them. At the end of the line was a red beacon signifying the safe house. Peter looked for the turn on the GPS, "Yeah, it's just about 200 meters to your right."

"Okay," The rain had stopped but the highway was still pitch black. Royal painstakingly scanned the edge of the highway for the exit.

"Put your brights on," Peter ordered.

"You think I haven't tried?" Royal snapped. He flicked the switch with such vigor Peter feared it would break off, however the lights never came on.

Peter sighed. *Piece of crap.* He consulted the GPS and peered out into the black, "It's gotta be... right..." A deer sprung out of the ditch. "Shit! Watch out!"

Royal swerved violently, causing Peter to grasp his hand rest and slam his eyes shut. *Jesus Christ!* The vehicle lurched back on course and continued smoothly. Heart shoved in his throat, Peter reopened his eyes. He looked over at Royal who was nearly hyperventilating. The two of them shared a static moment where Peter swore he could hear their heartbeats echoing through the cab. Initial shock over, they burst into uncontrollable laughter.

Hysterical tears formed in Peter's eyes, "Holy shit."

"Dude," Royal howled. "That was close!"

"Way too close!" Peter knew they weren't only talking about the deer. He turned in his seat to look at the unconscious parents. Life as they knew it changed at the gate; they had now entered a world of the unknown with countless possibilities for all six of them. They had been dangerously near to losing everything they had worked for.

Royal's laughter slowed and he was finally able to catch his breath, "Eyes on the road, Holloway. Help me find this turn."

Peter smirked and pointed to a small gravel path ahead, "You mean that one?"

Royal scowled playfully and steered the van off the highway.

Their sleeping passengers remained soundless behind them as the van bumbled down the single lane road. Cedars lined the edges, their branches batting the vehicle's sides.

Peter watched their little green dot move on the screen, "It's going to be a left, travel a few kilometers, another left, a right, and we should be there."

"Copy that."

The road was winding. It dipped down valleys and up hills. At some parts, it narrowed so much, Peter feared they wouldn't make it through. The rest of the ride was silent; the quiet of the wilderness echoed through the van. And finally, when the sky was changing from black to blue, the tablet flashed: they had arrived.

"Where is the entrance?" Royal parked and turned off the van.

Peter met him in front of the hood, his face alight from the tablet, "Uh..."

"That's fine, you take your time," Royal stretched his arms overhead. "We've only got our kidnapped parents in the trunk."

"Meh," Peter snuck a smile. "It's just a typical early morning activity for us."

"Peter!" he feigned shock. "Was that a joke?"

He smirked, eyes on the tablet, "I don't know what you're talking about."

"And at a time like this! It must be the stars!"

Peter instinctively looked up. He nearly gasped; the clouds had cleared and the stars were so bright despite the fading darkness. He swore that if he reached up, he could pluck one right out of the sky and hold it in his hands.

Royal snatched the tablet from Peter's grasp. He squinted his eyes at the screen, recoiled from the brightness, and chucked it back, "I have no idea how you read that thing."

Shaking his head in mock disapproval, Peter led him through some shrubbery, "It's here."

The rain mustn't have made it this far as the dirt here was still dry. The two of them kicked at the ground, clearing away overgrowth to reveal a hatch.

The handle was rusted but with a few good tugs, the latch groaned open. Peter held his breath. He anticipated a heavy stench of must to cloud up into his face, however he was met only by the smell of earth. He pulled out his flashlight and shined it down, exposing a descending metal ladder.

FOURTEEN

Royal peered over the edge, "Think we can get 'em down there?"

"We're gonna have to," Peter's flashlight didn't reveal more than the ladder and a small patch of concrete at the bottom. "Let's check it out first."

Peter swung his legs over the edge and climbed down. He hopped off, his landing echoing throughout the bunker. A small cloud of dust swirled around up his ankles as he walked forward, flashlight in hand. His immediate surroundings included a kitchenette and a living area, all coated in a fine layer of dust.

Behind him, a thump sounded followed by a metallic *snap*. All around, a pleasant blue light flickered then held strong to illuminate the space. Peter turned to see Royal beside a breaker box, the first switch flipped on. As he flipped more switches, the whole bunker came to life: the fridge began to hum, white fluorescent lights lined the underbelly of the cabinets, air blew from the vents. The walls were curved metal, like they were in a buried Airstream, piped with the soft blue lights. The far end opened to two bedrooms, joined by a washroom. Each bedroom had a queen sized bed, the sheets of which were slightly dusty too. Further exploration revealed interior cabinets that housed fresh, untouched linens.

Directly to the right of the ladder, a circular staircase led farther down underground. Peter descended, eyes widening as he entered a second living space. Giant leather sofas occupied the middle but what was on either side of them was what made Peter forget all about their clearing back home.

He took a look at Royal whose face was bright with glee.

One wall was a full bar, dust heavier on this level. On the other side, the entire wall was an electric screen that displayed the outside world in real-time: cedar trees backed by darkness. Peter walked up to it. The vent above the wall pumped outside air into the room, making it smell like the outdoors too. The air was delightfully cool on his skin. Royal flopped onto one of the couches and let out a sigh. Past the lounge, there was another pair of bedrooms identical to the ones upstairs.

Royal looked pleased with himself, "Did I do good or what?"

Peter nodded. He could definitely get used to living in a place like this. He kicked Royal's foot that was propped up on the coffee table, "We should probably go grab the kiddies before a cougar eats them."

Royal uncrossed his legs and hopped up, "Good call."

Together they dragged the parents from the van to the opening of the hatch. Peter then climbed halfway down and carefully supported each sleeping body while Royal lowered them. In the top floor bedrooms, they changed the bed sheets, laid the parent's down and tucked them in. They then went back up to the van and divided everyone's belongings. Royal began to unpack while Peter set the Christmas photo on his parent's bedside table. He had hope that it would be the first thing they saw when they came to.

They left the bedroom doors open, wary that if they were closed the parents would think they were trapped and being held hostage—not that there wasn't truth in that.

Peter's stomach turned, "I think we should lock the hatch."

He expected Royal to make some smart-ass comment but he only nodded.

Peter climbed up and pulled the hatch shut, discovering a keypad on the underside. He relayed his find to his partner.

"Is it reprogrammable? We were able to open it from the outside."

"I'll check," Peter entered in a four digit code and held down the lock button until it flashed. He re-entered the code and the latch opened. "Done."

"Same code as always?"

Peter hopped down, "You betcha."

Now that they were here, his mind began to still but anxiety still gripped his gut. There was nothing left for them but to wait and pray that their parents' reaction wasn't too deadly.

Royal was already half way down to the lounge, "Let's have a drink."

It was Peter's turn to sink into the comfy leather. *This is home, this is home, this is home.* He closed his eyes and repeated his new mantra.

"What can I get you, good sir?" Royal put on a stuffy accent and blew the dust off the bar top.

"Hmm," Peter animatedly scratched his chin. "An Old Fashioned, please."

Royal scanned the bar for any ingredients besides liquor but came up empty, "Scotch neat it is!" He pulled out a pair of dusty lowball glasses and rinsed them off in the sink, "Hey! The water works!" He chose a scotch Peter had never heard of and poured two fingers worth into each glass.

"Running water is definitely good," Peter took his drink.

Royal sat down across from him, "What do you think you're going to miss the most?"

"I don't know yet," he sipped his drink, pretending it didn't burn. "You?"

"Women, obviously."

Peter laughed, "Maybe you can find yourself a wild one that lives in a cave."

Royal raised his glass and winked, "Now you're thinking."

After a few moments of staring around the room, drinking in silence, Peter said, "This doesn't seem like your typical safe house."

"No, it was commissioned for some rich guy a few decades ago. I looked up his file, most of it was redacted, he holed up in here for a good long while but it seemed like the police's mission to keep him safe inevitably failed." Royal made a fake gun with his fingers and pointed it at Peter, pretending to fire. "The bad guys got him. Found him here and after that, it wasn't used again. I figure criminals possessing the location of this place kinda took the 'safe' out of 'safe house.'"

No kidding. "How long ago was that?"

"Five years. Couldn't well use it after the location had been compromised. They left it intact." Royal nodded to his drink, "Stocked and all."

"Food, too?"

"It will be a lot of dehydrated stuff and non-perishables. We'll have to go out and get fresh food eventually but we have what we need for now."

A loud thud sounded from above them, followed by a scream.

Royal's face fell. He stood, gripping his glass, "That'll be my mum. I thought we'd have more time."

Peter sucked back all of his scotch, "I really wish we could skip this part."

They mounted the stairs. Royal was silent but his mother's frantic calls for help grew louder as they climbed upwards.

Royal's mother had made it out of the bedroom. Her eyes found him as she stumbled forward, the effects of the drug still in her system. Arms weak, she couldn't catch herself and she hit the floor with a *smack*. Royal rushed to gather her up.

"Royal?" she flopped against him. "What is this?"

"Mum, you're safe. We'll explain everything."

Peter helped him lift her up and sit her in the dining booth, a long metal table with cushioned benches on either side.

"The others should be waking up soon now."

"Others?" Her eyes frantically jumped to Peter. He nodded, "Yes, my parents."

Her eyelids were heavy, "What is this place?"

"It's a safe house, Mum," Royal said.

Her head rolled, "Safe house? Are we in danger?"

"No," he soothed. "No, we're safe here. I'll see if I can find you some tea."

Royal sorted through some cupboards, nodding to himself when he located a stack of tea bags. He pulled a kettle out from a drawer near the sink. He filled it with water and placed it on the stove.

Peter sidled up beside him, his voice as low as possible, "Maybe we *should* tell them we're in danger. Like we're on the run from something."

Royal just looked at him.

"That way, they wouldn't try to leave, and we'd have a good reason for bringing them here."

"You don't think our real reason is good?"

"Well, *I* do, but I don't think they will."

"They'll just have to get used to it because I am not lying to my parents and neither should you. This is a chance at a fresh start."

The kettle started to whistle. Royal poured a cup and walked it over to his mom. She blinked rapidly, struggling to shake the sedation and wrap her head around this place.

A crash came from Peter's parents' room and his father appeared at the doorway. He took the room in and then settled a glare on Peter.

"Son, *this* is by *far* the stupidest thing you have ever done."

"I agree with your father," Anne emerged from behind him. Her words were slow and slurred. "Molly?"

"Anne? Frank?" Molly blinked, her focus sharpening. "What are we all doing here?"

"Is Matthew here too?"

"In the bedroom. He won't wake up."

"He will," Frank sat down beside her, still glaring at Peter. "It appears that our sons have kidnapped us."

Molly knocked her tea over, "Kidnapped? But why would they—oh..."

"Yup," Ann grabbed a towel and wiped up the spill, relatively coordinated compared to Molly.

"Royal Seamus O'Leary, you have *got* to be kidding me," her face was fully alert now, her glare worse than Franks.

"Mum," his voice wavered. "Please understand."

"I do understand," she was up now, hands planted on both sides of Royal's face, her eyes searching the room. "But this? What did you do to us?"

Anne was wringing out the tea soaked towel, "They drugged us." Her voice was stern.

Before Molly could react, Peter stepped forward, "We knew you would never come with us on your own."

"He's right, Molls," A gruff voice came from the bedroom. Matthew O'Leary's sleepy face appeared in the doorway.

"Matthew!" Molly ran to hug him, still clumsy.

"Quite the party yer havin' out here, eh boys?" He smiled and rubbed a hand across his ginger scruff. He place a hand on the wall to keep from staggering back as Molly embraced him. She held an arm around him for support and guided him to the booth.

Frank crossed his arms, "How about you two tell us what the hell is going on here."

This was the part Peter was dreading the most. He exchanged a look with Royal and tried to focus on what he had said about a fresh start, "Okay."

"Starting with where you got the drugs."

Royal exhaled slowly, placing one hand on the back of his head, "I stole them from the hospital?"

"Stole?" Molly's eyes looked like they were going to pop out of her head.

Matthew however, looked amused, "If I had to venture a guess, I'd say Midazolam?"

Anne's mouth gaped open, "Midazolam? Do you know how dangerous that can be? The respiratory depression alone..."

"I'm not unfamiliar," Royal interjected, his eyes fixated on the back wall.

"Oh, and how's that?" Molly crossed her arms as well.

"Uh," he cleared his throat. "You remember that nurse I was dating?"

"Jenna?"

Peter spun, "You dated Jenna?!"

"Yeah, I mean," Royal shuffled uncomfortably. "That's why you had to distract her instead of me."

Matthew chuckled. He seemed almost impressed. Molly hit him in the chest. He responded with exaggerated hurt, not unlike Royal.

"Continue," Anne looked at them expectantly, her tone still sharp.

"We waited till you were asleep, snuck in, drugged you, then drove you out here."

Peter prayed they wouldn't ask how they obtained a large enough vehicle to do so, but they did. He didn't answer them and neither did Royal.

Matthew looked at everyone, "Stolen, I bet."

Royal stared, unblinking, "We're police, right? If it's police property, it's not really stealing, is it?"

Frank glowered, Anne sighed, and Molly put her face in her hands.

Matthew chuckled again, "If I could, I'd toast you boys."

"Matthew!" Molly hissed.

"What! Ye gotta give 'em props for their dedication."

Peter could have sworn he saw his mother's lip tug upwards.

"Well," Royal clapped his hands together. "If you want to make that toast, there's a pretty sweet bar in the lower level."

"It is really awesome," Peter looked to his parents. Anne placed her hand on Frank's and smiled up at him.

Frank's face softened in response to hers, "I think we could all use a drink right now."

It was Peter's turn to have his eyes bulge, "Really?"

"Really." Everyone stood, even a reluctant Molly. "Now show us this 'pretty sweet' bar."

FIFTEEN

My girls are my only relief. Visiting them in the forest provides me with much needed refuge. I can feel their bodies decaying beneath me, enriching the soil. I bury my hands in the dirt, relishing in their essence. It's all I can do not to crawl into the Earth beside them. I feel blind if I don't go out there, I feel dead. Teaching has become nearly impossible; my body feels like it's stuck in quicksand, unable to move through the poses. Meditation doesn't help. The life has drained from me. I need to kill again but it's still too risky. I can't chance the police coming around and asking more questions. I've been smart. I've been careful—not one hair or drop of blood left behind for them to find. Yet, to kill anyone else at the Temple... it would only be a matter of time before they narrowed it down to me. I'm not an idiot.

Michael has certainly passed my test. The police have not come for me, not even for more questioning. He supported me like I knew he would.

And to be truthful, there is one other thing that helps: Selene. I've taken to watching her when I can't slip away to visit my girls. Right now she's in the Atrium and—it's easy for me to go unnoticed above her on the mezzanine. The Atrium is such a grand space, the roof arches high above us, but she doesn't look small—she takes up the whole room. My Moon. Her raven hair is pulled into a high braid that cascades down her back. She's only in a black sports bra and tiny matching shorts but that's okay, she shouldn't cover up. Her body is a wonder. How does she move like that? She's practicing the most breathtaking sequence: easing up into handstands, down into a plank, back into downward dog which she flips over into a wheel pose. Every motion is fluid. I think if she can move this easily, maybe I can too. Maybe I can be free of the quicksand.

Her flowing body puts me in a trance. She is my salvation. With her, I know I can survive until I can kill again. The Sun and the Moon working in harmony.

I think back to my girls and how they have brought me to this moment. They have brought me so much power. I touch my robes; they brought me my promotion. But it's a tease! A tease of what I can have if I pursue the lifeblood. My body aches for more. How quickly my gratitude turns to anger. My girls showed me a glimpse of glory then they took it away. Why would they allow me to suffer? Their little bodies weren't enough. They were pathetic in life and were pathetic in death. I need someone better.

SIXTEEN

Molly was the first of the parents downs the stairs. Her eyes skimmed over the bar and she walked straight over to the forest wall. She stood about an inch from the screen, her lips were parted, eyes wide.

"I knew you'd like that, Mum," Royal slid behind the bar top, resting forward on his elbows.

And then she touched it.

"Woah," Peter's jaw dropped. The wall changed, it now showed a meadow doused in daylight, wildflowers littering the ground. The screen illuminated the entire room, Peter's eyes struggled to adjust to the simulated sun. Molly touched it again and the scene changed to the view of the galaxy, like they were up in space.

"Hit it again," Royal cheered.

Molly tapped the screen, revealing snow-capped hills, an icy lake, and the northern lights overhead.

Peter smiled, "Leave it on this one."

Royal rubbed the dust off of a few more glasses and handed out scotch to everyone. They sat, O'Learys on one couch and Holloways on the other. Matthew raised his glass, winked at Royal, and swallowed it in one gulp.

Matthew refilled his glass, "I remember little Royal's first drink. He was fifteen and he had stolen some of my homemade liquor."

"Oh god," Frank cringed. "You're not talking about your moonshine, are you?"

"The one and only," he beamed. "You see, Royal took it to share with his friends. They mixed it with some sort of blue drink and boy did we have a fun the next morning watching him clean up our entryway. The whole thing was stained blue. Little shit puked for hours."

Molly nodded and rolled her eyes as she recalled the memory.

Peter thumped Royal on the back, "You never told me that!"

He pretended to blush, "Not my most shining moment."

"You didn't start out so smart," Matthew ruffled his son's hair. "But boy you've become pretty clever."

"Thanks, Da—"

Matthew talked over him, "Now, I understand you must have found this place in the police archives but the only thing I can't figure out," Matthew poured himself another. "Is what kind of cover story you gave the department so they wouldn't come looking for us?"

All eyes were on Royal. He too, downed his scotch. He opened his mouth to speak only to close it again.

"Well?" Peter wanted to know as much as everyone else.

"Uhh," Royal looked as if he couldn't breathe. He coughed into his fist, "Thing is..."

Matthew's face darkened, "I would like to retract my toast."

"You told me you had a plan!" Peter was in Royal's face. "Are you saying that you didn't come up with *anything*?"

His face paled, "I couldn't think of anything that would work!"

"What?" Matthew was on his feet, "You just figured they wouldn't find us?"

"Well, yea—"

"Look at how easy it was for us to figure it out! There is no question that they'd track us here."

"Maybe we ca—"

Anne said something but it was lost amongst the yelling. She raised her voice to cut through the noise, "We have to go back."

"No," Peter rushed to her side. "We've come too far. We can't."

"Peter," She address him with sad eyes. "They will kill all of us."

Frank put a hand on his shoulder, "We know that you boys meant well, but it didn't work."

Peter was near tears, "They're going to make *me* kill you. How is that any different?"

"You'll get to live," her voice shook. She held his hand in hers.

Molly was crying and hugging Royal. Matthew embraced both of them, his arms large enough to wrap all the way around. He nodded to the Holloways.

Peter's frustration was mounting; they weren't listening to him. "Mom, Dad, killing you would destroy me. It wouldn't matter that I succeeded you, I would be worse than dead."

"Peter, you knew this day was coming. Your whole life we tried to prepare you. We knew it was going to be hard, but you have to be strong. It's just the way it is."

He ignored her, "Am I a Catalyst?"

Frank flinched. He tried to hide it by rubbing his nose but Peter wasn't fooled.

"Who...?" Anne began, her hand coming to her mouth to support her head.

"Who told me? Is that what you're asking?"

"Peter, I..."

"It's true?!" He felt sick. "How could you let them do that to you?"

"We didn't have a choice, son," Frank tried to soften his face but was unsuccessful, his mouth curled in discomfort. "Please don't be angry that we didn't tell you."

"No," Peter's eyes flooded. "I'm not mad because of that. I'm mad that you didn't want children and they made you have me."

"You are the best thing that's ever happened to us. You know that."

Peter covered his eyes with his hand and wept. Everyone remained silent, waiting for him to compose himself. His chest felt like it was going to cave in. *We can't go back.* Hopelessness gripped him like a disease. It spread from his core until it consumed his entire body, making him weak. He racked his brain for a way to make them stay. *Keep them drugged? That would only work for so long. Tie them up? Force them to stay?* Anything he thought of made him feel worse. He knew there was nothing he could do or say that would keep his parents here.

Peter looked to the O'Learys and back to his parents, "I know that you have to go back. But I can't go with you."

Royal's face twisted, "Peter, no."

"It's the only way. If I stay, they get to live. No one will have to die because of me."

His parents were crying now too. "We'll never see each other again," his mother said.

"I know."

They nodded, "We can come up with a cover for you, pretend that you're ill."

Peter stared at his feet, "Maybe eventually people will forget about me and you can come visit," his voice dropped at the end; he knew how impossible it was.

"Are you fucking serious right now?" Royal was frantic, knocking the coffee table aside as he jumped up. "You're just going to let him stay here?"

Peter's parents nodded and hugged Peter, "He's made up his mind."

Peter hugged them back, "I love you."

Anne kissed his head, "I'm so proud of you."

"Can't you see what's happening here?" Royal backed away from them. "This is just typical Peter. He'd do anything for you. He'd die for you if you asked him to. I know he can't really want to do this. Not really, do you, Pete?"

Peter managed to look Royal in his desperate eyes, "I do."

Royal let out an exasperated groan and stormed up the stairs; the rest of them followed solemnly behind. Molly looked back at the northern lights as she ascended, catching Peter's eyes. Her face was full of sympathy but she too looked proud. *Good.* He couldn't deal with pity right now. Once they were at the top, she and Matthew embraced him.

"Good luck, Peter," they backed away to give Royal room.

"Dude," voice catching, he could barely look at Peter. "I have to go with them."

Peter shifted his feet, "I know."

"Come here," they squeezed each other tighter and tighter until Royal started laughing, "What are you going to do here by yourself? You're going to get so bored." Despite his laughter, his voice was hollow.

"Maybe there's cable on that screen down there."

"That'd be wicked," his chuckles subsided. "I'm going to miss you, buddy."

"Me too."

Royal headed up the ladder. The key pad beeped as he entered in the code and cool air cascaded down from the open hatch. Matthew and Molly followed him out.

Peter's parents held each other and pulled Peter into their arms. He expected that they should all be blubbering by now but they stayed calm, all of them smiling. They knew this was the right decision and Peter was glad they hadn't fought him on it. Peter felt elated to be able to save his parents and he knew they felt the same way, perhaps not for themselves but because it would make Peter happy. He fetched their bags and followed them up the ladder.

Early morning sun filtered down through the trees. The O'Learys were already in the van.

"Goodbye, Peter," his mother kissed him one last time. "Thank you."

Frank hugged him again, "Take care of yourself, son."

"I will. You too." Peter threw his arms around them. He wanted to thank them for being so supportive and giving him everything a son could ever need. He wanted to thank them for a million things but he needed to let them go. Any more words and he feared they might not let him stay. Any more and he may not be able to resist leaving, too. Besides, he wasn't sure he could speak again without falling apart.

They smiled, walking backwards until they were inside the van. Royal was in the driver's seat, his mother in the passenger seat. The rest all peered through the center to look at Peter. He waved at them as Royal reversed the vehicle and drove out of sight.

He stood there, waiting until he could no longer hear the van's wheels crunching down the road. All he could hear now was a soft rustle from the wind in the trees. He looked up to see the mountain peaks—a sight he had been longing for and realised nothing would ever be the same. The weight of the world crashed down on him. He fell to the ground, the dirt cold beneath him. His chest heaved as he held himself. Sobs assaulted his rib cage, deepening the dull pain from his bruises; he thanked the stars that no one could hear him.

He was alone.

SEVENTEEN

The police are here.

I don't understand—I was patient, I was careful. I have an alibi. I haven't killed again but they're here and they have a warrant. They say it's to search my room and I feel ill. It's Officer O'Leary who serves me the paperwork. He's with two other policemen but I don't see Peter.

"Where is Officer Holloway?" I ask.

He ignores me, his eyes looking at me like I'm filth. I am not filth—I am the Sun. The three of them prowl around my chambers, using chemicals on the floor and the wall. I've been so careful, they won't find anything. Not one hair or one speck of blood left behind. They fling my sheets off the bed and use a horrible blue light to search but I've burned those dirty sheets. I'm clean.

There's something different about Officer O'Leary. He looks how I feel—hollow, like someone's sucked the life out of him.

They don't find anything, of course. As they leave O'Leary whispers that he's 'Going to get me'. No, Officer, I think not.

I'm out on the terrace now, looking towards my girls. I want to go out there but I know I can't. The police could follow me.

I wish Selene were here. Perhaps I'll go and find her.

A dog barks from below. A dog? There are no dogs at the Temple. A man shouts, "Canine's got something!"

I look over the edge, the police are running into the forest. They're running towards my girls. No! They can't have them! I am running too. I am running down the stairs and into the woods. I hear the dogs barking and sniffing and panting. Even though I could outrun all of them, I force myself to keep my distance; I can't be found.

I redirect to a nearby creek and jump into the water. It's cold on my skin and my robe clings to me, heavy on my arms. Heavy like my heart. I rub mud on my body and my clothes, obscuring my scent. They'll never find me. I still hear them running, fainter than before— they're farther away now and I am safe to follow. Oh, my girls! They can't take my girls. The underbrush scrapes and snags at me, but I dare not slow down now for the dogs have stopped ahead. They are going wild, barking incessantly.

There's more shouting, "Here! Here! Someone get a shovel."

Oh, god, they've found them.

I can't stop them and there's nothing I can do. The Earth is tilting beneath me, my mind is spinning out of control. They are going to take them away. Gone forever. I am desperate to see them one last time. I head to the west and climb up one of the tall, tall trees. At the top, my soul lifts ever so slightly—I can see them from here. The police are reckless with their shovels, the bevels cut sharply into the dirt. They need to be careful! They'll hurt them.

And there they are, unveiled to the world. My first looks the worst, her skin mottled and grey. A wretched officer blocks my second, but my last is beautiful, so lovely and broken. Unwillingly exposed, their last bits of life escape into the air. I can't grasp it. Oh, god, my poor poor girls.

A new pair of faces emerge from the trees. Their voices carry, barking orders and calling Medical Examiners and Crime Scene Investigators. I feel weak and have to steady myself to keep from falling. They're going to take them away. How did this happen? How could I let this happen?

Time disappears. I watch them tape, number, and photograph my haven. More people arrive. I cling to my branch until everyone has come and gone. My girls are gone.

I can't stay here, I have to be with them. With a safe distance between me and the police, I follow. I know they are going to leave the Temple and take them for themselves so I will leave too. There's nothing for me here.

I've never left the Temple on my own before, I've never had a need. Now I have no choice. I don't know what to expect but I know that I cannot draw attention to myself. I need to leave my robe and clean up. I sneak into the men's change room to shower. A class has just begun so I know I have some time. I steal a student's black pants and hooded sweatshirt. It's strange, but I like it. The inside is soft against my cold skin. A small comfort to my own decaying insides.

I take the shuttle. Selene sits two rows ahead of me, content in her ignorance. I try to focus on her but not even the slope of her neck or the way her raven hair falls over her smooth, bare shoulders is enough to calm me. My sky is black and starless. Everything, even my Moon has been taken from me. I am careful to shield my eyes under my hood. They are full of anger and are sure to expose my intentions. The shuttle made quick

time down the mountain but now that we are in the
city, it moves excruciatingly slow. I have to clench my
jaw shut to keep from screaming.

The outside world taunts me with urban mockery. The
trees in the city are the same as the trees at the Temple
but the buildings are clinical and it is much more
crowded here. How can anyone breathe in a place like
this? The streets are poisoned with lifeless meatsacks
waiting for me to breathe for them.

The shuttle lurches to a stop and I almost puke. Eyes
still masked, I ask the bus driver for directions to the
precinct. I half remember from when they dragged me
here but I want to be absolutely sure. I do not have
time to get lost.

The precinct is close and I find it easily. I spot the
Medical Examiner's van being unloaded at the back.
My girls are inside black bags, their spirits choked by
plastic. I want to jump inside their body bags and zip
myself in with them. I am so close and it's physically
painful to keep my distance.

There is a park across the way. I take a seat under a
crooked cedar, my sit bones cradled by winding roots. I
secure my hood over my eyes and plant my hands in
the grass. I envision their bodies in that cold building,
being poked at and prodded by unworthy hands.
Glaring lights exposing their decomposing flesh.
They're mine! Who are they to wash them and cut them

open? And for nothing. They won't find anything to help them. I breathed death into them, not those worthless cops. Their lives are inside me. Not them. I stare unblinkingly at the front doors, willing my fate to change, however hopeless it may be. All I can do now is wait and see where this new road takes me. I will stay here all day and all night. This is where they are and this is where I shall be.

But what's this? The two detectives who ordered my girls away, they're walking out of the precinct. They took my life away and without a thought I am following them now. We walk east, heading towards a residential area. A cement walk-through takes us off the main street between a series of apartment complexes. We turn south and they walk up to a big two story house with a front porch. It's peach coloured with white trim—the epitome of boring. They unlock the front door. This is their house. They live here. Together.

They're married.

Everything clicks into place and I no longer feel bad about leaving my girls. This is exactly where I am supposed to be. I had faith they would help me find my way and they led me to this moment, a reward for my loyalty to them.

On my side of the street there's a bus bench with a perfect view of their living room. I pull a newspaper out of the dispenser next to the bench and sit down, pretending to read.

At first, I can't see them. The front light is on, but the living room is dark. I wait, breath held until they appear. A lamp illuminates the room and they sit on the couch. Their body language is strange—it's stiff, but they're still warm towards each other. Their expressions are hard even as the woman melts against the man's chest, lonely despite each other's company. She holds something in her hand—a picture? The two of them gaze at it, hypnotized, the world dead to them. What sort of existence is this? Stealing life and hope from others when they have none themselves. Just look at how sad they are! They need a purpose and I know exactly how to help them.

I sit here patiently. Eventually their eyelids droop and they begin to fall asleep there on the couch. I creep closer. The husband nudges his wife awake and they climb sleepily up the stairs. It's dusk now but the streetlamps have yet to come on. It's the perfect time to be invisible. I sneak up and around the house. They left their back door unlocked—stupid. I'm inside where they just were and I can see the photo that was in her hands now; it's them and a boy. Where is he? They clearly care very much about him and he's nowhere to be found. The only noise in the house is the man's raucous snoring, no footsteps or movement to be heard. Their boy has abandoned them. He isn't worthy of their life but I know that I can put it to good use.

I only wish I hadn't left my knife at home. Oh well, theirs will do.

EIGHTEEN

Peter's relationship with the lower level bar developed quickly from acquaintance to intimate friendship. He didn't dare touch the whiskey from earlier as it reminded him of his parents but there was no shortage of other liquors to choose from. He had located a cocktail shaker under the bar top along with varying glassware. Missing only lemon, a steady and increasingly more sloppy stream of gin martinis ensued. The more he drank, the less he cared, disregarding his glass and instead drinking directly from the cocktail shaker. *No one here to see me anyway.*

Peter wasn't sure how long he had laid on the ground that day after his parents left. His only indication of time had been the sun moving relentlessly across the sky. Intermittent shade had come from the low hanging cedar boughs as they did their best to break up the blinding sunlight. Dirt had dried to the side of his face, obscuring one eye and depositing a dusty taste in his mouth. When the shadows from the trees had become long and permanent, Peter had managed to pick himself up into a seated position. The mountains had been clearly visible then, their jagged edges cutting the scene Peter had longed for so dearly. A dark void had ripped open inside his gut and the fresh, free air could do nothing to stitch it closed. Dehydrated and numb, Peter had dragged himself to the hatch and let himself be swallowed up by the Earth.

Since then, Peter hadn't gone back up above ground. He didn't see a point; there was nowhere for him to go. Perhaps one day, after the booze was all gone, he'd venture out and explore. For now, he'd settle for trying to dull the ripping sensation in his chest.

Boredom wasn't shy to sink in, amplifying his loneliness; alcohol did little as a remedy but he drank on regardless. A plus was that the scenery wall did in fact double as a TV. He had to pull one of the couches back to be able to see the whole screen. The safe house only received a few basic channels but Peter found a cabinet containing a wide selection of 'USB's all labeled as either movies or TV shows. He had never seen a USB before but they proved easy enough to operate. He was working through watching all the movies he hadn't seen before, mostly old westerns and a series of comedic TV shows. However, today he let the screen display the snowy northern lights as he sprawled out on the leather couch, gin in one hand, family photo in the next. Four martinis deep, he was having difficulty concentrating on anything other than the picture before him. He studied his parents' faces; *they look so happy*. All three of them had been bundled up so tight, cheeks bright pink, hands shoved in their pockets. Peter hated the cold but there was something about snow that was so soothing. It made him feel content. He liked the way it quieted the world; he could always think more clearly in the winter time. He looked from the picture to his glass. The alcohol sure didn't help with clarity; perhaps tomorrow he'd be sober.

Peter wondered how his parents were doing. Would they be mourning him like he was mourning them? He hoped that whatever story they came up with to explain his disappearance would hold up. Anxiety began to bubble in his stomach. This was his last chance to help his parents, he didn't know what he would do if someone found out the truth. He tried to calm his nerves by sipping his drink and reminding himself that the lie would work for at least awhile. And besides, the precinct would be busy looking for the missing women, not him. The search warrant for Ari's room would have gone out by now. *Maybe there's been a break in the case.*

Peter turned the screen to TV mode and selected Channel Two for the evening news. News Anchor Ariel Nickel appeared along with the photos of the women. Peter sat straight up, nearly knocking over his glass. By the look on the Anchor's face, he knew she didn't have good news to share.

"Cedar Valley Police have discovered a burial ground containing the bodies of three young women. Autopsies are still underway but their deaths are being treated as homicides. They have been identified as the missing Melissa Grant, Madison Shaw, and Sarah Preston."

"No."

He froze, staring at the screen. He wanted to turn away, cover his ears, anything to make what he was hearing untrue. He didn't want to believe that they were dead. The picture frame slipped from his grasp into his lap. Breaking free of his shock, he caught it before it could fall to the ground.

"No suspects have been arrested at this time. The authorities are continuing to ask for the public's help. If you have any information regarding this matter, please call the tip line below."

Peter tried to read between the lines of what was being broadcast. *Does this mean that they didn't find anything to implicate Ari? Besides the bodies, did they find anything at all?* The rift inside of him split further; he couldn't help feeling like he had abandoned those women. *If I had stayed, would they still be alive?* He wrestled his guilt to the back of his mind, allowing anger to creep into the forefront. Whoever did this needed to be stopped; a dark pit in his stomach told him Ari was responsible. Peter had half a mind to call the tipline himself and somehow implicate him. Finding the burial site won't end the killing; he will keep hurting people unless he is caught. Helplessness consumed Peter. Leaving was the right choice, he knew that, but it couldn't keep Sarah Preston's face out of his mind. Every time he closed his eyes, he saw her. It was the not knowing that made it worse. Without actually seeing her or the crime scene photos, his thoughts grew dark—they twisted and splintered to fill the unknowns. He wondered if they had found them in one piece. *How did the killer snuff the life from these women?*

Peter saw Sarah's small frame lying on the ground between the cedars, scratching at the unequally strong hands that gripped her throat. He saw tears streaming from the corners of her eyes. He heard her choking and gurgling instead of screaming for help. And then he saw her give up; the light left her, her arms fell limp at her sides, dead.

He stood up to refill his glass but was accosted by a new thought. Sarah bound to a chair, rope digging into her ankles, chest, and wrists. Her ash-brown curls caught in a gag. Tears stained black. Big eyes pleading in desperation, whole body shaking as she strained to scream. A gun in her face. *Bang*.

Peter shook his head to rid it of the image.
Sarah dead.

Groaning, he pressed a palm to the middle of his forehead. He banged it against his skull to drive Sarah's gaunt, lifeless face away. Head spinning, he managed to make it to the bar. He needed fresh air but he still didn't want to go outside. Outside made everything real. He would hide out down here, drinking until he no longer remembered the world. Grabbing the whole bottle and forgoing his glass, he slumped down against the screen wall. Sweet, fresh air flitted down from the ceiling vents. The soft smell of cedars mixed soothingly well with the piney herbaceous burn of the gin.

　　　　　　　　　　　　ᛗ

A pounding in his head woke him. Peter limped his way to the sink where he filled a glass with water, drank, filled, drank, filled, drank, and flopped onto the couch. The screen wall was back to it's original—or what Peter considered to be original—state. The outside trees were bathed in sunlight; it had to be at least noon. He had just switched the TV back to the news when he heard a vehicle pull up above him.

　　They've found me.

　　Stomach rolling, he ducked back into his room and grabbed his gun. Barrel raised, he turned bleary eyes towards the stairwell. His stance wavered and he bumped into the doorframe. *Focus, Peter.* He steadied himself. *How did they find out so quickly? I was sure I had more time.* His headache threatened to split his skull open. The pain bled into every thought, dulling his ability to think clearly. He couldn't make sense of what could have happened back home. He couldn't come up with a timeline or scenarios or words exchanged. Everything bound together in his mind like a ball of barbed wire.

The hatch opened. *Didn't I lock it? I could swear I did...* He used the creak of the metal to cover his dash from the bedroom to the foot of the stairs. He disliked his vantage point; trapped down here, like a dog. Whoever was coming for him would have a leg up. He settled beside the wall, gun trained on the opening to the stairs. They would have to come down here if they wanted him.

A single set of footfalls came down the ladder, crossed the floor above, and began descending the stairs. Peter adjusted his grip on his gun, his breath caught in his chest. His finger had found its way to the trigger when a familiar voice called his name.

"Royal?"

"Peter?" The voice grew louder.

Peter set his gun down and embraced his friend as he rounded the corner, "What are you doing here?"

"Peter, I..." Royal's eyes were bloodshot and dark circles had formed below. His cheekbones protruded sharply from his sunken face. He looked how Peter had imagined Sarah Preston, standing before him like a spectre.

Peter frowned, "What is it?"

"I'm so sorry," he motioned towards the TV screen. "I'm so so sorry."

Peter spun to see Ariel Nickel with more breaking news. A picture of his parents appeared in the top corner of the screen.

"Early this morning, the bodies of Detectives Frank and Anne Holloway were found brutally murdered in their own home. The police are still..."

A low hum began in Peter's ears. It's volume increased until it was deafening. The edges of his vision darkened. He could see Royal standing high above him. *Am I on the floor?* Royal's mouth moved in silence. His vision darkened still and he felt his body being shook. He could no longer feel his limbs, everything was disappearing. And then like a flood his senses returned; his focus was sharp—everything heightened and cutting into him like knives. He could hear the television and he could hear his friend.

"There's..." Peter's voice was hoarse. He cleared his throat, "There's got to be some sort of mistake."

Royal held a fist to his mouth, unable to speak. Eyes brimming with tears, he shook his head no.

"But I saved them!" Peter was screaming now. His words drowned out Ariel Nickel and echoed off the walls. "I saved them, Royal!"

Royal crumpled beside him and held him, "I know you did, Buddy. I know."

His screams turned to hysterical cries, making his breath impossible to catch. He collapsed into Royal who absorbed every sob, silently mourning beside him. Peter fought to breathe, his chest racking until he could ask, "Will you take me back?"

Royal sighed and nodded, "Of course I will."

NINETEEN

Despite the cool evening, the air conditioning was on in full force in Pearl's office. Peter's hands were freezing and shoving them under the crooks of his knees did little to provide warmth. The ride back into the city had been excruciating. Every minute Royal drove them closer, the worse he felt. Now that he was here the car ride seemed negligible in comparison. Separated only by glass, bodies shuffled behind him, pretending not to peer in. He felt their eyes burning into the back of his head. He couldn't stand it.

Pearl crossed in front of the window, his back to Peter. "Eyes to yourselves," he barked at the bull pen. "This isn't a freak show."

He entered the office and closed the door behind him. He sat down at his desk opposite of Peter, his face pale and strained. Wrinkles carved lines at the corners of his mouth, deepening his worn expression.

He tried to distract his trembling hands by fidgeting with his cufflinks, never satisfied with their position.

"Peter, I cannot convey how deeply sorry I am—how sorry the whole precinct is for your loss."

Pearl had never called him by his first name before. Peter rubbed his hands together, breathed hot air on them then stuffed them back under his legs.

"Your parents were great detectives and even better people," Pearl's chair squeaked loudly as he leaned forward. "The entire force is dedicating to finding out who did this to them."

Peter freed his palms again, placing them together, his fingertips resting against his lips, "Is it him?"

"Who do you mean?"

"The same guy who killed Sarah and the others."

"We don't know yet."

The air felt thick and stagnant. Neither one of them dared to breathe.

"You must know something," Peter fought to keep his voice low.

Pearl cleared his throat and continued to jostle his cufflinks but said nothing. "Well we had better get to work, then," Peter stood and headed for the door.

"Peter, sit down."

"No," he shook his head. "We don't have time to sit. We need to be out there looking for whoever is responsible."

Sergeant Pearl's face was grim, "I don't think it's a good idea for you to be involved in the investigation."

Peter gripped the back of his chair, "What?"

Pearl looked from his cuffs to Peter, "You know it's a conflict of interest. Besides, I think it would do you good to have some time off."

"Sergeant," his eyes burned. "Please, you've got to let me help!"

Pearl's lips tightened, "I'm sorry, Peter."

The black hole opened up inside Peter's chest and it was tearing at his heart and lungs, growing bigger. It was sucking the air right out of him; he couldn't breathe.

"Is there anyone you could think of that would want to hurt your parents?"

"No," The black hole was tunneling into his gut. "Like you said, they're good people."

Pearl nodded stiffly, "Get some rest. If you think of anything, call me, but for now just go home. I don't want to see you in here for at least two weeks."

"Two..." The air grew thicker, choking him.

"Yes," Pearl stood, signalling their conversation had ended.

Leaving the office and entering the bull pen felt a lot like getting pushed out of a pressurized plane. He had been safe in there but out here the open space was tearing him apart. Cautious eyes tracked him, quickly evading his gaze if they made eye contact. *I need to get out of here.* He made for the exit, walking as briskly as he could. He pushed through the double doors, nearly tripped down the front steps and onto the sidewalk where he doubled over to dry heave into the bushes.

"It's him!" An unfamiliar voice sounded from down the block, high and grating. "Peter Holloway!"

Peter looked up to see a scrawny news reporter rushing towards him, a husky cameraman on his heels. *What the fuck is this?*

"Officer Holloway," the reporter had beady eyes and a face like a rat. He brushed greasy black hair out of his eyes and shoved a microphone in Peter's face. He stared at Peter intensely, like he was trying to pin him down. "Have the police found any leads?"

Peter knew he should turn and walk away but the black hole was churning inside of him, clouding his judgement. He balled his hands into fists, his knuckles cracking.

"Can you tell me how you're feeling right now?"

"How I'm feeling?" Peter's jaw clenched and he took a step towards the reporter. He towered over the scrawny man, glaring down at him but the reporter didn't falter. "How do you *think* I'm feeling?"

He swore he saw the reporter smirk. The back for Peter's neck began to burn and he lunged forward, fist raised. Someone stepped in front of him before he could make contact with the reporter's face—it was Royal.

"Leave him alone," he said, eyes boring into the news team. He tipped Peter's shoulder, encouraging him to turn away. "Come on, Pete. Let's go."

Peter followed him into the park. They sat on a bench and watched the pair slink back into their news van. Peter didn't take his eyes off of them, "Assholes."

"Fucking vultures, always out to get a rise out of someone." Royal studied Peter with a careful eye, "How'd it go with Pearl?"

"He took me off the case. Told me not to come back for two weeks."

He sniffed and rubbed his nose with his hand, "Huh."

"'Huh'? That's it?"

He shrugged, eyes avoiding Peter, "Maybe time off is for the best."

Peter's neck was burning again, "No, Royal, it's not for the best. You know I can't just sit around and do nothing."

"You're too close to it, Pete," his expression wary. "I know it's not what you want to hear but you wouldn't be able to see it clearly."

Peter's head was too loud. Blame and guilt shouted at him from every direction. He shook his head, sniffling, "How the hell did this happen? We did exactly what we were supposed to. It should have worked but they left."

"You know there was no way they'd stay."

"I could have made them stay! I should have tried harder. This is all my fault," Peter let his head hang. The blackness was prickling him from the inside out. "I have to fix it."

Royal sat there, his facial muscles flexing. Peter knew what he wanted to say. He wanted to say that it'd *couldn't* be fixed but instead he said, "What can I do to help?"

"You can get me copies of all the casefiles."

Royal froze, "Pete, you know I can't do that. If Pearl finds out..."

"I'll take the blame. I'll say I snuck in and stole them."

He kicked the ground, "You know that won't fly."

Peter shifted closer, "Please, Royal. I'm begging you. I need this."

Fear crept across Royal's face. He swallowed hard and played with his neck collar—he was hiding something. "What you need is to go home, Peter."

Peter watched him swallow again, "What aren't you telling me?"

"Seriously, just go home and let us handle it."

"Tell me." Being in the dark was driving Peter crazy. He didn't do well with the unknown, Sarah Preston was testament to that. So far, he had relied on high mental walls to keep his mind from wandering.

"You really do not want to see those files."

Peter sat back and looked towards the precinct. What Royal was really saying was that he didn't want him to see the crime scene photos. Obvious horror of dead parents aside, there was something in his tone that said it was more than that. Ariel Nickel's voice replayed in Peter's head:

"...brutally murdered."

169

Tears fell as he turned to his friend, "What did he do to them?"

TWENTY

I find myself back at the police precinct, lured here by my girls. However, I am not here to mourn them, I am here for reflection. The journey they took me on has been vital to finding my way; I know now that they weren't enough for me but they led me to my rightful path. The detectives' lifeblood is surging through me and I am on fire, burning bright for the world to see. I feel as good as I did when I killed my own parents.

Peter stumbles out of the front doors and I hide behind a news van. All the colour is gone from his face and he looks as though he's going to be sick. On the opposite side of the van from me, the sliding door crashes open and a newscaster and camera man rush towards Peter. The newscaster, weasel-like with his lanky limbs and slick hair yells Peter's name to get his attention. His cameraman looks like a buffalo in comparison ambling behind. I can't hear what they ask him but Peter's face is turning red and he's taking angry steps towards the reporter. He moves to bop the weasel but Officer O'Leary steps between them, like Peter's very own knight in shining armour coming to his defense. He steals Peter away to the safety of the park, sending the news crew back my way. I find cover behind another parked vehicle while the cameraman sets up to film the reporter.

The reporter holds a microphone below his pointed chin and looks into the camera, "Hi Ariel, I'm here at the Cedar Valley Police Department where I have just spoken with Officer Peter Holloway, son of murdered Detectives Frank and Anne Holloway."

What? Oh, my...

"He was unable to comment on the case at this time but it appears that the police are still without any leads."

I killed Peter's parents.

It takes everything in me to contain my joy. I want to run into the precinct and hug my girls. They brought me the greatest gift of all. Could it really be true? Peter's parents, dead at my hand. No wonder I feel so good.

I look into the park and I can see Peter's grim face but I cannot hear what he is saying. I need to get closer.

There is a chain link fence bordering the south end of the park, its links woven with green plastic to make it nearly opaque. I wait for the news team to pack up and speed off then I walk over to the fence. I get as close to Peter as I can.

They're talking about case files. Peter wants them but O'Leary won't get them for him. Why can't he have them? Peter sounds like he's about to cry and O'Leary doesn't sound much better. Peter's asking him what I did to his parents. I wait for O'Leary to tell him, to relive my work aloud for us to hear, but he doesn't. Instead I feel a darkness spreading between the two of them. I breathed death into Peter's parents and now it's making its way through their world. From Peter to his partner.

Can you feel it, Peter? The light inside of you is dwindling. It's fueling me instead, making me strong. And as for what I 'did to them', Peter? I can't wait for you to find out.

Your partner is taking you home. I suppose there's nowhere for me to go but with you; the more your darkness grows, the brighter my fire will burn. Oh, Peter, this is going to be fun.

TWENTY ONE

Royal pulled up outside of Peter's apartment and unlocked the car doors. He stared at him expectantly. It wasn't until he cleared his throat that Peter realized he was supposed to exit the vehicle. He mumbled his thanks to Royal who in return imparted one point of wisdom:

"Don't hit the bottle, just go to sleep."

Peter pretended to agree and slowly made his way up. Instead of sleeping, he sat in his sofa chair and poured himself a glass of the scotch he had taken from the safe house. It was the same bottle he had shared with his parents. The last drink they ever shared.

He grabbed the Christmas photo and sat it on the side table. He made the same promise to himself that he had made to Sarah Preston—that he'd find whoever killed them. Remembering how his last promise panned out, Peter quickly swallowed his drink.

He stared at the bottle, it was almost half gone. Were his parents really gone too? His vision blurred. He closed his eyes and swirled the whiskey in his mouth, trying to picture his mom and dad. He felt the safe house's leather couch beneath him, the soft air from the vents grazing his skin. He heard their voices. If only he could reach out and grab them, pull them into safety. Peter lurched forward, arms extended, desperate to grasp them. His eyes opened and the memory of them slipped away like grains of sand. The black hole inside of him gaped, like every ounce of light was being sucked away. Peter gripped his empty glass and threw it against the wall. It shattered, the pieces clinking to the laminate floor. A loud thump sounded from the other side of the wall followed by a gruff, 'Hey!'—his neighbour telling him to keep it down.

"Fuck off!" Peter picked up an empty beer bottle and threw it. When it shattered the darkness crept into his eyes, making him see red. Bellowing at the wall, he threw another one.

The muffled voice shouted back, "Knock it off or I'll call the police!"

"I am the police!" He grabbed the edge of the coffee table and flipped it. Half-drank coffee splattered on the floor. Loose papers flew into the air and landed amongst the sticky spill.

Peter wanted to pick up that scotch bottle and drink it all down but he couldn't bear the thought of going through all of it in one night. Buying another wouldn't be the same. It wouldn't be *this* one. He needed to savour it. Peter snatched up his jacket and gun and headed out, shoving the sofa chair down onto its back as he went.

It was raining again and cold wind whipped his jacket around him. His clumsy hands took multiple attempts to do up the zipper. The streets were slick and cars made a soft wet hushing sound as they passed, trying to quiet Peter's rage. He flung his hood over his head and marched forward. Footsteps sounded behind him. He spun around—no one was there. He kept walking, listening closely to the sound of his soles on the wet sidewalk. Left, right, left, right, left, right. It was just him walking. *But wait, what was that?* A twig snapped to his right. Leaves crunched. He drew his gun, flailing it towards the sounds. He squinted through the rain. Shapes appeared then disappeared. *Is that a person? No, a tree.*

"Who's there?" Peter's voice was lost in the wind. "I'm a Police Officer!"

He strained his ears but there was nothing but the pelting of raindrops on pavement. Peter tucked his gun back into his pants and continued on.

He was beginning to shiver, jacket no longer resisting the rain. The first bar he entered didn't have the right brand of scotch so he left. The second did. *Thank god.* The bartender was stocky but noticeably fit. He had a thick brown-red beard and slicked back hair which reminded him of Royal's father. He wore a white T-shirt with grey slacks and suspenders, odd attire for this end of town. Although his appearance was immaculate—even his mustache was groomed—Peter knew he was the kind of guy you wouldn't want to face in a fight. As he made his way over to Peter, his name tag became visible: 'Rick'.

Rick finished drying a pint glass, "What can I getcha?"

Peter's throat still burned from the scotch from earlier so he opted for a beer. Rick twisted off the cap and slid it to Peter. He nearly spat out his first swig; the damned thing tasted like ash.

Rick noticed his disgust, "Everything alright, sir?"

Peter nodded and began to choke down the rest of the beer, not wanting to make a fuss. That was something his father always rode him about; he could hear him now:

"Peter, you shouldn't be so self-sacrificing. You would rather suffer than inconvenience anyone else. The world won't bend to you in return. No one's going to look out for you except for you."

The black hole gripped his stomach. He waved Rick over, "Actually, could I get one of those instead?"

"Sure," Rick took the beer and walked over to the liquor display. "Which one?"

"I'm not sure how to pronounce it. The one with the green label."

"Gotcha. Neat or on the rocks?"

"Rocks," Peter's stomach twisted. "No, neat."

Rick's eyes narrowed as he poured the scotch, "Rough day?"

"You could say that," Peter swallowed all of it. "I'll have another, please."

The bartender didn't push him any further, he just kept pouring the whiskey. Peter was grateful for it. His head felt so loud, he couldn't make sense of all of the noise and confusion. He was completely lost. Without the case files he had no idea where he should go or what he should do—he needed to convince Royal to help him. There was no way they could keep him from looking for the killer. He didn't even know if it was the same one who killed those girls; they could have two psychos on the loose. If that's the case, they were going to need all the help they could get. Something evil inside of Peter hoped there were two killers; his neglect to stop the first would no longer mean he was directly responsible for his parent's deaths. But without the files, there was no way for him to know. Until then, his reality remained the same: Peter abandoned the women and now they're dead. He abandoned his parents and now they're dead too. He wasn't going to abandon anyone else. Never again.

Tonight, however, this scotch had Peter's full attention. He needed to wallow in this darkness and soak it all up. It seemed to be fueling him, like a dark horse carrying him forward. Succumbing to it didn't feel like failing; it felt like fighting.

Peter pushed his glass towards Rick.

"I'm sorry, mate. I've gotta cutcha off."

178

"Just one more," Peter worked hard to keep his words clearly enunciated.

"I've already poured ya more than I should've," Rick handed him the bill. "I'll call ya a cab."

Peter pulled out his card and gave it to Rick. He tapped it on a mounted tablet and returned it. The cab arrived quickly and took Peter home. The ride was a blur but he managed to stumble up his stairs and through his ransacked apartment to pass out in his bed.

TWENTY TWO

There's no view into your apartment from street level, I even tried different sides of the building with no luck. No matter. I know where you live now, Peter. I'll have to listen carefully, standing three floors below you in the shadows between the trees and the wall. There isn't a lot of movement in the apartments separating us but I listen carefully none the less. You're in there for a mere twenty minutes before I hear a crash followed by you yelling. More crashes and more yelling. It's the darkness—can you feel it? I can, even all the way down here. The crashing stops and there's quiet. I hear the front door of the complex swing open. I peek around the building—you're outside. Where are you going? Your legs are wobbly beneath you. My my, drinking already? You know that alcohol clouds your judgement, Peter. How do you expect to catch me with your brain so muddy? Well, not catch, *chase*. Those legs may be weak but I can see that you're on a mission. What could you possibly hope to find out here in the rain? You'll find no light out in these darkened streets. I thought I'd stamped out all your will, yet you trudge forward. Perhaps you're stronger that I thought. Good, you're going to need your strength.

I follow you away from your home and into the night. You're five minutes into your journey when you hear me behind you. You turn but I'm hidden; your bleary eyes look right through me. We keep going and I time my footfalls to match yours and then I don't, unsettling you. I can feel your fear, Peter. I throw a rock and it lands to your right. You thrash around like a hooked fish, brandishing your gun towards every whisper of the wind. I've hooked you. But for now I'll let you swim some more while that hook still hangs in your mouth, leaking blood so I can trace your steps. You swim through the rain and into a bar. Ah, little fish do you need a drink? Before I can enter behind you, you leave, sending me back into the shadows. What, this bar too dry for you, little fishy?

You try the next one and I wait for you to leave again but this time you stay. I wait for ten minutes and then I enter. I pick a spot down the bar from you, on the same side so you can't see me but I know where you are, Peter. The bar is U-shaped with a mirror along the back. I can see you perfectly. The darkness has wrapped you up so tight, Peter, that you can't see anything but yourself and that beer in front of you.

The bartender looks rough. He's dressed ridiculously like a poor boy with rich man's taste. He asks me what I would like to drink and I tell him that water is fine. I can't cloud my judgement like you, Peter. I need to be sharp. Tonight is a very important night for us and I am not going to compromise my mind. I wouldn't do that to you, Peter.

You give your beer back to the bartender and order something else. Whiskey. My, for a wee little fish you sure are picky. I'm watching you drink it down and exchange your empty glass for more when a girl approaches me. She asks if the seat next to me is taken. I have to say no, Peter, because I can't draw attention to myself. I don't want to but I have to. She tells me her name but I'm not listening. She leans closer, her breasts threatening to fall out of her shirt, hoping I notice them. Are all women this desperate? Thank goodness I have you, Peter, to keep me centered or else I fear I may slit her throat right here. She's yammering on about how handsome I am and she's touching my arm. *Oh my! What strong arms you have!* I know she's envisioning me fucking her. I can see it in her thirsty eyes. She thinks she can see it in my eyes too but I don't want to fuck her, Peter. I want to kill her.

But I won't. Not tonight. Not ever, maybe. My girls taught me that she wouldn't be enough. She would be a tease and I can't have that, Peter. I am worth more than the blood of a filthy bar rat. Besides, I have become quite fond of that couple in the corner over there.

They're sitting close, not first date close, but they're in love. I see wedding bands. They're perfect.

I send the desperate girl away. The bartender is pouring you another—you're almost starting to impress me. I never took you for a scotch drinker and by the looks of it, you aren't, your mouth is twisting every time you choke it down. You want more but he's cutting you off. It's for the best, don't fight it. You'll want to have a clear head tomorrow. Trust me. The couple is leaving, it's my queue to go as well. Get home safe now, Peter. I'll see you tomorrow.

The man helps his wife into her coat. She smiles at him as she frees her curls from the lapels. He holds the door for her while opening an umbrella—a gentleman. They remind me of my parents. They are so in love and complete servants to each other. I know with absolute certainty that they are exactly what I need. I am still buzzing from killing your parents, Peter, but I can feel it fading and I won't stand for that. I have no intention of becoming less empowered than I know I can be. When I have the means, why wouldn't I take advantage of this?

They leave on foot so they're easy to follow. They live in the opposite direction that you do but the community is very much like your parents', cozy and quiet. The rain is starting to let up yet they hold each other closer. They're too focused on each other to notice me. They aren't as paranoid as you, Peter. We come into a cul de sac. Their house is off-white stucco with dark brown wood trim. The front is flat and the top angles up; it reminds me of a dairy farmhouse.

Their window faces the backyard where I am. They don't turn on any lights until they are upstairs in their bedroom. I look around; there's no evidence of a dog—good; I don't have time for disruptions. The light goes off and I wait a while, letting the silence of night time set. When all I can hear is the soft patter of raindrops on tree leaves, I approach the back door. I am wearing gloves, of course, but the metal door handle is still cool in my grasp. It's locked which is unfortunate. Breaking a window would cause too much attention so I look around for another point of entry around the side of the house. Thankfully, one of the windows is open. I use my knife to slice the screen out of the frame and I lift myself inside. I do wish I could have used the door; there is something so satisfying about entering a home through its threshold.

I take my time and stroll through their living room. All of the pictures are of them and other adults. No children. They are not parents but that's okay. I don't want you to have to share your darkness with another orphan, Peter. That wouldn't be fair.

Ascending the stairs is nerve wracking. A mistake could cost me so much. Going back to my lesser self would be worse than death so I know I need to be careful. There is a familiarity one gets with their staircase. They know the sounds it makes on its own and how it sounds when it is being climbed. Traveling from bottom to top is a painfully slow process but I know that it is unavoidable. I place my heel on the next step and slowly bring my toes down until my foot is flush with the stair. Then the next, one after another until I am at the top. The second floor has a mezzanine that overlooks the front foyer. The banister is made of the same dark wood from the exterior and it runs up the stairs and across the terrace. It's perfect.

The husband snores like your father did, Peter. I can hear him from the stairs. I continue my heel-toe walk to their bedroom door. They sleep with it closed shut. I never understood that—if you're the only ones in the house, why do you need the privacy? It's a false layer of security, a door isn't going to keep out anything that truly wants to get in. I will prove that. I turn the knob and push it open with ease.

There they are. Their chests expand and their hearts beat before me. I will breathe death into them and they will breathe life into me. I want to savour this moment but the fire takes over and I know I have to begin. I cross the room swiftly. I pick up the lamp, solid and metal, and smash it into the husband's head. I strike him only once; I don't want to make him bleed too much. Not yet.

The wife stirs. I replace the lamp on the night stand. I rush to her side of the bed and I hold the knife to her throat. Her eyes pop open and I tell her that I'll kill her if she screams. She looks to her husband but she can't tell that he's been injured. I use the cord from the lamp to tie her wrists to the bed frame. She's crying yet I can see she's trying to be strong; a pointless attempt to spare her husband.

I lift a finger to my lips and remind her to stay quiet. I return to her husband and hoist him over my shoulders. I look up at the wife and smile—this is the first moment she realizes her husband is hurt and it is glorious. Her eyes grow wide and she's about to scream. I catch her by pointing my blade at her and I tell her if she makes a sound then she's next. I'm going to kill her regardless but I don't find any harm in lying to a dead woman.

I bring the man to the bathroom and slump him over the edge of the tub, a small trickle of blood oozes from his head. I make sure the stopper is in the drain. I tug his floppy head back and slit his throat. As his vessels are emptying into the bath, I go back to the wife. She is begging me to tell her what I did to her husband. I don't answer her and cut her ties. She tries to bolt for the door but I grab her by her hair. Her curls have flattened from her pillow. If not for her black mascara face she might even be pretty.

I yank her to her feet. The knife is to her throat and she's whimpering like a little lamb. I drive her to the hall. She's not fighting me, she's goes where I direct her. My puppet. We arrive at the bathroom and then she really does scream. I can't blame her. I shove her forward and slit her throat too, a silencing tactic that has proven useful to me. She's grappling at her spewing neck and I push her farther into the tub. I look around and I am impressed with how little blood I spilled on the floor.

After carefully hanging my clothes and removing my gloves, I lower myself into the bath. I roll the dead wife out. She doesn't get any of this—it's all mine. This reminds me of your parents, Peter. They offered up so much lifeblood for me. Just like them, the tub is filled perfectly. I wish you could feel how I feel right now; it's the most marvelous thing. I don't feel human anymore. I have wings and if I let myself I could just float right up, above the Earth, above the sky, and assume my rightful place as the Sun.

I stay in the blood as long as I can. I drain it then wash it off of me. I stay nude save for my gloves and drag the bodies into the hall. I find more electronics around the house and cut their cords. I tie up their ankles, anchoring them as securely as I can manage and toss them over the balustrade. Their bodies hang inverted above the foyer and blood drips onto the floor below.

I've been thinking you need a bit of a push, Peter, so I go to the kitchen and search the cupboards until I find what I am looking for: canning jars. I know the sun will be up soon so I have to hurry. I stand beneath the

DENISE WALKER

bodies and collect as much of the drippings as I can. I take a few pieces of stationery and a pen from their study before retrieving my clothes. Bleach in hand, I retrace all of my steps to ensure I haven't left a single unwanted clue behind.

I am done here and I am elated. There's nothing in the world that could bring me down. My good mood has me feeling generous so I'm on my way to your house, Peter. I have a gift for you.

TWENTY THREE

The doorbell rang. *How can something so tiny be so damn loud?* Peter held his hand to his head and tried to remember the last time he had woken up without a headache. Groaning, he opened his door to find Al, his spectacled neighbour from down the hall with a package in his hand.

"This was lying in the foyer," Al held a box out. It was plain, unwrapped but taped carefully along the edges. Small handwritten letters scrawled across the top. "Figured I'd bring it up for you."

Peter squinted against the harsh hallway light to read the writing on the box:

Attn: Peter Holloway
Apt 304

"Huh," Peter took the package from him. "Thanks, Al."

He retreated back inside and brought the box to the kitchen counter. He didn't recognize the handwriting and there was no return address; this had been hand delivered. Peter opened the lid. A piece of thick paper sat on top. There was a message on it in the same writing as the box but it was what was below the paper that Peter grabbed at.

Two mason jars of blood. Dizziness struck him. Someone had sent him two mason jars of blood. *Is this some kind of sick joke?* He reached for the message. His eyes barely scanned the words before his stomach turned, sending him across the kitchen to vomit into the sink. He ran the tap, washing away the rank whiskey laced bile. The stench made him sick again. He tried to concentrate on the sound of the running water but the message had already imprinted on his mind:

> *One whiskey, two whiskey, three whiskey, four.*
> *I bled them out and I want more.*
> *Five whiskey, six whiskey, seven whiskey, eight.*
> *Oh, Poor Peter, you're too late.*

Peter couldn't think. He couldn't move. He just stayed at the sink, head bowed and tap running. *This isn't real.* Two jars of his parents blood were not sitting on his counter. *Could they be? No.* The killer didn't send him anything. The killer didn't know where he lived or who he was. *He couldn't.*
No.

Water still on, Peter turned and slid to the floor. He couldn't see the letter or the jars from there. He stared blankly at the island cabinets and again tried to convince himself that the only thing that existed was the sound pouring from the sink; the metallic hush of water relentlessly pounding the steel basin and the dulled trickling of water falling down the pipes. His vision came in and out of focus. He knew there was no way he could stand again. He couldn't look—that would make it real. He pulled his phone out and called Royal.

He answered after the first ring, *"Hey man, everything alright?"*

Before Peter could reply, he saw something from the corner of his eye—the sticky note from the lasagna lay discarded on the floor:

'Love, Mom.'

"Royal..." was all he could manage. He feared he would lose his mind completely if he said another word.

"You're at home?"

"Yes," barely audible.

"I'll be right there," the phone clicked as the call ended.

༓

What a sight this must have been for Royal, furniture overturned, shattered glass everywhere, and Peter in a heap on the floor with his eyes glossed over like a mental patient.

"What the hell happened?" Oblivious to the blood, he ran towards Peter and shut off the faucet. Dishes had shifted and the sink had begun to overflow, water dripped off the counter's edge.

Peter gestured to the package, "Came this morning."

Royal turned to see the jars, "What the fuck?"

"Read the note."

"One whiskey, two whiskey, three..." his eyes grew wider with each word. "What the *fuck*?"

Peter pulled his knees up to his chest and lay his head on them.

"We have to get these to the lab. I'm calling my dad."

He lifted his head slightly, "Your dad?"

"Yeah, uh," Royal placed a hand on the back of his neck. "They..." he hesitated. "They've stepped in to take your parents place in the investigation."

"Oh," Peter said into his knees.

Royal snapped some photos of the evidence with his phone, "Did you see who dropped it off?"

"No, a neighbour found it downstairs."

The phone call was quick. He relayed to Peter that his dad wanted the package brought to the station.

"He's toying with me." Finally able to form more than a few words, Peter looked up from his lap again, "Killing my parents wasn't enough. He has to taunt me too."

"Sadistic freak."

Peter lay flat on the floor and stared up at the ceiling fan. He watched the blades turn in a slow, useless circle. *Focus, Peter. You'll need your wits about you. Focus.* He cleared his throat and sat back up, "At least we have that."

"What? How does that help us?"

"He's cocky and narcissistic. He wants us to chase him."

Royal frowned, "You think he wants to get caught?"

"No, I think he wants to prove he's smarter than us. It's a game to him," Peter was back on his feet. "Royal..."

He raised a hand to silence him, "You don't need to ask. I'll bring you the case files."

Royal left with the package and returned about an hour later. He wasn't alone; Banks and Alvarez strut in behind him.

Banks eyed the pile of broken beer bottles, "So this is where you've been hiding out."

"Not by choice. You know well enough I'd rather be at the station." Peter turned to Royal, "What are they doing here?"

He placed a box of files on the kitchen island, "They caught me taking these and insisted they come help." Catching Peter's incredulous expression he added, "Yeah, I know. I couldn't believe it either."

Peter studied his team members for any sign of confirmation. Banks ignored the exchange and proceeded to take in the disheveled state of the apartment while Alvarez only shrugged his shoulders and set a second box down.

Peter approached the counter and began opening the first, accepting his unanticipated help. "Two whole boxes?"

"Yeah," Banks sat himself down at a bar stool. "We got all the autopsies back from the three women. There was a lot of information to note. The second one is..."

"My parents," Peter nodded, spreading the women's files across the counter. He swallowed hard as he pulled photos of the burial site from the box. Whether he was ready or not, he would finally know what happened to Sarah. "Okay, catch me up with the women."

Alvarez started in, "All three had their throats slit and were bled out. That was it when it came to Melissa Grant but I don't know which was worse, Melanie Shaw or Sarah Preston."

"What do you mean?" Peter wasn't sure he wanted to know.

"Melanie had extensive genital mutilation—"

He fought the urge to puke again.

"—but the only part of Sarah he spared was her genitals."

Peter found Sarah's autopsy file. The pictures were grotesque; her limbs were deformed and rested unevenly on the table, dark bruising that never had a chance to heal painted her entire right side, and her face was completely unrecognizable. The damage to her body was depicted in detail by the Medical Examiner:

'Extensive unilateral blunt force trauma to right side consistent with a single mechanism. Trauma to the frontal bone resulting in a subdural hematoma. Multiple facial fractures to the mandible, maxilla, and malar bone. Laceration to the throat resulting in a severed carotid artery and jugular veins. Clavicle fracture, multiple rib fractures, hemopneumothorax, pelvic fracture...'

The list went on. Peter rubbed his eyes and tried to continue reading but his gaze kept shifting back to Sarah's pictures. Her death was worse than he had ever imagined. Hardly any of the words in the report made sense to Peter but it was the first line that confused him the most, "What does that mean, 'Extensive unilateral blunt force...'" he stumbled over the vocabulary.

"'... to right side consistent with a single mechanism'?" Alvarez regurgitated flawlessly. "It means that everything except the slitting of the throat happened at once."

Peter stared at him blankly.

"It means she wasn't beat up by him or assaulted with a weapon. The trauma here was caused by a single incident. Like the impact from a car."

"You think he ran her down?" *What next? Was he going to set someone on fire?* Peter felt faint as he remembered that there was a *next*—his parents. But he couldn't look at their file, not yet.

Banks pointed to Sarah, "She would have had to have been hit pretty hard to sustain these injuries.

You'd expect a second set from when she collided with the ground, but there isn't any."

"Yeah," Alvarez nodded. "And there are no markings to indicate she was run over. No tire marks or anything."

Peter didn't want to think about it anymore. The amount of fear and pain Sarah must have endured was crippling.

"The Medical Examiner also found traces of semen on Sarah's body. DNA is unidentified at this time—"

Peter felt tears line his eyes and he had to look away. He wanted to run, to scream, to end whoever did this.

"—which means we can't be sure it belongs to the killer. It could have been there before the murder took place."

Alvarez's reasoning did little to assuage Peter. He felt his apartment shrinking, like the walls wanted to smother him. After a few deep breaths he returned to the cases before him, reminding himself that if he wanted to solve this he needed to keep calm. He opened Melanie Shaw's folder, "She's the only one with genital mutilation? Why just her, do you think?"

"Hard to say. The stabs to her genitals could simulate intercourse." Banks skimmed the notes, "She was a bit older than Sarah and Melissa. Maybe she was more his age and would have been an appropriate sexual partner?"

"Or he's just a psycho," Royal chimed.

Banks closed his eyes, annoyed, "Humour me?"

196

"Fine," Peter felt more inclined to agree with Royal. "But if that's the case, if he truly just wanted sex from her, something had to have happened to make him lash out. He decided to kill her instead, why?"

"Because he's a psycho," Royal repeated, tapping his temple.

Banks ignored him, "What about impotence? Having trouble getting it up would have made him mad. Royal said you think he's a narcissist. Inability to perform would definitely be a stressor for someone like that—his image is everything to him, but I don't think killing her was a result of that."

"What do you mean?" Peter held out a photo of Melissa's mangled pelvis. "You don't think he meant to kill her?"

"Oh, he definitely meant to. I think *that* was the goal and the sex was secondary."

Royal snatched the photo from Peter and placed it face down, "He could have lured her with the promise of sex."

"She did have a boyfriend," Alvarez flipped through papers to find his statement. "We questioned him. They lived together and he painted a pretty nice picture of Melanie. She seemed like a nice girl."

"You're saying he tried to rape her then? Why would he go to the trouble if he could just kidnap and kill her like the rest?"

"Wait," they all turned to Peter. He was staring at the autopsy reports. "There's another difference. Melissa had blunt force trauma to the head, just like Sarah. It's not as extensive as hers but Melanie doesn't have any. He had to subdue the others but this suggests Melanie went with him willingly."

Alvarez sighed, "I suppose even nice girls make mistakes."

They all shared a moment of solemn silence. *Poor woman. She had made a mistake alright, one that led to the ultimate consequence.* Peter shuddered. His eyes wandered to the second file box, the one containing everything they had on his parents' murders.

"Do we know if it's the same killer?" Peter couldn't look up.

"Well," Royal began but struggled to continue, his eyes glued to the file box.

"The same knife was used on all three women," Banks took over for him. "Your parents were killed by one of their kitchen knives. The M.O. is the same but the victimology is completely different. But—" Banks shot a wary glance towards Royal.

"What?" Peter's throat felt tight.

Royal found his voice but it was thick with caution, "They think your parent's deaths may have been retaliation for disrupting the burial site."

Before anyone could stop him, Peter flung open the box. He steeled himself and pulled out the crime scene photos. There they were, necks slashed open and gaping like the black hole inside of him. The killer had strung them up, upside down, from the banister. His dad had a large head laceration while his mom had ligature marks around her wrists. A small amount of blood had pooled beneath them. He looked at the autopsy reports and scanned furiously though the medical jargon, trying to make sense of what had been done to them. Cause of death was exsanguination like the rest—they had been bled nearly dry. The only saving grace was that there was no sign of genital mutilation on his mother, and no semen either. Peter closed his eyes and exhaled slowly, determined not to break.

"Pete," Royal said softly. "You should tell them about the package."

Alvarez shared a look with Banks, "What do you mean, 'package?'"

Peter looked at them quizzically.

Royal cleared his throat, "I didn't tell them."

"Tell us what?"

Still trying to keep himself calm, Peter explained, "I received a package today containing two jars of blood and a handwritten note."

Alvarez slapped the counter, "Jeez, O'Leary! You should've led with that!"

Royal's phone rang. All he said was, 'Hello' and 'Thanks' then hung up. The colour drained from his face.

"What is it?"

"The blood doesn't belong to your parents and it doesn't match the women either. All we know is one is male and one is female."

"We have another set of victims?" Banks was standing now.

"We don't know that. There wasn't that much blood. They could still be alive."

"I don't think so, Royal," Peter's head spun. "Remember the message?"

Royal's voice dropped, "'*Oh, poor Peter, you're too late.*' What was the rest?"

Peter recited the whole message:

> "*One whiskey, two whiskey, three whiskey, four.*
> *I bled them out and I want more.*
> *Five whiskey, six whiskey, seven whiskey, eight.*
> *Oh, Poor Peter, you're too late.*"

"Why the fuck is he talking about whiskey?" Banks scrunched his nose as he looked around the apartment. His eyes landed on the scotch bottle.

"I went out to a bar last night and drank whisk—"

"By yourself?" Royal looked concerned.

Peter ignored him," I thought I was followed there but chalked it up to paranoia."

"It's a clue," Banks snapped his fingers. "He followed you there and chose his next victims."

"Let's go find them."

TWENTY FOUR

I wish I had been there to see you open my present, Peter. I bet the look on your face was priceless. I hope you're grateful that I've included you in this because even though I didn't have to, I wanted to. There are some things in life that are better shared, don't you think? Your darkness is still growing and it feels so good, even here at the Temple. Besides, our relationship is special; the more you hurt, the better I feel. I'll need to be there when you figure out my clue. I know it won't be for a while yet so I have time to keep up appearances—I can't very well abandon my duties here. I have an important job that the blood awarded me and I can't take that for granted.

There are no classes this morning so I take to the garden to practice. Well, If I'm being truthful, Peter, I came to the garden in hopes of seeing Selene. You would love her, you really would. She's here, thank

goodness, in her usual cedar grove. I pick a place with a
good vantage point and sit in lotus pose, my legs
crossed and my feet resting on opposing thighs. I close
my eyes and feel the Earth below me. I remember the
lifeblood I spilled and how it charged through the dirt
and into my body. I come onto all fours, flow through a
sun-salutation and then move into a wide-legged
forward fold. I place my palms to the Earth and like it
were nothing, I spread my new wings and lift up into a
handstand. My entire body is balanced, an extension of
the Earth.

I can see Selene. She too, is in a handstand, her legs
wrapped around her like an inverted tree. From here
it's as if she is floating in the sky and holding the entire
world above her head. That's how strong she is, Peter.
Just like my mother.

I practice balancing poses, trying to outlast her.
Though I am the Sun and the lifeblood has saturated
me, she is still my Moon. She's breathtaking and holds
every pose like it's her birthright.

I've returned to lotus and Selene is leaving. Her going
makes me feel like my sky is falling. It's nearly time for
class so I head over to my studio but I wish I could
follow her around all day instead.

The room is hot and I can feel my lungs expanding, my
muscles loosening, my soul opening. I relax. I like the
way my robes fall around me in the heat. I lower myself

down onto the mat my father gave me. This mat has life; I can feel it buzzing beneath me. I close my eyes and draw energy in from every corner of the room. My students are flowing in and joining me in *savasana*. When I no longer hear bare footfalls and hear only breathing, I move into a seated position and greet the room. My hands are at my heart and my eyes are still closed until something in the room tugs my attention and I bat my eyes open.

It's Selene. Selene is taking my class. My heart is racing and I am on fire. I am burning from my core and I feel like if I let myself, I could set the whole studio ablaze. I know I should feel nervous but I only feel excited. I've watched her and now it's my turn to be seen.

"I invite you to clear your minds. Let go of the day so far and become present. Let the energy of the Earth support you through your practice today."

I can sense a change in them as they obey me. Their breathing steadies and unifies with mine. We are becoming one.

"Start to roll the wrists and ankles. Find your breath then roll over into tabletop position. Hands under the shoulders and knees under the hips."

Watching them is mesmerizing; all of them moving together to my commands. They are extensions of the Earth, I am their Sun and right here is my Moon. My light is guiding them and this room is our whole universe. Our only purpose is to connect.

"Spread your fingertips wide and push back into downward facing dog. Peddle out your feet and send your hips high up to the ceiling. Spiral your biceps up. Send your heart to the back wall. Inhale through your nose and take a long steady exhale through your mouth."

Selene is in a perfect inverted V. Her heels are flush with the Earth and she finds a stillness that the forest would envy.

"Inhale: take a slow walk to the front of the mat. Exhale: forward fold. Lift the toes up and slide your palms under your feet. Massage the wrists. Keep your knees soft. Inhale: lift up half way to a flat back then exhale back into your forward fold."

I feel a giant ball of light expanding inside of me. I feel it shoot beams out to each of my students, empowering them. I guide them to inhale all the way up and stretch high above their heads. They are glowing with my light.

"Bring your hands to heart-centre."

Their entire practice is seamless. I feel like a proud father watching his children learn and grow. This is the first time I have ever given any thought to parenthood. I look to Selene. Her dark, perfect skin is glistening.

She's so beautiful. I picture our life together: the Sun and the Moon and all of our little stars. We could have as many children as we want because no one would dare to take them away from us. We are above even the sky.

We are all now in our final *savasana* and I want to remain here forever. This room is my creation. I know it cannot last but I am still saddened as they start to leave. Our beams of light disappear. Selene stays almost the longest—I cannot bear to stay once she exits our space. Outside, I take a seat on a flat, smooth stone and see off my departing students. We share smiles and thank each other. The light inside of me holds strong and I feel incredibly satisfied. I've never felt so right in my whole life.

And there she is: Selene. She has changed into a stunning yellow sundress. Her hair has been washed and it cascades down her back. It's much longer than I expected—a very pleasant surprise. Her hazel eyes are looking directly into mine. She sees me. And then she is right in front of me, smiling.

"Thank you, Teacher," her entire soul radiates when she smiles.

"You can call me Ari," I so desperately want to reach out and touch her.

"I'm Selene."

Does she want to touch me too?

"It's wonderful to meet you, Selene. Thank you for joining us today."

"Nice to meet you too. I really enjoyed your class."

I bow my head to her, "I hope you'll come again soon, then."
"I am sure I will," she tucks her mat under her arm and leaves.

In this moment, I could spread my wings and soar high above the entire world. Not even the exodus of oxygen would stop me.

TWENTY FIVE

Peter led them to the bar. The bartender, Nick, was working again and he frowned as Peter walked in the door. Nick's eyes moved to Banks and Alvarez who were in uniform and his brow furrowed deeper. If you took Royal's ratty T-shirt and added the amount Peter consumed here last night, to Nick they must seem like quite the group. Peter hadn't presented the most professional display yesterday and he had to admit that he and Royal looked sketchy compared to their sharply dressed team mates.

Pushing through the prejudice, Peter approached the bar top, "We need to see your surveillance footage from last night."

Nick cocked an eyebrow, "Tryin' to verify an alibi?"

Banks snickered, received by a dirty look from Royal.

"We're all cops," Peter tapped his badge that was clipped to his jeans. "Think you can help us out?"

"Sure, ya got a warrant?"

"Are you—"

Nick smirked, "I'm just jokin'. Follow me."

Peter was the first to follow, "We're looking for a murder suspect we think was here last night. Same time I was. Do you remember anything unusual?"

"Murder?" His face paled has he held the office door open for them. He looked back towards the bar top as if trying to envision the night before. "Can't say that anyone stood out."

The office was long and narrow, each wall covered with sturdy metal shelves that were piled high with glassware and linens. Nick led them past empty kegs and laundry hampers to the far end of the room where a computer sat atop a desk.

"This it?" Peter pointed to a surveillance recorder attached to the screen.

"Yup. You mind if I leave ya to it in here? Gotta mind the bar."

"Knock yourself out." Alvarez took a seat in front of the screen and began effortlessly navigating the surveillance program.

Nick left them and they crowded behind Alvarez. He rewound the footage to fifteen minutes prior to Peter's arrival. They watched the crowd, looking for anyone who looked out of place. The bar wasn't as full as Peter remembered; a group of corporate looking men shared a pitcher of beer in the corner and a few single people trickled in and out.

Royal pointed, "Here you come."

They watched Peter take his seat. A few minutes later, a hooded man entered and sat a ways down the bar from Peter. He kept his back to the camera. Shortly after ordering a water, a busty woman approached him. She touched his arm and laughed animatedly but they didn't appear to know each other. The man seemed mildly interested at best, his body language was stiff and he kept his eyes on the mirrored bar back.

Peter tried to sort through his cloudy memories but for the life of him, he couldn't remember either of them.

They kept watching. The recording showed a couple leaving through the front door. Less than two minutes later the hooded man dismissed the busty woman and followed the couple out the door.

Banks clapped Alvarez on the shoulder, "That's gotta be him."

Royal nodded. He poked his head out of the office and called for Nick to come back.

Alvarez invited Nick to come close to the screen. He rewound the footage to when the hooded man was at the bar, "Do you remember this guy?"

Nick peered closer, "Yeah, the bloke only ordered a water. Left me a fiver though."

"Do you remember what he looked like or did he mention his name?"

"Ah, y'know, he didn't say much. That woman there," he pointed to the screen. "She introduced herself but he never said anything back. I never really got a look at his face. Kept his hood up the whole time.

He was strange though, any guy I know would have left with that broad but not him."

Peter pinched the bridge of his nose. Last night, his parents' killer was sitting no more than ten feet from him. Something he noticed during the recording but hadn't said aloud, was that the hooded man seemed to have been watching him. He had stared at the mirror, head tilted slightly in Peter's direction. If only he hadn't been so wrapped up in his own drunken grief, he could have seen his face. Peter shook his head and did his best to stay focused.

Nick shuffled his feet anxiously. Peter wrote his phone number on a post-it from the desk and handed it to Nick, "You see him again, you call us immediately."

Nick nodded and headed back out looking grim, an expression that told Peter he was praying he'd never have to call.

Alvarez ejected the disc from the computer, "I'll take this back to the station and run facial recognition on the couple."

Banks followed him out of the office. Peter and Royal leant against the wall and stared at the blank computer screen.

Peter sighed, "He was right there, Royal."

"You couldn't have known," he put a hand on his shoulder. "Let's just hope they can track these folks down."

"Let's go back to my apartment. I want to look at the files some more."

"Lead the way."

魚

Peter was barely through the door before he dove back into statements and forensic reports. The clinking of glass sounded behind him. Royal was sweeping up the broken bottles.

"You don't have to do that."

"Someone's got to. We both know if I leave it to you, this glass will stay here for a month."

Clicking his tongue, Peter returned to the files, "What your parents think makes sense: that my parents disrupted his burial site and that made him angry enough to kill them."

Royal emptied the glass into the garbage.

"He was probably visiting them, the women. It's close enough proximity to the Temple for him to do that."

"Ugh," Royal shuddered. "Fucking creepy. You're still sure it's Sinclair?"

"Makes sense, doesn't it?"

"Yeah, but we didn't find any evidence in his room."

"Doesn't mean much." Peter laid out the pictures of all the victims, "The only thing I can't figure out is why his victimology changed so drastically. He started with young lone females—even one, maybe two if we include the semen found on Sarah, with a sexual component and moved on to an older, married male and female couple with no signs of sexual motivation."

"Maybe it's just that: he prefers the females but your parents' murder was fueled by rage. It was about revenge rather than pleasure."

"Then why did he follow that couple last night? And whose blood is in those jars?"

Peter's phone rang. It was Banks.

"We have an address."

ffl

It was late afternoon now. Royal drove while Peter scanned the info Banks had sent to his tablet.

He read aloud, "John and Laura Gibbons. 88 Charleston Way. Married for two years, no children. John is a Contractor and Laura is an Education Administrator. No criminal record and no connection to my parents that I can see. They seem like perfectly normal people."

"Here's their house," they pulled into a cul de sac. There were no other police vehicles outside, "We must have beat Banks and Alvarez."

The Gibbons' car was parked in the front driveway. A chill ran down Peter's neck, "Home in the middle of the week?"

Royal tightened his jaw, "Let's not assume the worst just yet. They could walk or take the bus to work."

They parked the car and approached the house. One hand on his gun, Peter knocked on the front door, "Mr. and Mrs. Gibbons, it's the police!"

Silence.

Royal peered in the front bay window, "I can't see anything."

"Are you getting déjà vu right now?" Peter's chest tightened.

"Yes," he tried the front door. It was locked, "Let's go around back."

Leading with their weapons, they opened the gate and headed through to the backyard. Along the side of the house, Peter noticed a sliced section of a window screen and tapped Royal on the shoulder, drawing his attention to it. They picked up their pace and tried the back door. It swung open easily.

Royal stayed glued to the spot, eyes lingering on Peter's chest, "Maybe we should—"

"Wait?" Peter snapped. "They could be in trouble. We don't have time."

His partner nodded quickly.

Guns raised, they split up. Peter entered the kitchen while Royal entered the living room. The house was quiet and nothing looked out of place, no overturned furniture or discarded household items on the floor. The scent of vanilla flitted through the air mixed with, *what is that? Bleach?* The chill in his neck traveled down his spine and gripped his stomach. Once Peter was satisfied the kitchen was clear, he entered the dining room. Everything in there was undisturbed as well but the smell of bleach grew stronger. He turned the corner into the front foyer.

"Oh, fuck."

Royal was standing with his gun lowered, his mouth slack. Peter followed his gaze to where John and Laura Gibbons were strung upside down on the bannister. Blood pooled below them from their slashed open necks. A note was pinned to Laura, the pin fastened through the flesh of her cheek:

"Good work, Peter."

Images of his parents, dead and bloody hit Peter like a brick to the face. "He told us we'd be too late," Peter doubled over. He couldn't breathe.

Royal eyed him, "You stay here. I'm going to check upstairs."

Sirens pierced the air. Peter opened the front door and sat on the front step, waiting for the cruiser to pull into view. He stared ahead, the world slipping out of focus. His head was spinning and he knew for sure he'd faint if he tried to stand. The sirens blared louder as they neared then switched off when they drove into the cul de sac.

Banks was the first out of the cruiser, "Holloway?"

Peter rubbed his temple, "You're going to need to call for backup."

Banks stared past him and through the open doorway, "Ah, shit."

Alvarez was on his phone, "Detective O'Leary? Yeah, the Gibbons' are dead. You'd better get down here and bring Forensics."

They began to draw their weapons but Peter held up his hand, "We cleared the house. It's okay."

"Are you okay?" Alvarez scanned him. "You look like you're going to be sick."

"Yeah, you go ahead. I'll be in in a minute," Peter closed his eyes and cleared his throat. He tried to slow his heartbeat—he could hear it pounding in his ears. His chest ached where he'd been shot even though the bruise had healed. Horrific images swirled in his mind: his parents dead and bloody. Melissa's decaying skin, Melanie's mangled pelvis. Sarah's broken body. His parents hanging and mutilated. Hanging and mutilated just like the couple behind him. *Fuck this asshole, he's probably watching us right now.* Rage flooded his entire body.

"ARE YOU WATCHING, ASSHOLE?" Peter yelled into the street. "ARE YOU GETTING OFF ON THIS?"

Neighbours began opening their front doors and peered out at him.

Peter didn't care. "YOU CAN'T HIDE FOREVER. I SWEAR, I'LL TAKE YOU DOWN IF IT KILLS ME."

More sirens. His eyes were red and snot poured from his nose. He didn't want Royal's parents to see him like this; once had been enough. Peter wiped his nose on his sleeve and hopped to his feet. The dizziness had subsided now but anger coursed through him like adrenaline. He re-entered the house. Alvarez was writing notes and inspecting a head wound on the husband. Banks was taking blood samples, swabbing each body before sticking the swabs into the sample port on his tablet. Both of them looked at Peter with blank expressions. He knew they had heard him yelling but he was grateful that they held their tongue about it. Heat collected at the base of his neck, already feeling embarrassed and regretting his outburst.

'Processing' flashed across Banks' screen in bright green letters. Peter held his breath. A soft *ding* sounded and Banks exhaled shortly. He turned the results to face Peter.

They were a match to the jars of blood.

"Pete," Royal called to him from the top of the stairs. "Come see this."

Squaring his jaw, Peter walked up the stairs and past the bodies. They were tied to the railing with electrical cords that under their weight cut deep into their skin. He was surprised that the cords held them so well. Blood streaked the carpet. He followed the trail into the washroom, careful not to step in any of it.

Peter wrinkled his nose—this is where the bleach smell was coming from. The floors were all splashed with blood. The pattern indicated that it originated in the bathtub however, the tub was pristine—not one speck of blood in sight.

Royal was taking photos with his tablet, "I doubt we'll find any DNA from the killer."

"No, we're not going to find anything he doesn't want us to find," Peter looked in cupboards. He found a near empty container of bleach under the sink. "The blood in the jars belonged to the Gibbons."

"So they were dead this entire time," Royal said solemnly.

Peter nodded. He followed a few drops of blood into the bedroom. One pillow had a small bloodstain on it. On the other side of the bed he noted another electrical cord tied around the bedpost.

Royal appeared beside him and pointed to the blood stain, "Your parents had identical injuries. Husband with a head wound, wife with ligature marks on her wrists. Seems he hit Mr. Gibbons over the head to incapacitate him. Why didn't he knock her out too?"

"Perhaps he's not strong enough to control both of them?"

"Maybe. He did that with Melissa and Sarah too and they were petit. It may just be for convenience. If the goal is to bleed them out as quickly as possible, I agree it would be easier to just to knock them both out."

"So why does he tie up the wives?" Peter frowned and walked over to the electrical cable. "He's sadistic, we know that." He looked towards the bathroom, envisioning himself in Laura Gibbons' position on the bed. The anger in him festered as an explanation slid to the forefront of his mind, "I think he makes them watch their husbands die. He doesn't care about the males, it's the females that matter to him. He enjoys their suffering."

"That's consistent with the first three women. We were wrong; the victimology isn't as different, it's just evolving. Individual women don't cut it anymore.

He needs to inflict more psychological torture before he kills them."

Peter stared back towards the balustrade, "I'm willing to bet that there will be no sign of sexual assault with Laura Gibbons."

"Agreed. I'm willing to bet that this," Royal gestured around them, "is the only thing that can provide him with sexual release." He paused, staring at the empty bed before them. "It's going to get worse, isn't it? The more he kills, the more sadistic shit he'll need to achieve the same satisfaction."

"You're probably right." Peter lowered his voice, "He's got to be watching us."

"You think?" Royal's eyes shifted to the open window.

"He knows where I live, he probably knows where all of us live."

Royal pulled out his phone, "I'll get a chopper up looking for him."

Peter shrugged, "Knock yourself out but I don't think we'll catch him that easily."

He stared at his cell then put it back in his pocket. Members of the Forensic Team streamed into the room, kits in hand. Peter watched them discuss what to collect: bedding, electrical cord, blood samples. He silently prayed that Forensics would come back with anything helpful, any little thing to point them in the right direction. He inched down the stairs past more people with kits. Royal's parents were standing in the foyer. Molly was looking up at Matthew who was talking on his phone.

She spotted Peter, "What in God's name are you doing here?"

He wasn't quite sure how to explain how he'd been investigating off-duty so he just motioned to the note pinned to Laura Gibbons' face. That seemed to be good enough for Molly.

Matthew was off the phone, "Next of kin has been notified. Jesus," His eyes looked from the note to Peter. "You have any idea why your name's on here?"

"Uh, yes?" Peter was confused. Royal had told him about the package earlier. *Hadn't he?*

Royal leaned into Peter's ear, "I didn't tell them about the note."

By their identically unimpressed expressions, it was clear that the detectives had heard his whisper. Before they could yell at him, Peter caught them up to speed. He told them about the note and how he agreed with their theory that all the murders were connected. He shared Royal's idea on the evolving victimology and their worry that the level of psychological torture may get worse with each new victim.

Molly shook her head, "Pearl is not going to like this."

"What's the significance of the blood, then?" Matthew moved out of the way to let the Medical Examiner through. "It's important to him. He bleeds them—not an easy task mind you—and he sent it to you as what, a gift?"

"If it's so important to him, it must've been a big deal to give some away," Banks had walked back to the foyer from the study. He was holding a stack of paper.

He held a piece up to the note pinned to Laura, "Looks like this is where he got the stationary."

"There's a whole bunch of jars in the kitchen, too," Alvarez joined them. "Just like the ones you got, Holloway."

"The bleach belonged to the Gibbons," Peter added.

"All objects of opportunity," Molly stared at the bodies. "Probably used one of their kitchen knives."

"I wouldn't be so sure," the Medical Examiner interjected. "Their wounds are much more consistent with those of the three first victims; the edges are slightly jagged. We won't know if they're exactly the same until I have them back at the morgue."

"So, he brought his own knife. That means that it was premeditated," Peter's knees wobbled but he fought to stay steady. The second line of the message burned in his memory, '*I bled them out and I want more*'. This won't end here, he's not going to stop. Peter was beginning to feel very small, there was too much information swirling around in his head, drowning him. He took a few slow breaths to try to settle his thoughts but he couldn't process anything. All he could think about was his mom and dad. "My parents were definitely killed out of rage, then. Their deaths weren't planned like the Gibbons'."

The M.E. gave the go ahead for Forensics to cut the bodies down and zip them into black bags. They wheeled the Gibbons out just as media vans began to arrive at the scene. The ratty reporter from yesterday was rushing towards the house. Peter clenched his fists and internally dared him to get too close. Royal held an arm across Peter's chest, allowing Alvarez and Banks to charge past them and out the front door. They barred the reporter from advancing further. It was dark out now and Peter had to shield his eyes against the media's spot lights to watch his teammates push everyone back behind the police line.

"We'll go make a statement," Molly sighed and led her husband out to the lions.

TWENTY SIX

I almost missed it but I am so glad I didn't, Peter, because it was better than I had imagined. I was particularly fond of how distraught you looked out on that front porch. And when you started yelling to me? I felt closer to you than I ever have. To answer your question, yes, I do get off on this. The darkness in you is becoming so thick, it's tangible and being here is like killing them all over again. The fire in me is roaring stronger than ever. Seeing you all run around like chickens is almost as good as the kill.

I can sense the darkness spreading to all your little friends too, Peter. It's like my own web of blackness, created in the shadow of my brilliance that sucks the life out of everyone you touch. How does it feel to be so contagious? I see Officer O'Leary's parents have slid into the position of your dead ones. That's very interesting. I saw that you ran to hide when they showed up. Not supposed to be here, are you? I'd take you off the case too, If I were them. I hate to tell you, Peter, but you're coming off as emotionally unstable. I get it though, it's been a rough few days for you.

Mr. and Mrs. O'Leary have noticed that you're here. They seem annoyed but they don't scold you. Remember that they're here to do a job, Peter, so don't get too attached. By the looks of it, Little O'Leary there isn't too far off from his twenty-fifth birthday. You'll both be orphans soon enough.

All of you are standing in the doorway, right within earshot. A bit reckless, don't you think? One might think it was on purpose, but I know better. You're not that clever, Peter, especially not now with that darkness clouding your eyes. What's really entertaining is your 'theory' on why I killed these two. You seem to think I did couple because I wanted to... torture her? Oh, Peter, that is so trivial. I don't care about her psyche— she's dead! I care about *your* psyche and how I can find ways to twist it until it breaks. You swore that you'd catch me even if it kills you and I can promise you, hunting me is going to do just that.

The media is arriving and that's my chance to sneak away. A spark ignites in my chest as they pull out their cameras and start rolling. I can no longer hear but I can see you're already distracted by that mess of a reporter from yesterday. Your bodyguards are ushering him away—too bad, I would have enjoyed watching you exorcise your frustration. Oh well, I'll be patient. One day soon I will have the pleasure of witnessing all that and more.

I am staying in the city tonight at a motel paid for by money I stole from the dead's study. It's terribly filthy and riddled with whores and junkies but fifty dollars isn't going to buy you much in this town. It's only for a night and I desperately need access to a television. The one in my rented room is tiny and breaking but it gets the news channel I want. It's past six so I have to wait for the eleven o'clock program. For now I'll take to sitting by the window. The rickety chair and table have a grainy texture to them from years of built up grime and the curtains smell like mold. There is a layer of dust on the window pane but I ignore it and stare out at the parking lot. The red motel sign reflects off the still-wet pavement. A rusty beater crawls into the lot and a bushy haired, leopard printed slut bends over to talk to the driver. Red pointy nails flick away an over-smoked cigarette and she flips her mane over her crack leached shoulder. My mouth feels dry. She'll take him back into her room here and I'll sneak in and kill them. They are scum and won't provide much release but it will be enough to keep me busy until eleven. She looks behind her, towards her room. My hand tightens around my knife. She looks back at the john then enters the passenger side. No. The car shifts into drive. No! The car pulls out of the lot.

"No!" I slam my fists onto the table. The hilt of my blade cracks the plastic. I am seething. How dare they leave! I'm scanning the exterior, is there another mark? No one. There is no one else outside. I want to run out and break down every door. I close my eyes and I am outside. I smash down the first door. It splinters with a loud *CRACK*. A woman who is no more than skin and bones is sprawled on the bedspread. A tourniquet lays limp under her arm and track marks create a constellation on the interior crease of her elbow. There's needles and lighters and fast food wrappers decorating the floor like a toxic meadow. Her pupils are pinpoint, stabbing into me like a knife. I grab her by her hair and drag her rag doll skeleton to the bathtub. She doesn't fight, she's not even here. Her skin is yellow and waxy. Her hair is grimy and matted and I can't wait to let go of it. Her teeth are rotting and her face is pitted with scabs and my stomach rolls. My saliva is thick in my mouth and I am having trouble swallowing. My hand is shaking and I dig my knife into her neck and drag it across. Her blood is spraying out with every beat of her diseased heart. I should feel release but I don't feel release, I feel ill. The smell of mold is overwhelming and I feel faint. The bathroom light is flickering and in its dim glow her blood looks black. No, it *is* black! It's tainted. I cannot bathe in her sickness. I shove her into the tub and her limbs fold around her like an awkward stillborn doe. Her blood is on me, on my hands, and my clothes. I need to get out of here.

I don't remember leaving her room but I'm in my own tub now. The shower is raining down on me as I sit with my knees pulled to my chest. My eyes are open but all I can see is black blood. I vomit on myself and bile stings my throat, choking me. The shower washes it away but then it fills again with black blood. I shriek and jump up to get away from it. I look down and it's gone. The bath is empty. I close my eyes and try to slow my breath. I run my hands across my shaved head and down my face. I open my eyes and my hands are covered in black. My heart stops. I look up and it's pouring out of the shower head. I slip and hit my side on the edge of the tub. Grabbing the curtain, I pull it down on top of me. Tangled, I twist and pain explodes through the back of my head. Black blood fills my eyes.

I wake in the motel bed. I am clothed in the hoodie and sweats from yesterday. Gasping, I check myself for her blood. My skin is dry and my clothes are clean. I check the washroom and it's as if it's never been used. My knife is—wait, where is my knife? I fling the sheets off the bed, nothing. I check under it, nothing. I am holding my head and trying not to scream. Where is it! I throw the shitty chair across the room. I rip the pillow cases off the pillows. I can't catch my breath. I am hyperventilating and I stumble forward, crashing into the TV stand. My eyes see a glint of silver—my knife! It was placed directly beside the television remote.

My knife. I clutch it to my chest like a lifeline.

It's as if my entire body exhales, every muscle relaxing.
My breathing immediately returns to normal. I killed
that girl last night, didn't I? I did. I am sure of it. My
mind must have shut down to protect me from the
tainted blood, blocking out the memories. The fire in
me must have taken over and cleaned up.
Subconsciously, I went to the laundromat next door
and cleaned my clothes. That explains the absence of
blood. I cleaned my knife and set it next to the TV
where I knew I would find it because I missed the news
last night and I knew I needed to tune in now. It takes a
few good shakes of the remote before I resort to turning
the TV on manually. The morning news is just
beginning.

*"Good morning and welcome to Channel Two
Morning News. I am Ken Woods. Yesterday evening
the bodies of John and Laura Gibbons were found
slain in their home. We turn to Greg Bridges who is
live on scene. Greg, do we have a serial killer among
us?"*

My breath quickens again and the frame switches to a
reporter in front of that wonderful dairy farm house.

*"There is compelling evidence that yes we do, Ken.
This killer is responsible for the deaths of* seven
*innocent people. The police believe there is a
connection to the murders of Detectives Frank and
Anne Holloway and the deaths of Melissa Grant,
Melanie Shaw, and Sarah Preston. I am standing here*

in front of the Gibbons residence where they were
brutally murdered two nights ago by the same
suspect."

The TV displays the pictures of my girls. Oh, look at them so pretty and perfect. I do miss them. A video clip of the police statement begins to play. Oh, Peter, look! It's your replacement parents!

"My name is Detective Matthew O'Leary and I am one
of the team leads on this investigation. We want to
issue a warning to you: this man is dangerous. We
believe he is responsible for the deaths of five women
and two men. Please do not walk alone at night and be
vigilant in locking your windows and doors. We are
doing everything in our power to bring this monster
to justice."

What's funny is that if they had swung that camera around with that spot light, I bet you'd see me. I was right there, Peter. I'll always be right there under your little nose. The camera was back on the primary News Anchor. The tip line number flashed across the bottom of the screen.

"Thank you, Greg. If you have any information
regarding these murders, please call the number
below. Now over to Wendy for the weather."

I turn off the television. I know I killed that girl last night, I know I did. I make sure I haven't left anything behind and I walk to a payphone to call the tip line.

TWENTY SEVEN

Royal called Peter at 0630. He apologized for calling so early but Peter assured him that he wasn't sleeping anyway. Every time he closed his eyes he saw his parents, dead, so shut-eye wasn't really high on his to-do list.

"We've got something."

"What is it?"

"A tip. I'll pick you up on the way."

"Your parents are cool with that?"

"It was their idea, actually."

"Huh," Peter tugged on a clean shirt. He pinned the phone to his ear with his shoulder and did up the buttons.

"Be there in five."

Peter wondered if the O'Learys' were taking pity on him or if they truly wanted his help. After a moment of contemplation, he decided that he didn't care. All that mattered was that he was allowed to participate.

Earlier this morning, Banks had forwarded the Gibbons' preliminary autopsy reports to Peter's tablet. Just like Peter had guessed, there were no signs of sexual assault on Laura. The M.E. was right too, the knife marks were identical to those used to kill the three women. Everything lined up but at the same time didn't provide any direction whatsoever. It was becoming increasingly more difficult for Peter to keep from getting frustrated. He knew the next kill would be worse and that it was only a matter of time before they found another body.

A loud *honk* from below told Peter that Royal had arrived. He grabbed his gun and made his way down, keeping an eye out for anymore 'gifts' as he went.

"Mind if we grab a coffee on the way?"

Peter shook his head, "Where are we going?"

Royal chewed on a bagel and replied with his mouth full, "Cedar Valley Motel. Room three."

"Oh yeah?" Peter leaned away from him to avoid any spat out food. "What's there?"

"No idea." Royal swallowed. "That's literally all the tip said, word for word."

"Shouldn't we get there quickly?" Peter couldn't believe his partner's lack of urgency. "What if he's there or someone else is in trouble?"

"Banks and Alvarez are probably there already."

"Like they were last night?"

Royal raised an eyebrow, "You really think something could come of this?"

"Yes, I do. He's never gone more than a few days between killing and there was only twenty-four hours between the last two."

Royal flinched, "Alright. No coffee."

The Cedar Valley Motel was situated off of seedy Westin Avenue, not too far from where their pepper spray incident had occurred. Peter hoped that Royal's willingness to go back resulted in some answers.

Banks and Alvarez *were* already there, both of them leaning against the back bumper of their squad car.

Royal pulled up beside them and rolled down his window, "So?"

"Nothing."

Peter could tell Royal was fighting hard not to say 'I told you so'. Exiting the car, Peter looked around. A few working girls were on their walk of shame back to their rooms; heels in hand, they'd earned enough to stay another night. He scanned the room numbers. Directly behind their cruiser was room three. The metal number had fallen off but a dusty silhouette remained.

"There's nothing in that room. It doesn't even look like anyone stayed there last night. It's clean."

Peter walked towards it, "Have you talked to the staff about who stayed there last?"

Banks crossed his arms, "This is one of those motels where they have an automated after hours system. You know, you stick the cash in and—"

"Yeah, it gives you an electronic key that works for as long as you've paid. I thought they were shutting shitpiles like this down?"

"They are."

Peter kicked at the ground, "Surveillance?"

Banks snorted but Peter wasn't ready to give up. He took a look inside room three to find that his colleagues were right, there was nothing there. He checked the bathroom—empty as well. *Least helpful motel room ever*. He ran his hand through his hair and scanned the parking lot. One of the prostitutes was having a cigarette outside her room. Peter walked brusquely across the lot to her. She jolted and began stamping out her smoke. She turned to open her door but Peter placed a hand against it.

"Excuse me, miss?"

"I got nuthin' to say to you, pig," her lips curled back in a snarl.

"I just want to ask you a question," he held the door in place. "No strings attached."

She let her bushy hair fall across her face, "Not interested."

Peter held the door shut and reached into his pocket, pulling out a twenty. "You see anything suspicious last night?"

She grabbed for the bill but he yanked it back. He held it close to his chest and waited for her to answer.

Huffing, she shook her head, "Nah. Everything was business as usual. Although, I was gone off and on all night."

"Anyone else say anything? Anything strange?"

It was her turn to look at him expectantly. He smirked and pulled out an additional ten bucks.

"No, nuthin'," she snatched the bills from his hand. She pulled back her leopard crop-top and tucked the money into her bright pink bra.

"Thank you," he released the door. "Now buy yourself a meal with that."

She feigned a smile, "Yes, Officer."

Peter walked back over to the team shaking his head, "I guess this was just another dead end."

"Getting pretty tired of those," Banks tapped his fist on his cruiser.

Royal had his hands in his pockets and was rocking back and forth on the balls of his feet, looking to Peter for the go ahead to leave. Alvarez was eyeing him like he'd lost his mind. Peter pat Royal on the shoulder and surrendered towards the passenger side, "Let's go get you that coffee."

TWENTY EIGHT

It didn't take you long to get here, Peter. I am a tad disappointed that your bodyguards arrived before you but I suppose there's nothing I can do about that. All that matters is that you came when I called.

This is my favourite time of day. The air is so crisp and cool on your skin but the low rising sun is so warm. It's the contrast that makes it so wonderful. One moment you're in the shade and you're almost shivering but then you get hit by a beam of light and it warms you so fast. It's the moment during the day where the Moon and the Sun meet. I wonder if you like this time of day, Peter. I bet you do.

Your buddies tell you that there's nothing here. You know how incompetent they are so you check for yourself. You even bribe that slut to tell you lies—the very same slut that I wanted to kill last night. Someone must have seen me but I doubt that my behaviour is anything out of the ordinary for this filth.

What's strange though, Peter, is that you don't find anything either. I led you straight here but you say it's a dead end. I must have cleaned up extremely well—my subconscious performed better than I could have ever imagined. My only question is: what did I do with her body?

I know I need to return to the Temple. I have classes to teach and I can't draw attention to myself by missing them. Yet, I know there's nothing there for me right now. I try to picture Selene and my class—that glorious moment of harmony and unity—it's no use. It wouldn't satisfy me now.

You know what's funny? I killed a woman—can you really call her that? I didn't take her lifeblood and I am not even that upset by it. I don't feel like it's draining from me anymore. I feel like it's finally made a home in me. What does give me pleasure though is knowing that web of darkness is growing. You and your crew seem annoyed that you didn't find anything but you aren't distressed. I miss that. I want that.

I'll get it.

What I love about this time of day is that the scum of the Earth have gone to bed and the champions of life have risen. This is when the athletes are out jogging, good pet owners are walking their dogs, good parents are waking up to ready their children for school, and hard workers are brewing their coffee to prepare themselves for their day. These are the people who deserve my attention. I am going to enjoy this beautiful morning walk back to the shuttle stop, my attention sealed on a jogger that's headed my way.

The streets are still so quiet. There's no one around but her. Didn't she see the news this morning when she was tying her shoes? Didn't she hear it broadcast over her alarm clock radio? It's really her own fault for being ill prepared. She even has her earphones in. Tsk tsk.

She's so close now, Peter, I can almost hear her heart beating. I can certainly hear her breathing. That elevated heart rate is going to make for a fantastic show. She's right in front of me and I grab her ponytail as she passes. She screams and I slice her throat open. I was right, what a wonderful display. I tuck my knife into my pants and keep walking. She's making the most precious gurgling noises behind me. I turn back to look at her. She's trying to crawl but the ground is slick from her blood and she falls, her face hitting the pavement.

It sickens me to see her blood just pouring away. It may seem like a waste, but it's not. The grief you'll feel from her death will cause that web of darkness to expand and all of that light will be mine. Not to mention that the Earth will return her lifeblood to me. Trust me, it will. It's not a waste.

TWENTY NINE

It was early enough that Royal's choice cafe was still quiet; only a few older folk and construction workers were in line. Most took their coffees and pastries to go but Peter made his way to the back of the room. Royal lingered at the counter as Peter took a seat in the corner—he liked this table; not only did it have a view of the whole shop but the surrounding lot and street as well. A good vantage point made Peter feel a little less helpless. Regardless, he couldn't stop himself from feeling like a failure. His heart was so heavy beneath his sternum he could feel it in his stomach. *We must be the most pathetic task force in the entire world. Here we are, me with my disgusting green tea I chose instead of coffee and Royal, who's up flirting with his nearly lost forever barista while some psycho serial killer is out there murdering people left, right, and centre. Yet, what the hell else are we supposed to do?* He had poured over the case files a million times. He had stared at the crime scene photos and lab reports until he swore his eyes would bleed if he didn't stop. He even had to admit that Banks and Alvarez had been helpful; they ran all the samples and interviewed anyone and everyone they could come up with but still, they had absolutely no leads.

Peter wondered about Ari. He had looked good up until recently but he wasn't so sure anymore. Royal said that Michael, the head cult leader *or whatever the fuck he was called*, came down to the precinct the other day to provide a character witness for Ari. He even provided him with a partial alibi—said he was meditating with him when Peter's parents were murdered. Michael seemed like the kind of guy who wouldn't even lie to a child about Santa being real. It wasn't in him to be false. Plus, Peter doubted he'd waste his precious cult leader time by trekking down to their lowly police station for shits and giggles. But still, why hadn't he corroborated Ari's story from the beginning?

Royal's phone was buzzing like crazy. He had left it on their table while he came over momentarily to tell Peter he needed more time to woo the barista. Peter tried to ignore the buzzing, figuring the onslaught of messages were probably from a slew of woman but then it began to ring.

The call display read, *'Daddy-o'*.

"Royal," Peter called to him, waving the phone for him to see. Royal brushed him off, holding up a finger to signal that he'd be a minute. "For Christ's sake."

The ringing continued.

Peter decided to answer for him, "Sir, it's Officer Holloway."

"Peter, you and Royal need to get down to the hospital right away," Detective O'Leary was talking a mile a minute. *"Light 'em up, just get down there as soon as possible."*

"Yes, sir. What's going on?"

When Detective O'Leary gave Peter the news, he jumped out of his seat and knocked over his green tea—*good riddance.* Royal spun towards the racket. Seeing the look on Peter's face, he knew they needed to run. Royal leaned over the counter and pecked the barista on the cheek. She blushed and held a hand up to where his lips had been, beaming as he and Peter rushed out the door.

The moment they were in the cruiser Peter smiled for the first time in days. "Light 'em up!"

Royal had peeled out of the parking lot, siren wailing, and was three blocks down the street before he asked where they were going.

"Hospital. We've got another victim." Peter's grin grew wider, "She's alive."

"No way!" Royal's face lit up with pure joy, something else Peter hadn't seen for far too long.

"Yes!"

"Holy shit!" Royal shook his head in disbelief.

"I know!"

Peter was buzzing. He couldn't keep himself from smiling. His adrenaline was spiked even further by the siren and the sheer speed of Royal's driving. To Peter, there was nothing more exhilarating than driving lights and sirens. Everyone stopped for you. *Fuck you, red lights! These streets are ours.*

Royal pulled into the Emergency bay. *Yeah, sure it's for ambulances but who cares, this is important.* They ran to the nurses station, Royal slowing as they neared the desk. A redheaded nurse carrying an armload of charts spun to face them. *Jenna.*

"Hey..." Royal tucked his hands into his front pockets and nearly retreated.

Jenna looked coolly from Royal to Peter, eyes narrowing as she realized they were partners, "I suppose you're here to see Miss White."

"Uh," Peter checked the details on his tablet. "Yes."

"She's just come out of surgery," Jenna set the charts down with a sharp *thud*. She turned her focus to updating patient notes. "You may wait in the third floor Quiet Room for her to wake up."

"Where...?"

Without looking up, Jenna pointed to her right, arm extended stiffly. They hesitated, waiting for more direction. It was apparent they would be getting no such thing, Peter and Royal darted down the hall. They came to a pair of elevators. Royal pressed the 'up' button and the doors slid open revealing a very packed lift. The gaggle of people attempted shuffling about to make room but Royal raised his hand to say they'd take the next one.

After a moment of waiting, Peter looked to Royal, "Do you think she knows?"

He knew Peter was referring to the drugs they stole. He shook his head, lips curling in a smirk, "I think she's just mad that you didn't call her."

Peter glared at him. The second elevator dinged and opened. They sidled in beside a pair of paramedics who had a sleeping elderly man on their stretcher. Peter watched the numbers light up: Main, 2, 3—they all exited on the same floor.

"Excuse me," Peter grabbed the attention of one of the medics. "Do you know where the Quiet Room is?"

"Yeah," he pointed, his sleeve sliding up to unveil intricate tattoos. "It's just down that hall and to the left."

"Thank you."

Matthew and Molly were standing in the hall. The Quiet Room was directly across from an ICU bed which Peter assumed housed Brianna White. He nodded to Royal's parents and peered into the room. Brianna lay in the bed, wires and IV's hooked up to every limb. Dark hair cascaded around her head and a thick bandage ran across her neck. It was difficult to tell how old she was; Peter could have guessed anywhere between twenty and thirty. A man sat next to her, holding her limp hand and scratching his red-brown beard. *Boyfriend?* Peter noted a ring on his left hand. *Husband.*

A man in a white coat approached them. Wrinkles at his eyes and mouth showed his age. He had a full head of grey hair that was beginning to recede at the temples. "Hello, I am Dr. Swanson."

They shook hands and exchanged introductions. Matthew asked him how Brianna was doing.

"She's stable. It was touch and go for a while there—she'd lost a fair amount of blood. She's extremely lucky that he was there," he motioned to the bearded man. "Came upon her while jogging."

"So, that's not her husband?"

"No, just a good samaritan. You'll have to excuse me, I need to finish my rounds. Hopefully she'll come out of the anesthesia soon."

They thanked the doctor and huddled closer. Peter asked where Alvarez and Banks were.

"They're at the crime scene collecting evidence and canvassing the area. We're hoping that they find something."

"Doubtful," Peter bit the inside of his cheek. "I'm going to go talk to this good sam."

Matthew nodded, "Use the Quiet Room. I'm going to head out to the crime scene."

"I'll stay here," Molly looked in at Brianna. "Having a woman here when she wakes up may be a good idea."

"Agreed. Let me know what happens," Matthew kissed her on the forehead and left.

Peter slid the ICU room door open. It made a soft *swoosh* that went unnoticed by the good sam. A loud rhythmic beep shrieked from the monitor above her, another noise the bearded man had completely tuned out. His eyes never left Brianna White.

"Sir?"

No response.

"Sir?" louder this time.

He straightened and looked at Peter, "Huh?" His eyes were light and kind but his face still held a tight nervousness. "Oh, hi."

"Hello, I'm Officer Holloway," Peter lingered in the doorway. "Do you mind if I ask you a few questions?"

"Sure," he didn't move.

"Uh," Peter hiked a thumb over his shoulder. "There's a Quiet Room across the hall where we can talk."

The man shifted in his seat, hand still holding Brianna's, "Do you mind if we stay in here with her?"

Peter cleared his throat, "Alright."

He slid the glass door, his eyes meeting Royal's as it shut. The blaring machine seemed louder now. He walked over to it and hit the *'silence alarm'* button on the screen. *Much better*. He pulled a chair close and took a seat, tablet at the ready.

"Let's start with your name."

"Andrew Summers."

"I thought they only let family into the ICU."

Summers gave a weak smile, "She doesn't have any. She's twenty-eight."

244

Peter jotted down notes into his tablet:

Twenty-eight, no next of kin, gone through Life Ceremony.

Peter felt a pang of jealousy, something he never thought he'd feel towards anyone who had to kill their parents. Brianna got her full twenty-five years with hers and as insane as it was to admit, she got to share a very intimate experience with them. Peter thought about how his parents' lives had been ripped away, just as hers almost was. Her dark hair made her look more pale and distant, more vulnerable. The jealousy subsided. In a way they were kindred spirits now, both traumatized by the same man.

"Tell me what happened."

Summers squeezed her hand, "I was out for my morning jog when I saw her. She was just lying there in a pool of her own blood. I called 9-1-1 immediately." His weak smile returned, "They say she's going to be okay."

"She's extremely lucky that you found her," Peter quoted the doctor. "Did you see anyone else around?"

"No, it's pretty quiet at that time."

"Did she say anything to you?"

"No," he looked at her, his skin tightened across his cheekbones. "She was unconscious the whole time."

Peter clocked his wedding band again, "Does your wife know you're here?"

"What?" He let go of Brianna's hand, "No, uhm, my wife died a few years back."

Shit.

"I'm so sorry," Peter's face softened. The three of them were now all linked by death. A warmth settled in his stomach. *Why is this so comforting?* He attributed it to Brianna White's survival. Finally, they had a win. Her face was as pale as the hospital sheets and her lips were so dry they were cracking, but she was alive.

And awake! Brianna White began to flutter her eyelashes open. Summers reached for her hand again. The moment he made contact, her eyes grew wide and she yanked her arm back. A hoarse rasp escaped her cracked lips as she tried to scream. She scrambled against her headboard and began to sob—or at least as close to sob as she could manage with a lacerated throat.

Summers was up on his feet trying to calm her down but that made her lose it even more. Molly and Royal had noticed the commotion; Molly rushed in, shooed Peter and Summers out of the room and pressed the nurse call button. Royal stood out of the way as the doctor and two nurses swiftly entered the room. Molly's soothing voice had begun to explain the situation to Brianna when the doctor *whooshed* the door closed, cutting off all sound. Summers had his face so close to the glass, his nose touched. The doctor closed the blinds, leaving Summers looking frayed.

"Watch him," Peter said to Royal. He pulled out his cell, "I gotta make a call."

Royal nodded, folded his arms and looked at Summers like he was a heartsick puppy. Peter rounded the corner and stuck his phone back in his pocket. The elevator was empty save for a lab tech. She exited one floor down, tugging her cart along with her. Peter stepped off on the main floor and weaved his way through the busy Emerg. Jenna wasn't at the nursing station so he pulled up a stool and took a seat behind the desk. He knew he shouldn't be back there but his sleepless nights were catching up to him and he needed the moment to rest. He pulled out his tablet and looked up everything CVPD had compiled on Brianna White and Andrew Summers.

Brianna White—28

Daughter of Patricia and Marcus White—Attorneys at Law.
Employed eight years as a Paralegal at Smith and Carr.

Peter wondered why she hadn't become lawyer like her parents. Perhaps she enjoyed the work-life balance ratio that a Paralegal had versus a full blown Attorney. However, her credit report indicated that she could use the extra income; seemed as though Brianna White had a bit of an addiction to high end fashion. No criminal record. Her medical records were clear, she was otherwise a completely healthy woman.

Andrew Summers—32

*Son of Theresa and Edward Summers,
Teachers.*
    *Employed twelve years by the Cedar Valley
School Board as a High School Teacher.*

Summers had a handful of parking tickets and
one ticket for Drunk and Disorderly from around the
time of his wife's death—something Peter could relate
to. Summers didn't have any children and he would
have seemed as boring as Brianna if not for one thing: a
sealed legal record. Peter sent it off to Alvarez to have it
unsealed.

Jenna appeared from the chaos of the
Emergency Room. She looked mildly annoyed when
she spotted Peter, yet settled in beside him and
continued to silently document patient vitals.
    "Jenna," Peter started but she didn't look up.
"Jenna, I had no idea that you and Royal knew each
other, let alone dated."
    She continued to ignore him.
    "I'm sorry that I didn't call you."
    Am I even talking out loud?
    "Jenna, I'd really like if we could start again. I'm
not really good at dealing with people being mad at
me—"
    "You're a cop," her words were clipped.
    "Yeah, well," he ran his hand along the back of
his head. "Listen, I never date. I'm not sure I ever
would have called you but my parents were murdered
and things have been—"

"Wait, murdered?" There was a moment of recognition in her face. "'Holloway.' Shit, I should have realised. Oh, god, I can be really tactless sometimes."

She bit her thumbnail and studied him. Peter expected her to offer her condolences but she didn't. All she said was, "Okay."

"Okay?"

She squared her hips to him, "Okay, we can start again."

"In that case," Peter allowed himself to smile. "I was wondering if I could get your number again."

Jenna tried to cover up a small sigh, as if she knew she'd regret giving out her number a second time. She wrote it down for him none-the-less.

His phone beeped. Instinctively, he looked at the screen—it was the unsealed file. *Jesus, Alvarez was fast.* He could feel Jenna's eyes on him but he couldn't look away from the email.

Summers had been involved in a criminal investigation: the suspicious death of Ava Summers, his wife. He was the primary suspect in her death. He scanned the email for the Cause of Death. When he found it, rage pricked the underside of his skin.

C.O.D.: Exsanguination; laceration to the jugular vein.

"I'm so sorry, I have to go."

Her face fell and again she tried to recover. It didn't work as well this time.

"I'll call, I promise."

His words didn't touch her. Jenna's face displayed a horrible combination of disappointment and frustration as if she had just been proven right about his character. Only a small part of him cared right now; there were more pressing matters at hand, he could deal with Jenna later.

As the elevator rose, so did his anger. *This can't be coincidence, can it?* Murder wasn't rare but it sure wasn't as common as it used to be. Life had become precious to all, well, to most. Summers linked two women whose throats were slit. Peter's stomach knotted as he charged down the hall. He nearly knocked Royal over as he grabbed at Summers. He yanked him across the hall and threw him into the Quiet Room. Summers stumbled back, caught the wall with his arm and tumbled down between a coffee table and a loveseat.

"Is this a game to you?" Peter growled at him.

Summers gaped at him, pale eyes wide. Peter pulled him up by his shirt and thrust him onto the loveseat.

"Peter," Royal hissed from over his shoulder.

Peter ignored him, "The thrill of killing your wife wasn't doing it for you anymore? You couldn't help yourself. You needed to kill more women."

"Wh—"

"And when THAT wasn't enough you had to kill MY PARENTS," he was yelling now, blood rushing to his head. Royal reached out to him but Peter smacked his arm away. "YOU FAILED WITH BRIANNA SO

YOU MADE UP SOME STORY SO YOU COULD FOLLOW HER HERE AND FINISH HER OFF."

"WHAT?"

"I saw how afraid she was of you."

Summers hands were raised, "That's not it at all."

"Then how the *fuck* do you explain that you're in the middle of two sliced up women?"

"Two, Peter?" Royal's voice was soft. "It's just Brianna..."

Peter chucked his phone at him, screen open to Ava Summer's case file. Royal frowned as he read it.

"Pete..."

"My wife killed herself," Summers looked tired. "It was ruled a suicide and I was acquitted or didn't you read that part?"

"I sure read the part that said her wounds were inconsistent with self-infliction."

Summer's exhausted features deepened, "That evidence was thrown out."

"Yeah, I bet it was. Along with all her blood you had on you, and your fingerprints on the weapon?"

"He's right, Peter," Royal had scrolled closer to the bottom of the file. "The first M.E. was stripped of his license due to an unrelated malpractice suit. He was replaced by the M.E. we have now and he reconducted the autopsy—he determined her death was a suicide."

Peter rubbed the bridge of his nose, "Gimme that."

"Just so you know, the fingerprints were there because I touched it—stupid, I know," Summers

251

continued, "And her blood was all over me because I held her in my arms as she died."

The report reflected everything they were saying to be true. Peter had jumped to the wrong conclusion and that made him even more angry. *How could this be another dead end?*

"I know it sounds crazy but when I saw Brianna on the ground, it was like a second chance to save my wife. I couldn't let her die again."

Peter reeled and slammed the Quiet Room door. Molly saw him from inside the ICU room and joined him in the hallway. She shook her head to say that Brianna White was unable to provide any useful information.

"Are you sure?" Peter's voice was strained.

"I'm sure. She was blitzed just like Melissa and Sarah."

Peter swung his fist against the ICU room glass. "She has to know *something!*"

Brianna White pulled up the covers around her face and began hyperventilating into her hands.

"Officer Holloway," Molly stared him down. "You will leave and get your shit together. *Now.*"

Peter didn't need to be asked twice. He marched towards the elevator. Royal tried to follow him but Molly held him back, "Let him go. He needs to cool down."

Peter bypassed the Emergency Department and walked out of the hospital. He found himself in a green space with a few park benches. Letting out a groan of exasperation, he kicked a sizeable dent into a trashcan. Peter slumped down onto a bench and held his face in his hands. To say he felt overwhelmed was an understatement. They were never going to catch this killer; he may as well lay down right here and wait for him to come along and slit his throat too. *That is what he wants, isn't it? To kill me? Just like the women, he wants to toy with his prey before slaughtering it.*

He rubbed his face and looked up. Jenna was sitting at another bench eating a sandwich. Her eyebrows were raised at him as she chewed silently.

"Have you been here this whole time?"

She swallowed, "Yup."

Peter sighed, "Shit, I'm sorry."

"You sure like to apologize," she said between bites.

"Apparently, it's my thing."

"So, she's related to all of these other murders?" Her tone was casual, the kind that came from years of working in the ER.

"Yup," he matched her cadence. "My parents included."

"Any leads?" She didn't skip a beat. Not having her flinch was refreshing.

Peter shook his head, "No."

Jenna threw out the crust from her sandwich and came to sit beside him. He would have commented on her pickiness but he didn't have the will to tease her.

She scrunched up her button nose, "You don't look so hot."

He exhaled, his breath catching in his throat, "It's been a rollercoaster of a day."

She nodded but remained silent. Despite the cloudless sky, the air was cool. A gentle breeze blew past and goosebumps raised along her bare arms. She fought a shiver. Peter felt an urge to end their awkward meeting. He began to make an excuse to leave when she interrupted him.

"Do you want to get a drink tonight?"

She had caught him so off guard that Peter almost asked her to repeat herself, "What time do you get off?"

"Six, you?"

"Same," he didn't mention he was technically not on the clock. "Why don't you text me your address and I'll pick you up."

"Alright."

"I honestly thought you wanted nothing to do with me."

The corner of her mouth twitched upward, "The jury is still out on that."

THIRTY

I had every intention of returning to the Temple. I was completely out of sight and nearly at the shuttle stop when I heard that idiot calling for help. Some worthless worm of man had come across my girl. Soon I heard sirens and an ambulance came and I couldn't just leave her, Peter. I killed her but the ambulance took her, took her bloody body away just like I took her life. But then why would they leave if she was dead? Isn't she part of a crime scene? I had to know if I had failed. I tried to kill her but that man, that worthless man ruined everything.

I follow my girl to the hospital and I am so anxious, I want to run through the halls and slice her again but I know I cannot be seen. I am invisible, just another face in the crowd. I watch them wheel her to the desk and the nurses say 'ICU'. She's still alive, Peter. I am shaking and sweating for I know I cannot fix my mistake, not here in such a public place but I follow her still. I get on the elevator and that's when I see you. I see you and your boyfriend run in all flustered towards the nursing station and I feel better. Your presence centres me. I can't hear what's being said but you have a very interesting interaction with the desk nurse; you're looking at her like a prince who has found his long lost princess but she seems to have a severe distaste for you. I think you're gravely misinterpreting the situation.

You two come rushing towards me so I press on the close-door button. Despite my efforts the doors open back up to you. Thank goodness this elevator is packed full and I'm pressed to the side because you look right in, eyes not noticing me, and wave us on. Being so close to you makes me smile. Excellent work, Peter. Excellent.

I beat you to the floor and her room is easy to find. I don't stop as I pass it but she's in there, Peter. She's in there with that worm and he's touching her and all I see is red. How did she survive? I slit her throat from ear to ear, I saw her blood fill the street. But she's here, alive and breathing.

I hear your voice behind me asking someone for directions. I keep walking away from you and away from her. A doctor is telling you that she's going to be fine. Fine? She's going to have a nasty scar for the rest of her life, one that will torture her with memories of what I did to her. That is not fine, that's perfect. I can feel the light in her seeping into me and replacing her hollow body with darkness. There is a vending machine at my end of the hall. I am faking interest in it while I listen to you and your merry band of men discuss me. Apparently, you still know nothing. You question the worm. I can't hear you but suddenly a rush of hospital staff blows past me and into her room. She's awake and she is so scared, she may as well be dying in the street all over again. A wave of adrenaline hits me and I can't help but beam in the blue glow of the vending machine. You leave to make a call so I finish my act by purchasing a water from the machine. I should make a call too. I find a free phone and dial the Temple. I let them know that I am feeling unwell and will not be able to teach today. This is far more important.

I've hung up and am now sitting on a bench, contemplating finding you, when I hear you yelling. You've returned. You're accusing the worm of murder and it's really quite precious. That darkness has taken you, Peter, and it's not letting you go. You're jumping to conclusions and trying to find answers where there are none. Officer O'Leary is looking at you like you just slapped him in the face, your darkness is confusing him. You are losing your fight and everyone can see. You scare my girl by attacking her window and I have to stifle a chuckle. Your superior is furious and she orders you to leave. You're smart enough to listen.

I follow you outside and your princess is there. You don't notice her and make a complete spectacle of yourself. She is a strange specimen; emotionless. But what's this? One moment you are assaulting a trash can and the next you're confiding in her and now she's asking you out for drinks? I'll admit I didn't see that one coming. I certainly must have missed something, Peter. Even I can't be everywhere at once.

You're going to take her out tonight. That's perfect. You being occupied gives me a great opportunity to have some fun this evening. Please have some too, Peter, as it may just be your last chance.

THIRTY ONE

The bar was dimly lit. She had chosen where they went: Delaney's, a rough around the edges pub on Dunluce Loop. When they had arrived, Jenna dragged him to a back corner booth. She slid in with the familiarity of a childhood haunt. This was her place. Peter half expected the wait staff to address her by name but they only interacted with professional politeness.

When Jenna ordered her first whiskey, Peter's jaw clenched. He had swallowed quickly to hide his distaste but by her third, he was unable to mask his unease. Jenna's eyes bore into him, demanding an explanation. He flashed her the biggest smile he could muster which he was sure looked more like a grimace and shook his head to say, 'It's nothing'.

It wasn't good enough. "Your dad drink?"

"No," Peter didn't know how to skirt the subject.

"I'm sorry. Like I said," she tapped her forehead, "tactless."

Peter sucked desperately on his gin and tonic, pausing only to change the subject, "How long have you been a nurse?"

"I did two years of training at eighteen and I've been in the Emerg for six years."

Peter did the math. Jenna was twenty-six.

"Yeah," she spun her glass in a slow circle. "We have some things in common."

Again, Peter felt that pinch of jealousy. He didn't want her to clue in on his inappropriate envy so he built a wall up in his brain—a compartment just for the jealousy. It worked well and all that remained was that warm gut feeling of kinship. The warmth felt a lot like trust—something that he rarely felt with anyone he didn't know well but he felt it with Jenna. She wasn't necessarily quiet or timid but rather intraspective; her gears turned constantly and every word she said had a purpose, however 'tactless' they may be. He wanted to see inside her brain, see what greased those gears and to his surprise, he wanted her to see inside of his.

"I'm a Catalyst," Peter blurted. *Did I really just say that?*

Jenna sat back in her seat, "Yeah, I figured it was something like that."

Peter detected empathy in her tone, not sympathy—It was dark and heavy, with the edge of personal experience. His eyes narrowed, "You, really?"

"I told you we had some things in common," she was smiling now, that smile that lit up her whole face;

it was like someone took all the stars and placed them inside of her. "I noticed this guilt in you that ran deeper than not calling me or being buddies with Royal. It was the kind of guilt that I've felt all my life except I feel like that's not the whole story with you."

He gulped the last of his drink down, "You're very intuitive."

"Apparently, it's my thing," her smile was still strong, disarmingly so. He wasn't accustomed to such a joyful reaction to this topic and it made him wonder if Jenna was feeling the warmth between them too.

"You don't have to tell me," she said, her eyes piercing right through him, stripping him of all his defences. They were somewhere between green and blue and so bright Peter was curious to if she were wearing coloured contacts. At any rate he was glad to let them weaken him.

"No," Peter took a breath. "I want to."

Their server came by and they ordered another round of drinks.

Peter lowered his voice, "I can't tell you everything."

"Of course."

"A few days ago Royal and I kidnapped our parents." He explained how they had left and how he had stayed. He told her how that was the last time he saw them and how if he had tried harder, they would still be alive.

"Wow," she folded her arms across her chest and leant back, sizing him up.

He expected her to be shocked or even disgusted but she seemed genuinely impressed.

"So that's what the midazolam was for," her eyes glinted in the dim light.

"Yes. Wait, you knew?"

"You two were not as sneaky as you thought, besides we keep a tight inventory on drugs like that."

"Why didn't you report us?"

"Royal's stupid, sure, but he's a good person. I knew there had to be a good reason for him taking it."

Their drinks arrived, "And was there?"

She nodded, "I think what you did was extremely brave."

"I got my parents killed."

"No," Jenna grabbed his hand. "The murderer did. You did everything in your power to keep them safe."

He kept his eyes cast down.

"Trust me, you did a lot more than most would do."

Peter knew she meant herself included. He wanted to pull her close and make her feel okay. If these last few days had taught him anything it was that life was fragile and could shatter at any moment. His phone was buzzing in his pocket but he ignored it. He wasn't going to hold back anymore.

Peter leaned across the booth and kissed her.

THIRTY TWO

I think the bartender has recognized me. Every time I glance his way, his eyes are locked on me and every time, he dips his ridiculous beige cap to hide his stare. He turns his back to me but I can see he's pulled a card from his pocket and he's dialing the number.

It was reckless of me to return to this bar but I knew she'd be here. Do you remember her, Peter? That damned flirt from last time. God, I wanted to kill her. I knew she'd be here.

I need to hurry but I don't think that's going to be a problem with her. Most rejected women would avoid their failed conquests, but not this one. She noticed me the moment I entered and it did not take her long at all to jump right back in.

She's touching my arm again and pouting her lips in a way some men might find sexy. To me she looks like a duck waiting to be shot by a hunter. Doesn't she know I can see right through her? She's saying how disappointed she was that I left without her the other night, talking like there was some sort of unspoken agreement that she belonged to me. She's right—she is mine, Peter, and she loves it. If I hadn't asked her to leave with me this time, I swear she would have jumped on my back, claws dug deep into my flesh. She wouldn't let me go again.

I'm taking her home with me, well, I'm taking her to your home anyway. She keeps asking how far we have to go and I keep assuring her it's not far at all. So needy. The walk is as short and lovely as I remember but I bet she'd lay down and hike up her dress right here if I let her.

Before you left for your date, Peter, I watched the building manager leave for the day. I bumped into him and lifted his keys; he didn't notice a thing. He won't realize that they're missing until the morning. After you left and I made sure you'd be out for a while, I came back and scoped out your building. I didn't want to be fumbling around later.

I grab her hand and lead her to the stairwell. She hovers close to my hip, too eager to reach your suite. Even though I mapped out where your apartment was, there were too many people coming and going earlier for me to determine the right key. I position her against the door and kiss her to distract her as I try each key from the manager's keyring. Her breath tastes like stale beer and I hate it. She's grappling at my clothes like a deranged koala. How can anyone find this attractive? Finally, one key fits and she stumbles backwards into the suite, nearly taking me with her. I shake her off of me. She looks around but I don't want her asking questions so I grab her by the chin, forcing her to stare at me. I spot crime scene photos on the kitchen island behind her. She can't see them. I direct her body back and turn it in my favour.

"Ask me where I want you," I command.

Her words are slurred and her body melts under my grip, "Where do you want me?"

"Shower," I tilt her ear to my lips. "Go warm it up for me."

I release her neck and shortly after, I hear the water running. I strip my clothes and hang them over one of your kitchen stools. All of my *victims* are laid out on the counter. It's so nice to see them again. I'm naked and my dick is erect but not for you and not for that slut in the shower. It's hard for them. There are tacky smiling photos of them—good ones too—ones where they're cut up and bloody by my hand. There are files and notes galore but you still don't have a clue. It's glorious being here; I feel so close to you and them all at once. Thank you, Peter.

I'm in the bathroom now.

She calls for me to join her, "The water feels amazing!"

Is she on drugs or something? Don't get me wrong, I am sure everyone enjoys a hot shower but I would never describe one as *amazing*. Well, not unless there's a bleeding girl in it.

I conceal my knife behind my back. I open the shower door—it is unfortunate that you don't have a bathtub, Peter, but I suppose this will do. I plan on approaching her from behind, wrapping my arms around her and slicing but just as I am lifting the blade she turns to face me. She sees the knife and screams. She pushes my chest with one hand and puts the other behind her to brace against the wall. It doesn't help her and she slips and falls. I am above her and she's begging through big crocodile tears.

"Please! Please don't do this!" Over and over.

I'm hacking at her, trying to reach her throat. She screams louder as the blade slices into her arms. Finally I get a leg on top of her and I pin her arms down. Her cries are desperate and she's thrashing under me. Every bit of strength she has is being used to fight me and by the way she's looking at me, we both know it's not enough.

Her blood sprays me and it feels *amazing*. Honestly, Peter, I was afraid that it was going to come out black like that junkie's blood but it doesn't. Even though this girl was just as despicable, it is bright red arterial perfection. I turn the water off and I take a moment to relax. I push her body out of the shower and take up the whole space with mine and soak up every ounce of lifeblood I can. It's like throwing gasoline on an open flame, Peter. I am burning alive and I owe it all to you.

I turn the water back on and let the blood wash from my skin. I don't bother with the splatter that decorates the walls and floor. I leave her crumpled body and return to the kitchen. I let myself take in the photos of my girls, your parents, the others. I redress as slowly as time allows but I know you'll be home soon. I do hope you're having as much fun as I am.

THIRTY THREE

Peter hadn't kissed many women but he'd kissed enough to know that this kiss was good. Hell, it was great. It was so great that he never wanted it to end. Jenna tasted like whiskey but Peter didn't pull away, instead he melted into it and let nostalgia wrap him up.

"Do you want to get out of here?" the words had formed before he could think about what they meant.

She nodded and pecked him again, her lips soft against his.

"Okay," Peter flagged down their server and settled their tab.

She was still close, "Yours or mine?"

"We can go to mine. I have a nice bottle of whiskey we can dip into."

Peter helped her into her coat. He had forgotten his but he was sure the booze would keep him more than warm on the quick journey home. Close proximity to bars was something he had considered when choosing a place to live and Delaney's was no exception. Going out for a drink or five after work used to be his favourite thing to do and it could be again if Jenna promised to be his company. He was twice as glad for the short walk tonight for he couldn't wait to get her alone.

As they walked, Peter was very aware of how close she was; every time her arm brushed against his, his chest fluttered with anticipation. He wanted so badly to touch her, to even hold her hand, but in the cool air she stuffed both hands in her pockets. It wasn't until they reached his building that she freed one to grab the door. When she released it, Peter took her hand immediately. She looked surprised but it quickly dissipated into that bright smile of hers. He led her up the stairs.

"No elevator?" She teased.

"I happen to like the exercise, thank you very much."

"I suppose as a nurse," her breath became heavy as they hit the top. "I can't argue with that."

He steered her down the hall, "You probably don't want to argue with me anyway, being a cop and all."

Jenna gave him a sharp poke in the ribs. He responded by throwing her up against his door, their faces less than an inch apart. Her breath tickled his cheek and heat spread down his neck. She moved her head forward and kissed him deeply. He quickly unlocked his door and brought her inside. He unzipped her jacket and slid it from her shoulders. Her hands hurriedly untucked his shirt and touched his bare back, they were freezing but Peter loved the feeling against his warm skin. Her fingers traced down his spine, caressing the goosebumps she created. He tried to stop her before she reached his gun but he wasn't quick enough. Grazing the top of it, she giggled against Peter's lips.

"What?"

Still giggling, she shook her head, "I have no idea."

"You're ridiculous," Peter unlocked the door and walked her inside.

"Oh, yeah?" her hands were travelling across his chest, unbuttoning his shirt.

"Yeah."

Her breath was hot on his skin. She nipped his earlobe and whispered, "What ever will you do with me?"

Peter slid his hands over her ass and lifted Jenna around his waist. Her skirt hiked up and her lace panties grazed his stomach. Yearning to take them off, he ran his finger under the fabric and felt himself grow against her. With one hand on the small of her back, he used the other to pull his gun from his belt line and set it on the counter. Lips never leaving him, Jenna unbuttoned her blouse and threw it on the ground. Peter carried her to his bedroom and tossed her onto the bed, producing more giggles. With a coy smile playing on her face, she removed her bra. He climbed over her and secured an arm between her shoulder blades, lifting her up and back so her head was on a pillow. Jenna hiked her skirt up higher and began to remove her panties. Peter took over, lifting her legs straight up as he slowly slid them off, kissing her skin as he went. Her skin was cold against his lips and he longed to warm her up. She lay back, thighs spread. Peter had removed his belt and barely his pants before she tugged him back on top of her. She reached down, peeled down his boxers, and pulled him into her.

It was as if her body was made to fit his, and his hers. The amount of pleasure coursing through Peter was indescribable, he couldn't get enough. He marvelled at her. Unable to keep his hands off her bare skin, he traced the contours of her body, pausing to graze her nipples. Jenna's back arched and she groaned into his neck, asking for more. Her moans made him crazy and turned him into an unstoppable force. He pinned her arms above her head and thrust faster, deeper. She needed him and Peter loved nothing more than being needed. He rolled her on top of him. Looking up at her, he knew this is exactly where he wanted to be. In this moment, there was no black hole inside of him. She had the light of a thousand stars and it was enough to brighten the both of them. Jenna braced herself against his chest. Her touch alone caused his heart to race. He grabbed her hips to guide himself even deeper and her moans grew louder and louder until they peaked. Peter was right there with her and she collapsed on top of him, their ragged breath falling in sync.

"I may have to rethink this no dating thing."

She laughed and nuzzled closer. The corners of her mouth were still turned up but for a moment, Peter saw a darkness slide across her eyes. He kissed her forehead and wrapped both arms around her. He thought back to their conversation at the bar and the reality of Jenna's hardships finally sank in. That jadedness he'd sensed before didn't just come from working in the hospital, it came from a deep rooted grief that would never let her go. He wanted kill her grief and takes its place, and he wanted to hold her just as tightly. Peter had always avoided becoming attached; there was always a fear holding him back, a fear that if he got close to anyone, they'd be taken from him. He wasn't scared with Jenna. He had never felt so known by another person; she had more insight into him in one night than most had in a lifetime.

Jenna rolled out of Peter's embrace, "I'm going to go freshen up."

"I thought girls only said that in movies."

She stood, "Yup, just me and movie stars." She winked.

He chucked a pillow after her, "I'll grab us that whiskey."

Jenna disappeared from his room. Peter lay back and enjoyed the lingering warmth of the sheets; they smelled like sweat and vanilla. He closed his eyes and let himself be happy. Just for a moment.

Jenna screamed.

It wasn't a small scream either, it was sharp and true with terror. Peter ran towards the shriek. Jenna was standing in the hall halfway between him and the washroom. Her face was drained of colour and she had her hands raised up around her face, frozen before they could touch her skin.

"What is it?" He searched her for signs of injury.

"I honestly thought girls only did *that* in movies," her eyes were wide and staring down at herself as if she were looking for an explanation for her behaviour. "I really shouldn't have been so surprised," the words spewed so quickly from her mouth that he had a hard time keeping up. "I mean, I see trauma and death and blood and everything all the time but I did not expect to see that in here, I mean, I saw all the photos on your counter but that's expected right? You're a cop and that's expected," she said the last part quietly and more to herself than Peter.

He grabbed her hands, "Jenna, what are you talking about?"

Her face returned to its natural state, soft but emotionless. She let her hands rest against Peter's grip. She spoke as easily as if she were reporting on the weather, "There's a dead woman in your bathroom."

🏛

Peter's team arrived within ten minutes followed shortly by Forensics. He and Jenna sat on the couch while everyone else took photos and collected evidence.

Jenna was angled towards him, apologizing profusely for 'acting irrationally'.

"You acted rationally," Peter assured her. Her hands found his, yet she felt very far away. "You had a normal reaction to the abnormal," he regurgitated words he'd heard at work a million times. He looked to the washroom, "The extremely abnormal."

"How are you not more rattled by this?" The gears inside her head slid into place and she pulled back a little, "Sorry, dumb question."

"Not dumb," Peter felt unnaturally calm. "You're right, I should be freaking out right now. Horrible shit keeps happening and I think I've switched to autopilot. It's like I've reached my terror quota or something. For example, the killer left me jars of his victims' blood—"

She didn't react.

"—it was only a matter of time before he started leaving me whole bodies."

Royal approached them. He sat in the adjacent sofa chair and pulled out his tablet.

"So," he wiggled his eyebrows at Peter. "What happened?"

Royal's ability to continually make light of this was inconceivable. Peter glowered back, "Maybe someone else should conduct this interview? Alvarez or Banks?"

Royal scoffed, "Banks? Really?"

Jenna pat Peter's hand, "It's fine."

"You sure?"

"Yep." A firm nod.

Royal leaned forward, expectant.

Reluctantly, Peter dove in, "We went out for drinks and came back then..."

Jenna cleared her throat, "Then I found her in the bathroom."

"I see," Royal tried to mask a smile, his cheek twitching. "Did you notice anything weird like, tool marks on the door or anything?"

"Everything was normal, you know that," Peter was growing tired of questions with no answers. "It's always normal."

"He could slip up."

Peter raised an eyebrow.

"Okay, so what then? How did he get in here?"

Peter sighed, "I have no idea. That woman sure wasn't here when I got home at six-thirty. We left at seven and got back around ten."

"By the amount of blood, I'd say she was killed here," Jenna said matter-of-factly. "He cleaned the shower but the rest of the bathroom is a mess."

Peter kept his brow raised and exchanged a look with Royal. He let his smile break free and shrugged his shoulders.

"So he brought her here and killed her, cleaned up all traces of himself, and left within three hours," Peter sighed. "And before you ask, my building doesn't have surveillance."

"At least we have a lead," Alvarez walked over, snapping off a pair of latex gloves.

"What do you mean?"

"You know who this woman is, right?" Banks snapped, exasperated that he had to ask.

Peter had no patience for Banks' attitude. He matched his tone, "To be honest, I was a little distracted by everything else."

Royal wiggled his eyebrows again.

Alvarez punched Royal in the arm, "It's that lady from the bar. You know, the one that was flirting with the killer?"

"No way," Peter was on his feet, pushing past his colleagues to confirm the corpse's identity. "Jesus, he's right. I'm going to call the bar to let them know we're coming."

"You think she was there tonight?"

"It's a starting point, at least." Peter retrieved his cellphone to realize that the buzzing from earlier had been missed phone calls. He recognized the number, "Shit." He listened to the voicemail, "Shit, shit, shit, shit."

"What?" Royal was behind him.

Peter slammed his phone onto the counter, uncaring if it was damaged and played the message for everyone:

"Hi, uh, Officer Holloway? This is Nick Maier from Woodvine Tavern. I could be wrong but I think that guy is here. You know, that one you told me to call you about if he came in again? He's talking to that same girl."

Everyone displayed degrees the same fallen expression; Royal's eyebrows crowned, a vein expanded on Banks' temple, Alvarez shook his head, and Jenna bit her lip as she pieced the puzzle together.

"Wait, there's another."

"Officer Holloway, you might want to get down here. He just left with that woman."

"Fuck me," Royal threw his hands in the air.

"Why didn't you answer your phone?" Banks snapped.

"I—" Peter didn't have a good answer. The black hole was gaping inside of him, threatening to pull him in. This was his fault.

Banks advanced, fists balled, "If you had just done your job, we could have prevented this."

Peter was speechless. Banks was completely right. *Another death on my hands.* Peter didn't want to defend himself; he shut his eyes and waited for Banks to punch him. At this point, he deserved more than a fist to the face.

"Hey," it was Alvarez who stepped between them. "Let's not forget that Holloway's not even supposed to be involved in this at all."

From the corner of his eye, Peter saw Jenna's body stiffen. He offered an apologetic grimace in her direction. Alvarez was still staring down Banks, who didn't relax but walked away.

Peter called Nick to tell him they were on their way over. He let Jenna know that he'd have an officer take her home. She nodded and collected her things which included a clandestine stashing of her panties in her purse. Her starlight brightness had dimmed, darkness spreading between them. All Peter felt now was the raging guilt Jenna had described. *This* is why he didn't date. Nothing was more important than preserving life—not laughing, not kissing, not even fucking. Tonight he chose wrong and it got a woman killed. Death was following him like a curse.

As they drove, Peter felt like the chase was pointless; he wanted more than anything for it all to be over. He badly wanted to grieve in peace without another body turning up but he was losing hope that the end would ever come.

"What took you guys so long?" Nick was shooing out the last of his customers.

Peter's guilt swelled, "When I didn't answer you should have phoned the police."

Nick's eyes narrowed, "I thought I *did*."

He wanted to argue but he knew it was a waste of time, "Show us the tapes."

With Alvarez still back at the crime scene, working with the computer was slow-going. Technology had never been Peter or Royal's forte. *Thank goodness we only need to rewind a few hours.* Peter set the recording to 1900 and watched: the bar was full with post-work customers looking to unwind. Their latest victim was already there, leaning over the bar and chatting with Nick. After forty-five minutes of her flirting with various patrons, a new subject entered the bar. She latched on immediately; it was the same man from before—hooded and camera avoiding. Backs turned, they sat and chatted for a mere ten minutes before they left together.

Peter was ready to smash the computer, "He never shows his face."

"Wait," Royal rewound the tape. "There! Oh, my god that's..."

He froze the image. The killer's face was staring right at them, his head turned for a fraction of a second; a taunt he wasn't able to pass up.

"Arun Sinclair."

THIRTY FOUR

Oh, how I wish I could have been a fly on the wall when you found that slut. Was it you or was it your date? Doesn't matter. Either way it had the same effect, I am sure. I'm curious if you even realize the wonderful repercussions yet? For example: I've displaced you from your home. Where are you going to go Peter? Everywhere you hold dear is now a crime scene. You can't even go to your parents' house. Then there's the grief associated with your desperate need to save everyone, that's always fun for me. But my personal favourite? The real cherry on top? The fact that every time that little redheaded girl even *thinks* about spreading her legs for you, all she'll see is my work. This has been my best move yet.

The moment I return to my room at the Temple, Michael comes by to invite me to midnight meditation with him and the other Elders. Of course, I accept! This is what I have been working towards, Peter. This is my chance to show them that I am worthy now. I am relieved that that slut's blood wasn't tainted. I needed that extra boost to be noticed. Every nerve in my body is firing and I feel like a human firework—sparking and lighting up the entire nightscape around us. The twinkle in Michael's eyes tells me he can see it too. He was waiting for me to burn this bright. Is this how it feels to be a god? I tell him that I will see him soon and he leaves. I am closing my door when I hear him say something.

It sounds like, "You had better show us how dedicated you are."

"I'm sorry?" I say.

Michael turns back, he looks confused, "I didn't say anything, Arun. I'll see you soon."

But he did say that, didn't he? I shake my head and retreat into my room. My sparks have dimmed but I try to feel happy that I'm back here. I stand out on the balcony and pour myself a glass of cool, clean water. It washes through me and I feel refreshed. My burgundy robe flows around me as I look out over the darkened valley. It looks like a deep black ocean filled with wonder. I remember my girls and how they were way out there and how now they could be anywhere, buried in the Earth or rotting in a metal drawer. I try not to get upset, I need to keep my composure. Tonight is my night.

To stay centered, I sit down in my empty tub and close my eyes. I remember every moment of each kill and I relax. I can feel their blood on my skin. I sink lower into the tub and then I'm drowning. I open my eyes to see black blood all around me. It's in my mouth and my nose and I can't breathe. I throw myself out of the bath and lay heaving on the floor. I reach to rip off my tainted robe but when I touch it, it's dry. I twist to peer into the tub, it's empty and clean, just as it was before.

I want to scream. What is happening to me? That tainted blood has poisoned me. I must fight it, I must get past this. Meditation will help. I get back on my feet and leave to join the Elders, consciously leaving my visions behind.

But I am anxious. Every little noise startles me. I try to control my breath as I climb the steps to the Elder's tower. The hardwood creaks beneath my feet. The curved, stone walls are lined with large windows that are open to the outside air; I concentrate on breathing in the breeze. Below I see Selene and my chest softens. I feel better instantly. She is heading towards the gazebo for midnight meditation as well. Ah, maybe I'll be able to find her afterwards. I reach the top of the tower and I am smiling as I walk into the dark circular room. The air is cool and the walls are lined with candles that provide the most welcoming glow. Several of the Elders are already here and seated. I find a spot in their circle and sit down, legs crossed. This is where I belong. I follow their lead and close my eyes, letting my hands rest palms up on my knees. I take my first slow inhale and picture it like a cool wave flowing up my chest and as I exhale, it flows down my back. In, out, up, down. My mind settles into nothingness. This is exactly what I need.

"Who let this tainted worm in?"

My eyes shoot open. Everyone around me is silent and their eyes are shut. No one appears to have said anything. I return to my breath. I just need to get back to my center and ground myself then everything will be fine. In, out, up, down. All that matters is the natural ebb and flow of the breath.

"Filth like you is not welcome here."

Again when I look, all the Elders are still. No one has moved, no one has reacted. I close my eyes and try to breathe deep but I am shaken. Am I losing my mind?

"Ari."

I keep my eyes closed. I squeeze them tighter. It's not real. It's in my mind.

"Ari."

Peter, is that you? Is that you who's calling me?

"Ari, open your eyes."

They are open and the Elders are on top of me. They knock me back. I am screaming for them to get off of me.

"You must be cleansed, Ari," they all say together.

My arms are pinned by two of them. My god, they are strong. Stronger than I. They pin my legs.

"Peter!" I am screaming for you. I know you were here, warning me. "Where are you?"

"Stay down, worm! We must drain you of this demonic blood!"

They are holding a blade to my chest. Even in the dim light, I can see that their eyes are black. It's not me who needs to be cleansed—it's them! The Elder who holds the blade is kneeling at my head. He's cutting at my robe. I jerk my head up and my forehead collides with the underside of his jaw. He loses his balance and falls into one of the others, freeing my right hand. I hear the clatter of the knife hitting the wood floor. I reach in its direction and my hand secures around the handle. Its owner flails for it but it's too late and I thrust it up into his belly. I twist the blade as I yank it out and black blood pours from the wound. I scramble away from the

284

bleeding Elder but the others grapple onto me. I swing
the blade wildly, coming in contact with various limbs.
Black blood springs from all of them. It's covering me.
It's going to infect me and they won't let go. I slash
deeper and faster. I'm screaming.

"Peter! Peter help me!"

They're falling away from me. Is it you Peter? Are you
killing them? I look at my hands—they're stained black.
Elders surround me, their bodies shredded and leaking.
Are they dead? I don't have time to check. I have to
run. It isn't safe here.

I nearly slip down all the stairs; my body is so slick with
the poisonous blackness. Dear god, is this the darkness
I've been spreading? Has my web finally reached me?
Maybe I am strong enough to hold it off. Yes, of course
I am. I'll be fine but—oh god, Selene. I know she is
strong but I don't think she could withstand this. I have
to find her.

I run to the gazebo. It's empty; their session has let out.
Are you gone? I have to find you. Oh, Selene, where are
you? I scan the grounds and I see your yellow sun
dress. I could spot that dress from anywhere. I have to
stop you. If you leave you'll be swallowed up.

"Selene!"

You turn and you're so frightened.

"Don't be scared, Selene."

"Ari?" Her eyes her wide. She knows that she's safe now, with me.

"We have to leave."

"Ari, you're covered in blood! What happened?"

"We have to go," I reach for her hand but she pulls away.

"My god, is that a knife?"

"I'll protect you, let's go. It's not safe here."

She is backing away from me. She's shaking her head, "What did you do?"

"Selene, no, you don't understand," I reach again. She looks like she's about to scream, "I know this is scary but we have to go!"

She turns to run but I grab her. She's yelling for me to let her go but I hold on tighter. She is squirming in my grasp, my god, it feels so good to hold her at last. Her hair smells like the Earth. You are my Moon, Selene. She hears my thoughts and relaxes.

"Good, let's go," I loosen my grip and go to take her hand but she slumps to the grass. "Selene?"

Sirens wail. She isn't moving. I crouch down and I realize my knife isn't in my hand. It's in her side.

"Selene!"

The sirens are getting louder.

I pick her up and cradle her in my lap. Oh, Selene. Why wouldn't you just come with me? Her blood is red. She isn't breathing. She isn't breathing but her blood is red. She lived pure and will die pure. I pull the knife from her flesh. I take her blood and smear it across my face and my chest—it will protect me.

The sirens are so close now. I wish I could take you with me, Selene, but I'll never be able to carry you. Not like this. So I leave you.

And I run.

THIRTY FIVE

Peter exited the cruiser so fast he almost forgot to turn the sirens off. Molly and Matthew were setting up a command post at the makeshift barrier between the parking lot and the Temple gardens. Peter headed down the path flanked by Royal, Banks, and Alvarez. The night was quiet, like the entire Temple was holding its breath. He'd never been here at night. *Was it always like this?*

Reading his mind, Royal shone his flashlight around, "This is fucking weird."

Peter nodded.

Ahead of them, a small figure emerged from the arched entry way. It was a young woman. She was turning around frantically as if surrounded by invisible attackers. She spotted Peter and the others and began to sprint towards them, careening her neck to look back at the Temple in fear. As she neared, Peter could have sworn that she looked exactly like Sarah Preston, wrapped in a light coloured robe and mousy hair flying around her face.

"Help!" Her eyes wild. "Please!"

They drew their guns.

Not slowing, she collapsed into Royal, "They're dead!"

He looked past her towards the archway, "Where?"

She pointed upwards, "The Tower."

Royal steered her back to the command post. Molly began asking her questions while Matthew called for backup. He turned to the four of them and gave them their assignments: Banks and Alvarez would head to Ari's room while Royal and Peter took the Tower; they didn't have time to wait for reinforcements.

They ran through the entrance and down the main hall into the Atrium. Peter nodded to Banks as they split off north and west. A few curious residents lingered in the hallway. Peter held a finger to his lips and motioned for them to get back into their rooms. "Lock your doors," he whispered.

A burly, bearded man in a burgundy robe lingered in his doorway, "What's going on?"

"Sir, I'm going to need you to get back in your room."

He eyed their guns and nodded then retreated calmly.

"Wait," Royal stopped him and frowned towards the end of the hall. "Where's the best access to the Tower?"

"Just keep going, the hall turns into a staircase."

"Thank you."

They pressed on. The hall began to curve and then took a tight turn that spiraled upwards into wooden stairs.

"Someone came down these stairs and out here," Royal pointed at blood that trailed from the steps and out a side door.

"From that woman?"

"She looked clean."

Peter wedged the door open and peered out into the darkness, "Up or out?"

"Out," Royal didn't hesitate.

They pulled out their flashlights and carefully followed the blood trail. It led past a candle lit gazebo and back towards the parking lot.

"Shit, it stops."

Peter scanned the grass with his flashlight. Nothing. Nothing. Still nothing.

"Let's go back—"

"What's that?" Peter's light fell onto an object that cast a long shadow over the ground.

They hurried towards it.

"Ah, shit." Yellow sundress, dark skin and even darker hair, all marred by the mangled wound in her side. Peter knelt down to check for a pulse, "She's dead."

Royal hopped on the radio, "We're going to need some backup to the west perimeter. We've got a body."

Before, Peter would have felt something for this woman but all he knew now was darkness. It was a void that swallowed any feeling and rendered him empty. "Let's head back up."

Careful to preserve the blood trail, they ascended the steps. Goosebumps rose on Peter's arms but they weren't from the open windows. The blood was becoming more abundant, it was nearly impossible to avoid stepping in it. A large dark wood door faced them at the top and blood pooled out from under it. Royal grabbed the handle, shared a stretched look with Peter and turned the knob.

Five bodies. That's what Peter guessed. It was hard to tell with them all bloody and folded on top of each other. Lacerated limbs pointed every which way. The sharp smell of copper caused them to wrinkle their noses.

Their radios went off:

"Holloway, it's Banks."

"Go ahead."

"Sinclair's room's empty. What do you two have over there?"

Peter couldn't even begin to sum it up, "You guys had better get up here."

"That bad?"

"Worse."

Royal was creeping around the edges of the curved room. He leant forward in an attempt to see if any of the Elders were alive. He shook his head and muttered, 'Jesus Christ' over and over.

Peter called Matthew, "We've got five dead up in the Tower. The blood trail led us to another body outside. He's out there somewhere."

"Alright, I'm sending everyone your way. I'll get on the horn right now and dispatch the chopper and the K-9 unit."

"Okay."

"Sit tight, we'll find him."

"Yeah, thanks."

Peter's nose still stung from the copper. Dead eyes stared at him from every angle. The closest to him was familiar—Michael. Michael who had spoken so highly of Ari. *What a fucking idiot; he vouched for a psycho and now he is dead.* Peter knew he should feel grief or sorrow but he only felt frustrated. He wanted to bang his head against the wall and teleport himself back into the forest, back to the safe house.

"What's the point?"

"Hmm?" Royal snapped photos with his phone.

"What is even the point of catching this guy?"

"Uhh, to stop him from killing more people?" More photos.

"He's just going to do it anyway," Peter crouched down. He couldn't stand it anymore; he wanted to give up. "We are always ten steps behind."

Royal gestured to the pile of bodies before them, "This literally just happened. You heard my dad; they're sending everyone. Ari's out there and he isn't getting away this time."

Footsteps and hurried voices echoed from the stairwell.

Peter stood, "I wish I could believe you."

Shock, disgust, sadness—all the *twisted* expressions exhibited by everyone around him seemed so pointless. *Yeah, he's a monster, we fucking get it. How can they still be so surprised?* The room filled with depressing chatter about how 'god awful' this whole thing was and how 'we had better stop him soon'. Peter's head was pounding and the smell of blood was choking him. Flashing lights from the cameras were blinding. He needed to get out of there.

"Pete!" Royal called after him but he was already running down the stairs. A Forensics worker yelped as Peter slammed into her and knocked her down a few steps. Muscle memory told him to apologize but no sound came out. He didn't stop, he just kept going. Peter didn't know where he'd go. He couldn't go home... he couldn't go to Jenna—*showing up wrecked to her house when we've only had one date? Not a good idea.* He found himself walking towards the gazebo. The M.E. had a team collecting the dead female in the grass. Peter blew out all of the candles in the gazebo and watched from his perch. He felt exhausted and numb. *This is absolute bullshit.* Ari would kill as long as he's out there whether they followed him or not. They didn't have the manpower. People will say, 'He's just one guy—how could one guy do all of this?' It didn't matter if there was one of him, or one hundred of him; it only takes a second to take someone's life.

More sirens pierced the air. Their reinforcements were arriving. *Won't do much good.* The *whump whump whump* of the helicopter blades cut through the wailing. The chopper soared overhead and towards the valley, sweeping the forest with bright spotlights. Howls and barks flooded Peter's ears as the K-9 unit rushed past him and into the trees. *Was Ari really stupid enough to try and hide in there?* They had found his burial site without issue. *Taking cover in the trees would be absolutely idiotic.*

Peter decided to leave them to their wild goose chase and wander under Ari's terrace and past the rest of the North Wing. There were eight separate balconies along the wing and the path led progressively deeper into the valley. Tall cedars blocked out the rest of the world and the Temple disappeared into a grassy cliff. The dirt trail Peter followed was moderately travelled and the sounds of the search quickly faded as the smell of earth took over. It was peaceful down here. The cliff curved and the sound of rushing water hit Peter's ears.

A river flowed from the woods and cascaded down into pool after pool, finally settling in a small dark lake.

Climbing down the rocks, the only thing he could hear was the crashing and babbling of the water. The world had been left behind. Peter edged his way to the shore of the little lake. Water rippled slowly towards his feet and before he knew what he was doing, he was knee deep. It was cold and numbed his skin. It was a pleasant feeling, having his body and his mind feel the same. He waded farther. For the first time, the pain and anger were gone. He let himself sink below the surface. Silence, glorious silence surrounded him. He let his body sink down, down, and deeper still. The water pressed against his chest. It burned but he stayed under. There was nothing in the world he wanted more than this beautiful silence. His throat seized, forcing him to breathe. Water flooded his lungs. He tried kicking for the surface but he couldn't tell which way was up. Peter's mind darkened and he lost control of his limbs. The silence won.

THIRTY SIX

What in the hell are you doing, Peter? Has the darkness taken you over completely? You were clever to follow me down here. Only a handful of Temple residents know about this spot. I knew you would like it but I didn't expect you to make it your final resting place. Jesus, you of all people should know it's not your time. Why would you save me from the Elders if you were just going to drown yourself? No, there's more to this than that. You're just letting me take my turn. Well played.

I slip into the water and dive down. I grab you under your arms and haul you to the surface. God, you're heavy; did you really have to wear your clothes? I get it, it added to the challenge. I'm soaking wet but I drag you onto the mossy rocks. You're not breathing. Really, Peter?

I give you a shake, "Open your eyes, Peter."

Nothing.

"Peter, it's not your time."

I shake you harder and you spit up water. You're coughing and sputtering. I want to take you with me, Peter, but I can't. Not yet.

I'll see you soon.

THIRTY SEVEN

Sweet, cold air slipped its way into Peter's lungs. His body choked out lake water and he rolled onto his front, trying to expel all the fluid from his airway. His entire system was waterlogged and soggy. He flopped back onto the ground. *How the fuck did I get onto dry land?*

A blurry memory of a voice entered his mind:

"Peter, it's not your time."

Frantically, Peter scanned his surroundings. There was no one there. He listened intently but still, the only sound was water. He must have imagined the voice, a trick of his subconscious. Somehow, he was alive, but he had yet to decide if he was happy about it or not.

Shivering, he trekked back to the Temple. As he came up the incline, it was evident that the search was still on. In the distance, dogs barked and officers shouted. The chopper whirred above them, sweeping back and forth. Peter walked under the balconies, into the Atrium, and out the arched entrance. There was a sea of law enforcement vehicles in the parking lot. The command post had expanded into a triage zone for the dead. *Not much of a triage zone if they're all black tags.* The M.E. was walking around with a clipboard, making notes. His hair was a ball of frizz and his face was drawn; Peter suspected he'd never seen so many bodies at once. The Examiner's minions were following him around, zipping up the body bags after he'd finished his notes. Peter blew past them. Royal was walking towards the M.E. when he spotted him.

"Hey! Peter!" he jogged to catch up. "Hey, man, they found Ari's bloody robe. The DNA from the skin cells matches him and the blood is a hodgepodge of the Elder's and the—Dude, you're soaking wet, what the fuck happened to you?"

"Can I have the keys to your apartment?" Peter pictured himself back in the lake. He envisioned Royal pulling his bloated corpse from its depths. That's what would have happened if he had stayed down but it didn't upset him. Not like he thought it would.

"Why do you—" Royal took in Peter's stance. He saw his face and without hesitation he handed over his keys.

Peter didn't say another word and he walked to their cruiser. He turned off the flashing lights and threw the car into reverse. Molly and Matthew's heads shot up from whatever they were so focused on. They looked each other, alarmed, as Peter peeled out of the parking lot.

He thought a hot shower was what he wanted but Peter couldn't fathom rewarding himself now; he didn't deserve to feel better. Fidgeting with Royal's keys, he decided that if he couldn't go home, and he couldn't go to Jenna, he could go somewhere to continue his path of self-destruction. Peter returned the cruiser to the station lot, left his badge and gun inside and started walking. He had no idea how long it would take him to get there. Hell, he spent previous car rides wishing he was going anywhere else, let alone timing the trip. At this point, he didn't care if it took him all day and all night. He made sure to purchase bottle of scotch before he hit the industrial zone.

He wanted to ensure he stayed numb so he concentrated solely on tilting the bottle, taking a mouthful, and embracing the burn as he swallowed. Tilt, drink, burn. Tilt, drink, burn until the walk became more about one foot in front of the other. Left, right, left, right, left, right, until that red glowing sign bathed over him.

Cedar Valley Motel.

Peter swayed in front of the key dispenser. The display showed room 1 through 20 as individual push buttons. Unoccupied numbers were lit up. By some sheer miracle, Peter was able to select the room he wanted: 3. He slid his bills into the slot, pressed the room button, and took his key.

"Hey there, handsome," a ratty blonde leaned up against the machine. Her skin was waxy and dotted with scabs. She grinned in an attempt at seduction but her teeth were black and cracking. She didn't even look eighteen.

She held up a key, "You sure you don't wanna stay in my room?"

"Run along, Tawny," a low sultry voice came from behind him. "This one here's a cop."

'Tawny' scattered like a startled cat. Peter turned towards the voice. The bushy haired, leopard clad hooker he had bribed before was standing not five feet from him.

She took a long drag of a cigarette, "Couldn't stay away, could ya?"

Peter stared at her. He gestured for her cigarette. She handed it over, head tilted back in curious apprehension. Peter inhaled deeply from the lipstick stained edges. He savoured the ashy taste of smoke in his mouth before he slowly exhaled. She watched him, unblinking. With one hand, she slid away her coat to reveal her tight lace top that did little to contain her large breasts. Peter took another drag, handed it back to her, and walked towards that faded '3'. He swiped the key and opened the door. Heels clicked after him. Tilt, drink, burn, and he let her in behind him.

Her moans were loud. No, they were obnoxious. The way she was yelping, one would think she was climaxing every ten seconds. Peter wished she'd just shut up and let him finish. She was like a fucking monkey; up, down, here, there—never staying in one spot for more than a few thrusts. Couldn't blame here too much though, it was the coke's doing. The moment Peter came, she dismounted him and pulled a baggie from her bra.

"You mind?" she began emptying the contents onto the coffee table. *Ballsy bitch.*

Peter tugged off the condom and flushed it, "What's your name anyway?"

"Maxine," she was dividing the coke with a razor blade. *Where did she get that from?* "But I let good fucks call me Max." She said it in a tone that made Peter question if she was mocking him. He decided that he didn't care.

He pulled on his boxers and sat down on the couch beside her. He watched her shakily but meticulously create perfect lines. Her ass nearly off the edge of the seat, she bent over and snorted one. Rubbing her nose, she sat back and relaxed. Now she was truly satisfied.

"Can I have some?"

Max looked at him like he had just slapped her. "What?"

"You ever done blow before?"

"No, but I hear tha—"

"You hear nothing," she bore into him. "Don't ever start this shit."

"I'll pay."

Peter expected her to at least hesitate and consider his offer. She didn't. She hopped up on the couch, perched with her feet under her, gaze intense, "This will rob you of everything you have. It will take your life away and you'll never get it back."

"Sounds familiar," Peter grumbled.

"I'm serious...uh..."

"Peter," he startled himself by using his real name. "My name's Peter."

Max began shoveling her coke back into its baggie, ruining all her neatly sorted lines.

"What are you doing?"

She pulled her tank top back on, "You got what you paid for."

"Stay."

Max kept grabbing her things.

"I'll pay. Is that something you'd be willing to accept payment for?"

She stopped buttoning her denim skirt, "No more coke talk?"

"No more coke talk."

She dropped her jacket back onto the floor, "Alright."

THIRTY EIGHT

I figured that I would be safe coming back to this hell hole. Believe me, I didn't want to but you haven't left me with many options, have you? Besides, there's something to be said about returning to the familiar. I've retreated to my cracked plastic table and chair in room 2. I am staring out into the foggy lot, watching john after john get picked off by the lingerie clad hyenas. Right now, there's a drunk trying his darndest to select a room from the machine. You should see his, Peter. He's trying so hard to focus but he's being circled by the vultures, they're picking at him with their talons. A young one is swooping in but that leopard print bitch is taking over. She must run the operation here. Prostitute Hierarchy. The drunk turns, bottle in hand, towards me.

It's you.

Oh, my god, Peter. This has got to be the black blood talking; it's confusing me, making me see things. It has got to be because that *cannot* be you that I am seeing. What are you doing here, Peter? You are in rough shape. Understandable, sure, but is this really how you want to spend your new lease on life? That fucking whore is following you to your room. Your room, which happens to be the same room I sent you to after I killed that junkie. Did you choose it on purpose?

So, here we are, me right next to you and I am discovering just how thin these walls are. Are you aware that I can hear everything? *Everything.*

How could you do this? She is absolute filth, Peter. She is going to infect you; there is no doubt in my mind that she is filled with that black blood. You'll be infected and it will be too late. I won't be able to save you this time. The darkness brought you here and by the sounds I am hearing, you'll soon be consumed in full.

I can't go in there. I can't stop you. I am listening and it's too late. It's over. I have my ear pressed to the wall, waiting for her to leave but I don't hear your door creak open. I shudder and walk to the TV—I need a distraction. And what a perfect distraction it is. The anchor looks rattled and his voice is higher than normal. Joy flows through my veins. I feel electric.

"We're coming to you with breaking news. The Cedar Valley Slasher—"

They've given me a name? This is amazing.

"—has struck again in a gruesome attack that took place at the Temple this evening. At least six people are dead in the largest mass murder we have seen here in The Valley."

A jolt of electricity runs through me, tickles me. The largest? Oh, my. My smile is back.

"While we haven't received an official statement from the CVPD, our sources say that the suspect has not yet been caught. However, an extensive search is underway."

Of course I haven't been caught. One of CVPD's finest is *right next door* and I still haven't been caught. They're all up there playing hide and seek in the woods and I'm nowhere near. Oh, look! They're showing a picture of me.

"The police have identified the killer as this man: Arun Sinclair—a twenty-five year old teacher from the Temple. If you see him, call 9-1-1 immediately and do not approach him. He is considered armed and dangerous."

They know it's me. I thought I would be upset when the time came but I feel even more exhilarated than before. Finally, the world can see me for who I am. They know all this power belongs to me. The video pans to a spotlit line up of black body bags. It zooms in on one—it's Selene. I miss her but I know she's safe now. The world isn't safe but now her pureness is a part of me. My Moon will be forever safe this way. Her face is zipped away and I say good bye.

It's late and I should sleep but as soon as I turn off the TV, all I can hear is you and that thing conversing.

First you, "*What happened to them?*"

Then her, "*I'm not sure. I figure they OD'd somewhere and were never found. They were always disappearing to go shoot up.*"

Pity. They could have been used for so much more.

"*I'm sorry. My parents are dead too.*" Before she can answer you continue, "*They were murdered.*"

"*If you're looking for empathy, you won't find it here.*"

"*No, I—*"

"*You were just looking to even the playing field.*"

"*Yeah, something like that.*"

Jesus, don't try to befriend a prostitute, Peter. I hear a faint buzzing then she asks, "*You gonna get that?*"

"*No.*"

"They've called like, five times."

It's probably your boyfriend, Peter. Should have told him not to wait up.

"Still not answering."

"You're on the run, huh."

"Something like that."

"You in trouble?" She sounds worried that your 'trouble' will spill over onto her. You should know, Peter, it's hers that has spilled onto you.

"No, it's not like that." You sound dead; there's nothing there in your voice. I doubt you've convinced her and she doesn't reply so you ask, *"You ever wish you were someone else?"*

"No, I don't."

You don't know it but where you are now is worse than dead. You have lost your light and you have hit the bottom. The Peter I knew would never be here. And it's me, I did this to you. I told you I would, don't you remember? Yes, of course it brings me happiness to know that I succeeded but I know in my heart that our story is not over. I've made you so fragile; it's up to me to help you through this part and between watching the news and listening to you dance with the Devil over there, I've made a plan.

Get Ready.

THIRTY NINE

The sun had become Peter's enemy. It broke through the tattered motel curtains and tore him from his whiskey-deep sleep. He turned away from the window and prayed to God that the last twenty-four hours had never happened. This was the worst wake up Peter could remember. Max was gone which was good; it helped his denial. *A prostitute? If only my parents could see me now.* He tried to blame his drunken stupor but he couldn't disregard the fact that his choice to come here had occurred before he started drinking. If anyone had seen him and reported him, he'd be sacked immediately—it was only a matter of time. Although, at this point, Peter wasn't sure if police work was what he was cut out for. The death was too much. He didn't think it would ever affect him this intensely, he thought he was strong. *Fuck that. I'm not strong, I'm exhausted.* He didn't care about getting fired, let alone catching Ari, the 'Cedar Valley Slasher'. *Fucking media, always glorifying violence.* He knew they had made Ari one happy psycho by naming him that.

Peter put on last night's still damp clothes. He looked to the bathroom and sighed. He couldn't be paid to shower in this dump. Ignoring his six voicemail messages, he called Royal back.

"Dude, where the fuck are you?" There was no jovial nature to his voice.

"I'm on my way over, I need to use your shower."

"From where?"

Peter hung up and dialed a cab. It was his turn to take a walk of shame. All the hookers were still asleep after their busy nights. *Thank god.* He deposited the room key and met with his prompt taxi.

卌

He took Royal's keys and unlocked the townhome. Royal was in the foyer to greet him, arms crossed. A vertical line carved deep between his eyes.

"Jesus," Royal eyed him, his voice tense. "You look rough."

Peter tried to walk past him but he was blocked by an arm.

"You know I had to break into my own place last night?"

"Sorry," he ignored Royal's anger and pushed against his arm.

"That's it? That's all you're going to say? No explanation at all."

"Right."

"Come on, Pete!" his arms and forehead relaxed but his voice was still tight. "What's gotten into you?"

"Nothing." *What am I supposed to say? 'Oh, I just drowned myself but was then saved by a mystery person and/or ghost only to spend my night with a prostitute?' Not likely.*

"Alright," eyes narrowing now. "Get ready, they need us at the station."

"I'm not going," Peter shut and locked the bathroom door.

Royal banged against it, "What? What do you mean?"

"I'm not even supposed to be there," Peter stripped out of his uncomfortable clothes.

A pause. Royal continued softly, "We need you there. We need everyone we can get."

"Won't do any good," he turned on the water and drowned out his friend's protests.

The rushing water reminded him of the lake. It wasn't silent, but the lack of other noise was welcomed. He didn't know how to get Royal off his case besides hiding out in here. Peter couldn't go to work. He couldn't face all the pictures and the news and the victims' families. He didn't really have anywhere else to go, so he was trapped, subject to interrogation. It was too much. Hopefully Royal would clue in to that and leave him alone.

He was prepared to face Royal and skirt his questions but when he exited the washroom he found the house empty. He looked outside, Royal's car was gone too. Peter relaxed. He went to the fridge and warmed up some leftover pizza and cracked open a beer. The lager went down smooth despite his pounding head. He plugged his phone into Royal's charger and waited for it to come back to life. He contemplated turning on the TV but figured that was a bad idea. Peter selected a random movie from the TV's virtual library and hit 'play'.

He rubbed his temples. Thinking back to last night, he hoped he hadn't contracted anything from Max. *Jesus, I'm now on a first name basis with a hooker. Great.* His phone lit up but he had no new messages. He hoped Jenna was coping alright and not avoiding him. A small, miniscule, nearly-not-there ball of warmth appeared inside of him when he thought of her. He messaged her:

"Hey, I had a great time despite, you know. I hope you're doing okay."

It wasn't even a lie. He really did have an amazing few hours with Jenna which made him feel even more guilty about Max. That guilt snowballed with how he had treated Royal just now. He decided to text him as well:

"He buddy, I'm sorry for acting how I did. There's no excuse for stranding you last night."

Peter leaned back to watch the movie. He didn't expect either of them to text back right away but by the time the movie ended, he still had no new messages. He called Royal, no answer. *That's strange.* They had been busy at work before, granted not this busy, but Royal had always returned his call. He was probably just getting back at him for screening his calls last night. *Asshole.*

Thirty minutes later, Peter's phone rang—it was Molly. *Shit.* Royal had sent in the big guns to get him into work.

"Ma'am?"

"Have you seen Royal?" Her voice was strained. The rapid rustling of paper and chaotic background noise told Peter she was more impatient than worried.

"What, he's not there? He left his place at around eight this morning while I was in the shower."

"I thought he might be with you. He hasn't come in or checked in at all today. We could really use him here."

Peter checked outside again to be sure, "His car is gone."

Molly huffed into the phone but didn't say anything. He could feel her stress level rising through the phone.

"I'll check his regular haunts."

"Thank you. Call me when you have an update."

314

"I will."

He expected her to hang up without a goodbye but she spoke again, "Peter?" The background noise disappeared. She must have shut herself in an office or maybe the conference room. "Are you okay?"

"Yeah, I will be," he was unsure if that was true. "Thanks."

Peter dialed the café where Royal's barista worked. There was rarely a day where Royal went without his coffee but they hadn't seen him either. A sinking feeling crept into his gut.

He shouldn't have said 'haunts', plural. Besides the café, Peter couldn't think of anywhere else that his friend would go. If he wasn't with him, he was home or out with a girl. He called Jenna, no response. *They're just dodging my calls, right? There's no other reason. Royal's mad at me. Jenna's at work. That could be it, couldn't it?*

He called the hospital.

"Cedar Valley General, how may I direct your call?"

"Emergency Department, please."

"One moment."

Horrible, taunting hold music played while he waited for the line to be transferred. Peter shook his leg impatiently.

"Emergency, Joyce speaking."

"Hi, may I speak with Jenna, please?"

"May I ask who's calling?"

He sighed involuntarily, "It's Officer Peter Holloway."

"Oh, uhm, Jenna never came back after her lunch break."

"Is she sick?" His stomach dropped lower.

"No, she just didn't come back. No one has seen her and no one can reach her. Pretty inconsiderate if you ask me; we're really sho—"

Peter's heart clenched. *This can't be happening.* He began dialing Molly back, pulled on a pair of Royal's pants and swung open the front door. The line connected and he nearly tripped over two jars of blood.

FORTY

Having everyone know my face has proven to be a bit of a challenge. I haven't been able to move as freely, constantly suspicious of onlookers. I saw you leave this morning and although it was tricky, I followed you to Mr. O'Leary's house. I listened from an open window, stuffed behind some bushes as you pouted your way into the shower—good idea by the way, you definitely needed that—and then Royal left without you. Subduing him was easier than expected. You cops are not as vigilant as you make yourselves out to be. I threw a bag over his head and kicked the crap out of him. I threw him in his own trunk and took him back to the Cedar Valley Motel. It was bit of a squish—he should really think about getting a larger model. Maybe you can trade it in if you inherit it from his death. Thank goodness your boyfriend is a slob, I was able to find a whole new outfit of discarded clothes in the back

seat. This baseball cap is a bit snug but it will have to
do; I cannot chance being recognized today.

After dropping O'Leary off, I waited until your little
redhead took her lunch break and grabbed her from the
courtyard where she asked you out. You know me,
always a sucker for consistency. And to be completely
honest, I am still surprised by that whole situation.
You'll have to let me know how your date went before I
completely destroyed it. I didn't use the bag with her—
too obvious at this hour. I walked up to her and told her
my son was unconscious in my car. When she got there,
I knocked her head against the vehicle and shoved her
in the trunk like Royal.

If I had the chance to choose again, I would not have
the Cedar Valley Motel as my 'home base' but here we
are. Ha, you see what I did there? This baseball hat is
rubbing off on me. Anyway, we both know how filthy
this place is, the walls ooze despair. But sometimes we
don't get a choice, do we, Peter? You would know better
than anyone. It shouldn't be hard for you to find me but
we should at least make it fun, right? I owe us that.

I'm not going to kill them right away. This whole time,
all my kills have been so rushed and I think it's time I
slow down and smell the roses. However, I need to
scare you—I need you to believe they are dead or at
least in immediate danger, which I suppose is true!
These flimsy chairs definitely wouldn't hold the
redhead, let alone Officer O'Leary, but the beds are

nailed to the floor so the posts will do nicely. I am a fan of those electrical cords but they are few and far between at his motel. Alternatively, I was able to get some zip ties from the hardware store down the street. I kept my head down and I limited human interaction as much as possible. I don't think anyone recognized me.

One good thing about this motel is that it's got this lovely 'don't ask, don't tell' quality. You know what I am talking about. That young hyena from last night saw me hauling the nurse out of the trunk, but by the way she was jittering around there's a good chance she'll chalk this up to a hallucination. Predictably, she turned away to greet a john. At one in the afternoon! Does no one have self-control anymore?

I closed the trunk and helped the awake but obtunded redhead into room 3. When Royal saw us enter the room, he yelled into his gag and fought against his binds. His face burned red with frustration. I had to giggle at him, his efforts were quite entertaining. I tied her to the bedpost just like him; arms zipped behind them, mouths gagged, and their legs zipped together at the ankles.

The nurse was coming around now and the moment she realized the situation she was in, oh my, you should have seen it. It was in her eyes, the terror that I'd instilled so far had made a home in her. She looked to Royal, her gaze seemed to ask, 'Is this him?'. He nodded back to her and tears just streamed down her face. I had to take a seat and soak it all up. Wow.

Now, as I was saying, I didn't want to kill them right away. I took my knife and sliced vertically up the nurse's inner forearm. She squealed into her gag and Royal was straining towards her, trying to yell for me to stop. I rolled my eyes, as if *yelling* was going to stop me. You two really are the worst cops ever. I collected the spilling blood into a jar. I left it under her arm as it drained and walked over to him. He stiffened and prepared for my blade but she began squirming. She squirmed so much she knocked over the jar.

"What are you doing?!" I slapped her. I looked at the spilled blood and it was black. I scrambled back, "Do you know how reckless you're being?!"

She didn't reply, she just cried. I tiptoed around the spill and sliced her other arm. She squealed again and I yanked her ear up to my mouth, "If you knock this one over, I'll slit your throat."

She was sobbing. She looked to Royal again and he nodded. That seemed to calm her for whatever reason. I sliced his arm and he made nothing more than a grunt, thank god. I could not take any more of this whining.

Once the jars were full enough, I capped them and set them on the table. I wrote you a few notes. I was preparing to leave when my anger got the best of me, "I wasn't going to say anything but what kind of friends do you think you are?"

They looked confused, as they should; how would they know what I am talking about when they are so wrapped up in their own petty whiny shit?

"While you were busy *not* making sure Peter was alright, I was busy saving his life."

Their confusion increased. They looked at each other, each shaking their heads to signal they both still had no clue.

"He was so upset that he needed to get wasted and come here. He had to sleep with a whore in this very bed you're tied to."

Nothing. No reaction.

"That's fine, don't believe me. But you remember Maxine, Officer O'Leary? Big bushy hair and all that awful leopard print?"

The recognition settled into his face, which paled and his eyes widened. That was a small victory for me. I took Red's keys from her chest pocket. I picked up the jars and the notes.

"I'll let you stew on that while I deliver these."

And I left them.

FORTY ONE

Fuck not caring. Peter's body was in overdrive. He knew that these blood jars could only mean one thing: Ari had new victims. Royal and Jenna were missing and it couldn't be a coincidence. *He has them, but are they alive? There doesn't seem to be as much blood as last time. It's possible they're not dead, right? They have to be alive.*

Molly and Matthew looked just as distraught as Peter felt. Their faces were drawn and drained of all colour. They circled the jars on Royal's steps. Molly buried her head into Matthew's arm as he breathed deeply and turned his eyes to the sky. It was nearing noon. Royal could have been missing for as long as three hours now.

"Tell me again," Molly looked to Peter.

"I told Royal I wouldn't be coming in today and he was trying to change my mind. I hopped in the shower to get him off my back and when I got out, he was gone."

"Well, it sure worked didn't it?" Matthew's voice was razor sharp.

Molly scolded him but his words had already cut Peter, "You don't think I get that? I feel fucking awful right now."

"It's possible that it's not even his," Molly's voice didn't reflect her hopeful words.

Matthew shook his head and walked back down the sidewalk. He peered down at the cement, "It looks like there could have been a scuffle here. There are drops of blood that lead to the curb then disappear."

The forensics team was getting out of their vehicle. Matthew waved them over and directed a few techs over to Peter and Molly. They took samples of the blood and inserted them into their tablets.

Molly looked at Peter, "It's possible that it's not theirs."

After a long, breathless moment the tablet *dinged* and the tech's face fell. "It's his," he said.

Molly fell to the ground but she didn't make a sound. Peter could tell she was trying to hold herself together but the fear was leaking through. She kept placing her hand to her mouth then removing and shaking it. She shook her head too, trying to play off her tears as irrational.

Peter held his breath. *Okay, it's Royal's. Royal can handle himself. He'll be fine. But Jenna?*

"It's hers," the other tech held up his tablet. The screen read, 'Positive Match'.

Peter punched the door, leaving a dent. Paint chips stained his knuckles. Silence followed, everyone remained quiet so that they could collect themselves.

Molly reached over from her heaped position on the ground, "What's this?"

She held the note in her hand.

Peter took it from her. He recognized the handwriting, "A clue."

"For what?"

Peter pinched the bridge of his nose, "To where they are."

Her eyes drew wide, "Well, read it!"

"'This is where it began. Not for me, but for you.'"

"And?" She was on her feet. Matthew was listening from the sidewalk.

Peter flipped the note, "And that's it."

Matthew called over, "Blood over here is his too. Sinclair must have taken Royal from here. Used his car."

"What does it mean?" Molly snatched the paper back.

Peter knew exactly what it meant. His chest seized. *That sick fuck.* Exhaling sharply, "My parents' house."

Her brow creased.

"It wasn't his first kill but it's what brought me into all of this."

"You sure he's addressing you?"

He nodded, "Oh, yeah."

She held out her backup sidearm, "You'll need this."

There was nothing Peter wanted less than to go in that house—a circumstance Ari had designed on purpose; another game. Peter steeled himself against his reeling mind and swore to himself that he wouldn't give in. He wouldn't give that son of a bitch what he wanted.

Guns raised, they entered through the front door, breaking off the police tape. They swept the main level. Nothing. The carpet under the stairs was still stained with blood. Holding his breath, Peter tried to keep his eyes off of the ground as he made his way to the second floor. The hallway carpet was stained through with red from wall to wall. His stomach rolled, nausea swayed him. He propped himself against the bannister only to yank his hand back when he realized this is where Ari had strung them up.

They cleared the rest of the house. Still nothing. The whole place was empty.

Peter rushed towards the back door. *Maybe they were in the yard? Or the garage?* He glanced up at the family photos on the wall, nearly missing a note that was stuck over his parents' faces in one of the pictures. Peter ripped it off.

"Wrong!

I do wish I could have seen your face when you realized I sent you here.

Now, I need you to do the next part alone.

If you bring the rest of your team, I will kill them.

If you notify them in anyway, I'll kill them.

Now think, I killed your parents in their own home;

Where would I kill this ginger bitch?"

Peter looked behind him, no one could see him from where they were. He took off out the back door, into the alley way, and dialed a number on his phone.

"Banks."

"Hey, it's Holloway. Listen, can you get me Jenna's address?"

"Why?"

"One of the jars had her blood in it."

"Oh, shit."

"Yeah, the other one was Royal's."

There was a silence then, *"Are you serious?"*

"Yes," Peter looked around to see if anyone had followed him. He was still alone, "Banks, the address?"

"Fuck, yeah, gimme a second. I got it here, It's number 4, 8813 Creekside. Do you want—"

Peter hung up the phone. He fished around on top of an exterior garage light until he located the spare key. As quietly as possible, he unlocked the garage and approached his Father's car. His father had always insisted on leaving the key on a hook inside the garage, no matter how much his Mother nagged it was unsafe. He claimed he could never find them unless he did so, and besides, 'Who would steal from a cop?' Peter opened the garage door and turned the key. If anyone heard and came running, he couldn't tell; he was already speeding away.

Jenna's house was easy to find. It was a townhouse like Royal's. Peter pulled out Molly's weapon and approached the front door, listening for noise within. All he could hear was the low roar of pre-rush hour traffic behind him. He tried the door—it was unlocked. He pushed it open and led with the barrel of his gun. It was quiet inside too.

Jenna's living room was completely white with grey accents and dark wood furniture. The couch was white leather, laden with oversized pillows and faux-fur throws. He pictured himself on that couch, Jenna on top of him, fur enveloping their naked bodies. Armed and fearing for her life was not how Peter had envisioned his first visit here.

He crept through the kitchen. Pristine white tile backsplash led to dark granite counters which housed shining chrome appliances. Everything was neat and tidy, not a crumb in sight. Peter made his way upstairs. The smell of bleach slipped into his nose. *No, no, no, no.* Flashbacks of the Gibbons' dead bodies and reeking home swirled through his mind. *Was Ari lying? Was she already dead?* He couldn't grip the thought. *She can't be dead.* He ran down the hall and slammed open the bathroom door. Nothing but clean. No blood. Just clean. Nose stinging, he crossed the hall into her bedroom. More fluffy throws and cloud-like pillows, but no Jenna.

Another piece of stationary lay folded on her white sheets.

> *"I had to make sure you were alone.*
> *She's not here either.*
> *She's where you were last night.*
> *Room 3."*

The motel. *Really?* There was no mention of Royal. Peter prayed he was there with Jenna. And more so, he prayed that this was the last leg of the hunt. Despite what Ari may believe, following his demands was easy. Coming alone was not a disadvantage but rather exactly what Peter wanted. These clues would have caused nothing but a slew of unwanted questions from his coworkers, all of which would delay the search. Explaining what he was doing in that motel room last night would only end badly. Ari obviously knew he had been there, how exactly Peter was unsure of. The more Peter tried to formulate a cover story for himself, the more everything seemed to fall apart. His priorities were all mixed up. *How can I be worried about keeping my job right now?* Anger exploded inside of him. He hated Ari for toying with him. Peter's rage was the main reason he was glad to be alone in this for he planned to give Ari exactly what he deserved. Jail was too good for him. Peter needed him gone. *Destroyed*. If the soliciting charge wasn't enough to fire him, murder would certainly do the trick.

He was going to put him down for his parents, for Sarah and the other women, for Royal and Jenna, and for him. *No more. This ends now.*

Peter saw that he had a few missed calls from various members of his team. He put his phone on silent mode. *Sorry kids, no time for chit chat.* He fingered his gun in his lap as he drove, itching to pull the trigger. Ari had given him his chance; he wasn't going to miss it.

The motel was in full swing. Hookers hung in their doorways, cigarettes in hand, awaiting their next clients. Peter could even see Max desperately trying to tame her hair, black eyeliner smudged under her eyes. He parked his father's car by the registry and closed the door gently. Peter considered warning Max—telling her to run, that this place wasn't safe, but the faded number '3' was staring him down and locking him in. He stormed straight for the room. When he reached the door, he paused and mentally kicked himself—*if Ari's watching, he now knows I am here. Of course he's watching, he's been watching the whole time.* Futile as it was, Peter stayed out of the view of the window, inching closer so he could get a look inside. Through the grimy pane and dusty curtains, Royal and Jenna were on the floor, both bound to the bedposts.

They're alive.

No sign of Ari inside. Peter's hand was sweating along the grip of the gun. He grasped it tighter. Shifting over, he turned the door handle—locked. Taking a step back, he looked around the motel lot, no Ari out here either; no one but the prostitutes were visible. He squared himself and kicked the door in.

"Oh, thank god," Peter lurched forward. Royal looked beat up, but okay. Jenna looked fine too save for the makeup streaking down her face. He loosened her gag and slid it out of her mouth, "You okay?"

She nodded, fresh tears brimming her eyes. To his right, Royal began yelling into his gag and thumping his legs against the floor.

Jenna's eyes bulged, "Peter!"

A foot collided with his back, sending sharp pain up his spine. He fell forward, gun clattering out of his sweaty palm. He scrambled forward to grab it but a hand clutched his shirt and yanked him back. Peter sent his arms behind him, attempting to grasp his attacker. The hand spun him sideways and a fist slammed into his jaw. His vision blurred. Squinting, he saw Ari standing before him, hands raised and ready.

"How nice of you to finally join us," Ari smiled and swung at Peter.

He ducked and charged at Ari's midsection, drilling his shoulder into his ribs and knocking him into a wall. The dresser shook, a vase fell and shattered on the ground. Grappling each other, they toppled onto a plastic chair, its flimsy legs splintering under their weight. Ari was now on top of him. He was laughing. Peter groaned against him, struggling to free himself. Ari sent a fist against the side of Peter's face and then the other. The edges of his vision were turning black but he fought back harder. He wouldn't let Ari win. He slipped his arms free and secured them around Ari's neck and squeezed. Ari's olive skin turned red as he scratched at Peter, trying to get air. Peter felt the surge of his fighting heartbeat beneath his hands. Ari's mouth gaped like a fish searching for breath. Peter tightened his grasp. Royal yelled, cheering him on.

Jenna screamed too, but it wasn't a cheer. Excruciating pain exploded through Peter's abdomen. His hands fell away and Ari pulled a knife from his gut. Ari's eyes were fixated on the dripping blood as he climbed off of Peter. He touched the blood and smiled, examining it on his fingers. His shoulders relaxed and he placed his hands in a prayer position, muttering, 'Thank you' to himself. Peter grabbed his wound, blood covered his hands and spilled out onto the carpet. He felt sick.

"Oh, god," Jenna sobbed.

Ari was still staring at his fingers. One hand pressed against the bleed, Peter used his other to slide himself towards his gun. It was surprising how hard moving had suddenly become, every breath sent burning pain through his torso. *Just a few more feet.*

Crunch.

Peter cried out and closed his eyes against the pain. Ari had stepped on his outstretched hand.

"I don't think so, Peter," he picked up the gun and placed it on the dresser. "I hate guns. They're like cheating, don't you think?"

He grabbed Peter under the armpits and dragged him to the register. He yanked his hand away from his stomach and zip tied it with the other. Peter looked down, his shirt was soaked with blood. He feared he may vomit.

"You've got to let me help him," Jenna begged.

Ari looked at her, then at Peter, "You'll infect him."

"No," she shook her head wildly. "He needs medical attention. He could die."

Ari's eyes widened with her last word. He stared down at Peter's wound, "This wasn't supposed to happen."

And was that supposed to be an apology?

"Then let me help him!"

Ari hesitated then walked to her, "You promise you won't get any of your blood on him?"

Why is he helping?

"I promise."

Ari used his knife to cut a few strips from the bed sheets and tied them around her wrists. She had one long slice on each that Peter hadn't noticed before. Royal had one too. Peter's rage coursed through him stronger than ever before. He fought the urge to lunge himself uselessly at him. *Save your strength, Peter.* Ari cut her ties and let her come near. Her eyes were red and swollen. Gingerly, she lifted up his shirt, frowning when she visualized the wound.

Her voice shook, "May I have some more strips, please?"

Peter could tell how much it pained her to play nice. Ari obliged and cut more from the sheet.

"What is he talking about," Peter tried to focus. He kept his voice low so only Jenna could hear, "Infecting me?"

She shook her head ever so slightly, "I have no idea."

Jenna folded a strip over the wound and then wrapped the rest around Peter's abdomen. Her hands were ice cold. He yelped out when she tied the knot.

"Sorry," she muttered. "It has to be tight."

Ari walked over, "What are you two love birds whispering about?"

Peter addressed him, "Why do you think she'd infect me? She's not sick."

"Oh, Peter," he took the hilt of the knife and drove it into Jenna's temple. She crumpled to the side, crying into her hand.

"Hey!" Peter snapped his head towards Ari but he didn't even flinch.

"Look!" He pointed to the blood oozing from her head, "It's black!"

But all Peter saw was red. Ari had clearly lost his mind. He was crazy, delusional. "It's red, Ari."

"No, look," he grabbed Jenna by the hair, making her cry out and shoved her head closer to Peter.

Peter shook his head. *Could I convince him he's wrong? Would he let us go?* Peter knew it was pointless. He knew Ari wouldn't keep them hostage like this for long. If they didn't find a way out, they'd be dead within the hour.

"You don't believe me?" Ari's face saddened. "After all that I've done for you? That hurts, Peter."

"All that you've *done?* Are you fucking kidding me?"

Ari scratched his chin, "I saved your life or did you forget already?"

"You..." *The lake.*

"Yes, Peter. I couldn't have come this far for you to just kill yourself. That wouldn't be fair, would it?"

Royal's face twisted. He looked at Peter with pained eyes, searching for the truth. Peter looked away.

"Don't you feel that darkness inside of you? It's growing and it's spreading. It's already reached little Jenna here. I gave you another chance, Peter, and what do you do? You come here," he spread his arms wide and looked around the room. "And fuck some filthy slut named 'Max'."

Royal and Jenna looked at him in disbelief.

"He's lying!" *How did he know this?*

"How do I know this?" It was as if he read Peter's mind. He pointed to the wall that neighboured the next room, "I was right there, listening. And could hear everything, Peter. I know how she lets you call her 'Max' instead of 'Maxine' because of your ability to perform. I know you tried to get her to give you cocaine

335

and I know that you paid her to keep you company after she got you off."

"Fuck you!" Peter pulled against the register. Rage overtook his pain. He visualized himself grabbing his gun and putting every bullet he had into Ari's face.

A smile played on his lips, "Why would I lie? What purpose would that serve? Here, I'll prove it to you."

Ari grabbed Jenna by her hair and pulled her to her feet. She clawed at his hands, her knees buckling beneath her.

"What are you doing?" Peter's stomach turned. "Let her go!"

Ari dragged her towards the bathroom. She dug her heels into the ground but he flipped her over, making her trip. Royal tried to use his outstretched legs to help her, he uttered what sounded like a muffled, 'Hold on!' She rolled onto her belly and crawled frantically, grabbing Royal's pant leg. Ari was laughing again. He snatched her by her ankles and pulled. Royal was yelling, Peter was yelling, and Jenna was yelling the loudest.

"No!" her hand came loose, her face and chest sliding across the floor.

"Come here," Ari gathered her up in his arms and hauled her into the bathroom.

"Peter!" Jenna kicked and screamed. "Peter, help me!"

Ari pushed her forward. Her ribs cracked against the bathtub. She gasped, winded.

"Ari, you son of a bitch! Let her go!" The radiator groaned against Peter's struggles. Sweat poured from his forehead. More blood seeped from his abdomen. "Let her go!"

She put her hands on the tub, bracing against Ari's shoves. Her elbows collapsed and she fell forward. Eyes bright red, she fought to find her grip. She sobbed harder, her screams piercing the air. Trapping her against the tub, Ari grabbed her chin and exposed her neck. He placed his knife to her skin.

"I can't let her go, Peter," Ari held her as she thrashed. "I need to make you believe me."

Royal strained against the bed as hard as he could. Peter's vision slid out of focus, distorting the room.

"I believe you!" Peter felt a screw come loose on the register. "I believe you!"

"Then you know this is the only way to keep us safe," he slit her throat, bright red blood spraying the tile.

"NO!"

Jenna's body arched forward. She held onto her neck but she couldn't stop the bleed. Blood surged out around her fingers.

"No, no, no, no, no," Peter shut his eyes. *This isn't real. This is just a horrible horrible nightmare.*

"Open your eyes Peter," Ari sat down in front of him and gestured to the dying Jenna. "Don't you see? She was tainted."

Peter spat in his face, "No, she Isn't! You're insane. You're fucking mad."

Ari calmly wiped the saliva from his cheek, "I did this for us."

Royal hung his head. He stared at the floor, unblinking.

"This world's lifeblood is swiftly being poisoned, Peter, and we have to stop it. I've bathed in enough pure blood to be safe but you're not."

"What the fuck are you talking about? You killed all these people just to...?"

"I don't usually like to share but if you are to live, I'll have to. Consider yourself lucky, Peter. Now, I've seen Royal's blood and it's still pure. We can bathe you in his."

"What!" Peter kicked out at Ari, red hot pain shot up towards his sternum. "If you fucking touch him—"

"Yeah, yeah, I get it. You'll kill me. Well, there are worse things, Peter."

Ari bent down to untie Royal when sirens pierced the air. Through the window, Peter saw a sea of police cars swerve into the parking lot.

"Huh," Ari stood, leaving Royal tied to the post. "I suppose our timetable has been moved up on us. Very well."

FORTY TWO

It's true, this hasn't gone according to plan. I am not worried, though. I am adaptable. This will still work. Peter, it's evident that you can't see it but I have put a lot on the line to save you. That's alright, I suppose. Maybe in another life you'll be able to appreciate my efforts.

The police are outside. They're all in position behind their cars with their guns raised, all yelling for me to come out. Hands behind my head? I think not. My hands are busy. I bet they even have snipers out there, how exciting! However, I am not overly sure where they would put a sniper in this dump. Never-the-less, it's perfect.

I look at Royal. Poor chump, he had a chance to be useful to you and he won't get to take it. At least I was successful with the nurse. You were too blind to see but she would have tainted you and then this would never work. Perhaps it was my doing all along that kept you safe. The black blood avoided you thus far because you are already so dark on the inside. Your whole world is black and that's thanks to me. If you think about it, I've been saving you from the start.

"Are you ready?"

I crouch beside you and lean a hand into your wound. Sorry, but I need to weaken you some more. You moan from the pain but you don't pull away. I slice through your ties and help you to your feet. You're wobbly and you make it worse when you try to fight my grip. I retie your hands behind your back and you relax. That's good, Peter. I hold you close as I open the door and face the crowd, knife to your throat.

Bright lights are blinding me. I hear my audience gasp.

"Put down the knife, now!"

I'm afraid that's not going to happen. I take a step forward, guiding you with me. The blade nicks your neck and it produces a trickle of red, pure blood. I smile.

"Drop the weapon and let Officer Holloway go!"

"No, thank you."

CEDAR VALLEY

I drag the knife across your throat, blood spilling over us. You collapse to your knees and I follow you as bullets rip through me. We're on the ground now. You are looking at me while blood gushes from your neck. You don't try to stop the bleeding and neither do I. You lay there looking at me and I looking at you, together. Our blood mixes on the pavement and I know now— Selene was not my Moon, you were. Two halves of the whole, Peter. We are finally safe as we exit this world true and pure. I can see it in your eyes that you understand now. It wasn't Selene, Peter.

It was you.